AFTER

YOU

DIED

AFTER

YOU

DIED

DEA POIRIER

The following is a work of fiction. Names, characters, places, events and incidents are either the product of the author's imagination or used in an entirely fictitious manner. Any resemblance to actual persons, living or dead, is entirely coincidental.

ISBN 978-1-951709-41-9
eISBN 978-1-951709-63-1
Library of Congress Control Number: available upon request

First trade paperback edition July 2021 by Polis Books, LLC
44 Brookview Lane
Aberdeen, NJ 07747
www.PolisBooks.com

POLIS BOOKS

Trigger Warning
This book contains elements of sexual violence, physical abuse, emotional abuse, psychological trauma, struggles with mental health, bullying, and suicide.

*This book is dedicated to every child who suffered
at the hands of the Dozier school.*

I believe you.

And I hope one day you find peace.

If you're anything like me, you never wondered what your girlfriend would look like as a corpse. For the record—she was just as pretty. Even though I remember nothing else from that night I remember her face, as beautiful in death as it had been every single day of her life. There were a million things I expected to happen once Olivia was my girlfriend, but murder never crossed my mind.

1

BEFORE
January 1st, 1968

Her long white dress whips behind her as she disappears into the trees. It lashes, like a flag caught in a hurricane. Instead of devastation, she leaves the flowers that she wove into her hair in her wake. The hot afternoon sun bears down on us. We've been out here so long, sweat glues my hair to my face. The wind carries the scent of a brush fire on its wings. My heart races as I chase after her, excitement buzzing in my veins.

"Olivia?" The word seeps out of me, as slow and tired as I am.

"The time to hesitate is through." Her voice is high, beautiful; it rings through the trees. She's been singing The Doors all day, thanks to my t-shirt. Somehow, even though she taunts me with songs, she manages to remain hidden.

The trees swallow me. In the shade, the temperature drops a few degrees, but I still feel like I'm being boiled; that's Florida for you, hot enough to smother you even in January. Masses of brown, green, and gray stretch before me, blurring into an endless expanse. Strangled beams of light root their way through the twisted branches above me; the sandy soil dotted with a patchwork of spots.

Twenty feet in, there's no sign of her—she's vanished into the forest. I search between the trees for her white dress, her blonde curls. My heart thrums with excitement. When I run, the Spanish moss dangling above catches my hair.

She sings again, but her words are lost amongst the trees. Between the words her laugh echoes in the distance, as high and delicate as a bird's song.

She loves this game. She's always loved when I chase her. I'll chase her forever. Deep down I know I'll never catch her, never have her. I've been after her since we were little, but she'll never be mine. Mom says the first time I ever said love, it was to Olivia. Three years old and she already had my heart. Fourteen years later, and every-single-beat is still for her.

I slip in-between the trees like a whisper. For a moment, I see her, the hem of her dress catches my eye, then disappears again so fast, I'm not certain I actually saw it. I stop to catch my breath. With my back against a tree I gulp down air. The heat and humidity threaten to suffocate me.

"Our love become a funeral pyre." Her laugh sings through the trees. "Come on Asher," she says in a playful voice. "You can do better than that."

Thirty feet away her round face pops out from behind a tree. Even from here, I can see she's panting, but there's a smile on her wide face. Her curls are limp, heavy with sweat, a few of the small flowers remain tangled in them. I push off the tree and dart toward her again. As soon as I move, so does she. She melts into the forest, disappearing as easily as a jaguar. I curse myself for not being faster.

"Come on, baby," she starts again, but her song dies.

My chest is tight, a cramp tightening up just below my ribs. I open my mouth to call out, but to my right, a hint of movement pulls my attention. Someone runs beside me. A figure pops in and out as it weaves between the trees. I slow to get a better look, but only foliage stares back. Though I resume my chase, a tingling feeling claws its way up my neck, the heat of eyes burn against my skin.

We're being watched.

A twig snaps behind me, I turn.

Nothing.

"Olivia?" My words are uneven, muted by the thunder of my heartbeats.

A creeping feeling works its way through me and settles in my stomach, something bad— no, something *terrible*—is about to happen.

Whoever is out there, the forest is keeping their secrets, for now. Slowly, I move between the trunks, over the protruding roots, and take the moment to catch my breath. Bark digs into my flesh, through my thin t-shirt, as I rest against a tree. My heart is unsteady, uneasiness floods into me.

Another snap.

Instead of looking, I push off from the tree. Olivia is painfully quiet. My breath catches in my throat, and worry strangles me. The air bites at my wide eyes, my mouth goes dry. *Where is she?* It's rare a moment that passes without a giggle, or at least her egging me on.

In the minutes since her laughter died, a pit has formed in my stomach, pushing a bitter taste into my mouth. Knots tighten in my guts, every second that ticks by is painful. My breath catches in my throat, my mouth opens, but I can't find my voice to call for her.

The air is cut by Olivia's scream. Long, terrified, haunting. Whoever was watching me must have caught up to her. I have to find her.

"Olivia!" The humidity rushes into my open mouth, the air thick in my throat. I swallow hard to clear it. Cold sweat beads on my flesh. Sickness wells inside me.

She has to be okay. She has to. Has to.

My feet pound the earth. A yelp slips through my lips as my shoulder smashes into a tree.

Where is she? I have to find her.

In the distance, I hear sobbing. I slow. Carefully, I walk until the sound grows louder. I find her huddled on the ground against a tree in a clearing. She hugs her knees. Her white dress dirty, gathered up against her, like a wilted flower.

The trees group together in a circle, leaving an opening nearly fifteen feet across. They grow into one another; I can't tell where one ends and another begins. Above us, the Spanish moss is woven like a net. Soft tendrils of light pour in from above. I creep closer.

"Olivia, are you okay?" I ask. My voice is low, my eyes take turns, surveying her and the tree line. My body is so tense, I feel like a rubber band stretched to its breaking point. I'm still painfully aware that someone is still out there. Someone watching us.

Her hands muffle her cries. I lean over, and touch her shoulder gently. My gaze follows hers. That's when I see what upset her. Atop the blanket of moss and leaves behind me, there's a dead doe. She's cut clean, opened up, skin peeled away from her organs. The entrails and blood spill onto the forest floor. Beside the mother, two pink preterm foals are decapitated. Shimmering splatters of red cling to the decaying underbrush.

I've never been able to handle hurt animals, though I've seen butchered deer a thousand times; my dad has a penchant for hunting. I move in front of her to block her view, and my own. Pulling Olivia gently, I stand her up, making her face me. Brushing her hair out of her face, I lift her chin. Her lip quivers, and red veins snake through her eyes, making her irises an impossible shade of blue. Though I feel as uneasy, as unsettled as she looks, I hold myself together—for her.

"Are you okay?" I ask again.

Her full lips quiver. Pallor taints her features. The tears make her eyes puffy, the lids are tinged pink. She wipes her cheeks on her dress. Though she nods, it looks forced. All I want is to get her out of here. Away from whoever might have done this, whoever is still hiding in the trees. I put my arm around her, and urge her out of the clearing.

Heavy footsteps creep closer; dead leaves crushed beneath their weight. I turn, and step in front of her, guarding her. That's when I see Dominic's wide goofy smile. His red hair glows, even in the dim light.

"Hey, man!"

I'm so tense, I nearly jump. I fall back slightly, brushing against Olivia. Next to Olivia, Dominic is easily my closest friend, but seeing him out here makes me uneasy. I exhale, anxiety escaping with my breath.

"What are you guys doing out here?" He walks around the corpses, as if he were avoiding a rock. His gaze doesn't move toward the bodies.

I eye him carefully, trying not to see the gore. *How does that not bother him?* He didn't kill them, there's not a drop of blood on his clothing, though it still seems strange he's not even a little bothered. Guilt swells inside me as questions about Dominic swim in my mind. *Stop it. He's your friend.* Six months ago, right after school let out for the summer, Dominic's family moved to town. We became fast friends—he has the same penchant for cutting class and sneaking out that I do.

"Nothing, just out for a walk," I say after far too long.

Olivia reaches for me, her fingers curl around my hand. She

pulls me gently. Somehow, even in this heat, her fingers are as cold as bones. The way she tugs at me, there's an urgency, I don't want to be around the deer any more than she does, but I'm tethered here between them.

"Did you see who did this?" I ask him, scanning the trees before my eyes rest on him again. Something about the way that he stands only inches from the corpses tugs at me, but I ignore it.

He shrugs, "Nope."

"It's pretty fucked up." I start to turn to Olivia, cowering behind me. The way she looks at him, it makes me ask, "What are you doing out here?"

"Nothing, and come on man, it's just a deer." His voice has an argumentative edge, he kicks some of the underbrush toward the corpses and the thoughts swell in my mind again.

Olivia pulls my hand again, the way she tugs, there's panic in every movement. I look back at her, her light blue eyes are saucers. For a moment, her eyes move to Dominic, then she tenses. She flashes me a look, and I know what it means: *we need to leave, now.*

"Later, Dom," I say as I turn, but his hand wraps around my forearm, holding me back.

"Where are you off to?" His words have more snap than a firecracker and he narrows his eyes.

"Olivia and I have plans." I jerk my arm out of his grip, and I give Olivia a little push, so she'll start walking.

He glares at me. "Of course you do. Have fun." The way he hurls the words, he may as well have said, "fuck you."

I'm on edge as we walk back through the woods. We've walked these paths a thousand times, but this time feels different. Though I don't hear any more steps behind us, I still feel like we're being watched. Like we're being followed. I hope Dominic doesn't stumble on whoever hurt that deer, whoever is still out there.

After we've made our way to the tree line, Olivia stops me. She looks back like she expected someone to follow us. Her skin is pale, a sheen of sweat clings to her brow, she won't look at me when she says, "I think you should stay away from Dominic."

"Why?"

"There's something off about him." Her voice drops. "I think there's something *wrong* with him." Her voice shakes, and she clears her throat while wringing her hands.

I shake my head. "No way. He can be weird sometimes but he's great, really. He's harmless, I promise. Okay?" Though I say the words, the way Dom acted—didn't act—it gnaws at me.

"Why do you always have to see the best in everyone, even when the evidence is right in front of your face?"

When I say nothing, she looks at her feet. I can see she's not satisfied. But she says, "Fine," anyway.

When it comes to Olivia, fine *never* means fine.

We walk back to my house, the light fading behind us. Tonight she's got to go home, we can't spend the rest of the evening together, like we usually do. She heads toward her house, and I head toward mine. Before I reach the door, someone runs up behind me. My heart jumps, I turn. She grabs onto me, giving me a quick hug. With her face against mine, I feel the warmth of her breath on my neck.

"Good night," she whispers as she nuzzles me. A kiss nearly as soft as her whisper grazes my cheek. It was barely a kiss, barely anything really. But it's the first one. To me it feels like mountains moved, the world shifted. As her footsteps lead her back to her house, I stand in shock.

Before I head inside, I take one last look toward the tree line. I swear, for just moment, I see a face and red hair watching us from the woods.

I wish I'd known in a week, Olivia would be dead, and I'd be a murderer.

2

After
March 16th, 1968

The tension in the room is as thick as blood. It makes sense though, when you think about it. After all, it's what covered me when they found me. Every part of me was sticky, heavy with death. My white knuckled hand gripping a bloody knife—at least that's what they tell me. In my mind, that night is a void. Since losing my memories of that night, something else in me has shifted. My mind is tainted by visions, memories that aren't my own.

Even though I know I'm losing it, I still didn't do it.

I couldn't have killed her or anyone else, could I?

It changes nothing, though. After all, they have *evidence*. Even if they didn't, they'd still find me guilty. Someone has to be guilty.

But there's no way I killed her.

Five voices ricochet around me like gunshots; I'm caught in the crossfire. While they shoot back and forth, negotiating my fate, my mouth is a thin line of nothingness. The parts of me that aren't numb from emotional exhaustion feel like they've been wrung out, beaten down. The insides of my mouth are chewed raw, and my mouth tastes like copper. I try to tune out their voices, to count the ticking clock on the wall, but it's impossible.

My mother, father, and lawyer sit on one side of the table, next to me. On the other side, the district attorney and assistant district attorney stare daggers at me. After each and every offer they make to my father, they glare at me, as though I should thank them for letting me live. My appearance here is a formality. A frustrating one at that. No matter what I might say, or not say, they'll make a decision for me.

I'd rather have the electric chair. When offered the option of rotting in prison, or living each day crushed beneath the questions—death would be a welcome escape. Living the rest of my life with this guilt, with all these questions, is not an option. Each second I'm awake, I feel like I'm one second closer to ending it myself.

"You can't send my baby to prison. I've already lost William to 'nam. I won't lose Asher too," my mother wails in hysterics. Her beehive is expertly plastered to her head, and though she's flailing her arms as she speaks, it doesn't move an inch. Her baby blue dress is perfectly pressed, the white collar stiff against her shoulders. There isn't a single thing about her life that's amiss—except me. It hurts to see her like this, her eyes puffy, nose running. I can't imagine what it must be like for her, the possibility of losing two children to situations she's unable to control. Thinking about it makes the weight of the guilt turn from cement in my stomach to lead.

Ever since my brother was drafted, my mother has spoken of him like he's dead—lit candles in the window, a flag at half-mast in our front yard, she even wears a black veil every week to church. She's a woman in mourning—but my brother isn't dead, and he isn't going to die. He writes her every week, though she doesn't tell us about it. I've seen the letters she has squirreled away in a box with his picture. I don't call her on it, how can I? One son in 'nam, the other in a cellblock. If this is how she copes, if this is how she holds herself together, I won't take it from her.

My father glares at her as he snuffs out his cigarette. Her eyes meet his for a brief moment. Cheeks flushing, she straightens her dress, the collar around her neck, and sits down. Her eyes fall to her folded hands in her lap. At least this time, he said it with his eyes, not with his hands. With my wrists shackled, I won't be able to intervene. If they send me away, I won't ever be able to protect my mother from him again.

"Please excuse my wife. I'm sure you understand how women get when it comes to their children." My father speaks slow, his drawl seeping into every word. He tugs on the sleeves of his beige suit, his plaid tie, and leans forward with his forearms on the table, hair so thick with pomade it shines like a highway in a summer storm. "Here's what I was thinking, he pleads guilty, but as a juvenile with no priors, you send him to the Dozier school until he ages out."

My stomach drops, and my face goes cold when he mentions Dozier. Some might say it's worse than a death sentence. Prison, death row, they would at least grant me a swift death—a fast escape. Everyone in Florida has heard the whispers about the school at some point. They've investigated the reports of abuse hundreds of times, but nothing ever comes of it.

Even behind his thick glasses, I can feel the rage in the beady little eyes of the assistant district attorney. My father's mention of Dozier must have been the last straw. The air is bitter with his hate. His face glows red, even the tips of his ears are tinged. He spits out a half-cough, half-laugh. "You think that's going to fly? He murdered an innocent girl." His eyes lock on me, face screwed up like he's smelled sour socks. "We should just take you out back right now."

"Go ahead, put me out of my fucking misery," I almost say. I think better of it and keep up the mute act. My lips press together, and I eye the glass of whiskey in front of my father.

I understand the A.D.A.'s frustration—to those who don't believe the stories, Dozier school would be a laughable punishment for murder. But from our end of the table, it's the only thing in this state with a reputation worse than mine. Dozier is a reform school in the sticks of the Florida panhandle. It's buried so far in the middle of nowhere, they don't even have fences around it. They don't need to. They know if you escape, chances are you'll get eaten by a gator. Even if you manage to avoid the jaws, there are a million other ways to die in the swamp. Besides, maybe no one bothers to escape because there's nothing to escape *to*.

Why couldn't they have left me in my cell for this meeting?

"Arthur, can you give us a minute?" the district attorney asks, but it's clear in his tone that it's a dismissal.

The A.D.A. huffs, slams his fits on the table, and storms out. I can still feel his anger, and smell his bad cologne lingering after he's gone.

My lawyer, the beetle of a man, perks up. Large eyes searching, thick moustache curling, he clears his throat. "Thank you, David, now we can get to business. I think we can come to an…" he pauses and swallows, "an agreement."

My father reaches into his suit pocket, pulls out a thick envelope and slides it across the table to the D.A. He takes it, thumbs through it for a moment and stuffs it into his suit. A smile creeps across his face for just long enough for me to notice, but it disappears into the shadows as he lifts his head.

"He will go to the Dozier school until he ages out. After that he will be free to go home, but on probation for three additional years. If he commits any crimes after his release, he will go to prison," the D.A. explains.

Fear coils inside me, though I try to swallow the dread, each time my heart beats, it flares up again. Every breath I take drags in another thread of panic, my eyes drop to the table as I shift. The metal cuffs bite into my wrists.

"We understand," my father confirms for our side of the table. He doesn't look at me, or my mother for approval. Instead he just says, "We agree."

"Great, I look forward to seeing you again, Judge Flemming," he says, extending his hand toward my father.

Today, I discovered if you're eighteen and the lead suspect in a murder case involving the girl you love, and your dad is a judge, you can avoid jail time. No one in this room cares she's dead, except me. Worse, no one cares if I killed her, except me. I should be happy my father was able to bail me out. He spared my record today. In the end, I know he's protecting his own image—he wants to run for governor.

Everyone stands, shaking hands, lighting cigarettes, clinking glasses, like this is some kind of fucking celebration. This is as close as I'll get to Olivia's funeral. My downcast eyes refuse to meet anyone else's. I don't even stand. Guilt weighs me down, and their looks will only make it worse. They'll think I should be happy, celebrate this. After all, in a few years we can forget I ever possibly murdered someone and move on like it never happened. *Joy.*

One day I might get out of Dozier, go work with my dad's race horses, and count the days without Olivia. When the days without her pile up in my mind, I twist my wrist against the handcuffs until the metal bites into my flesh. The only thing that dulls the agony of her absence is physical pain.

While my mother and father schmooze and booze, I sit at the table digging my thumb into the fake wood. The clock ticks down the seconds until I'm in a cell again, until I'm in Dozier. The thought of that place turns my blood cold. Stories have littered the news for years. Murders, beatings, disappearances, the place has a sinister past, it's enough to make the bile creep up the back of my throat.

It's even worse that my dad is responsible for sending me there. He paid off the D.A and *that's* the place he chose to send me. There's only one reason he'd send me there.

He doesn't want me to come back.

3

BEFORE
Date Unknown

I've been walking for three hours, that's my best guess anyway. The sky is black, there's not a single star, even the moon is gone. Behind me the gas streetlamps still flicker in the distance, but it's what's ahead that's important. Trees creep over the road, their ancient bowed branches form archways. The sharp drill of crickets rises with every step I take. As I walk deeper into the swamp, the crickets die and give way to the slow, rolling croaks of bull frogs.

My pockets are heavy. The liquid sloshes inside the vials I carry. Though I made up my mind to do this weeks ago, guilt is still heavy on my heart. I have to press on. I've already gathered the supplies, and I've set the date.

The water from the river laps at the sides of the dirt road. The wind carries the sweet, woody scent of a burning herb. *Sandalwood.* I thumb the hilt of the blade in my pocket, energy buzzes through the metal and tickles my skin. It's a risk being out here, without the decoys. *Just in case.*

When I break through the weeping, knobby trees, I see the shack at the edge of the swamp. Beside me I sense the heat of life radiating off the gators. But I don't stop, they don't even flicker fear inside me.

I knock twice on the slotted wooden door. Though I can feel her inside, it takes longer than I'd like for her to come to the door. Something rustles inside, and her dark eye pops into view through the gaps in the worn wooden boards. Her lips are pursed, and her brows drawn as she glowers at me. Clearly, she thought I'd back out, that I wouldn't come.

It takes her so long to push the door out, that a bad feeling brews inside me. When she finally lets me in, I dig in my pockets for her payment. I drop the rubies and gold coins on her table. Though I offer her a smile, she doesn't return it. Her aged face is creased into a perpetual frown.

"That's more than we agreed on," she says with a thick Cajun accent.

I shrug. "It's not like I can take them with me."

She eyes me and a hint of a smile crosses her dark lips. In her hands she's got a bowl of paste, she drops a handful of new herbs into the bowl and begins to stir. Her back turns on me as she sweeps across the room.

I take out the dagger and set it next to the coins. "I don't want that," she spits the words at me.

I slip the blade back into my pocket. I wasn't trying to offend her. But it'd make me feel better if I knew she'd be around the next time I need her. She'll have to warn her grandkids about me. There's pain in her eyes when she turns back to survey me. She thumbs something in her hand. Under her breath she mutters harsh words that are foreign to my ears. She thrusts a necklace in my direction.

"What's this?" I ask as I turn the green gem over in my hand.

"Put it on so I can bind the magic to the necklace."

"And what good will that do me?" I ask as I drop the necklace onto the table. I'll die soon, and it's not like I can take anything with me to the other side. She knows that. We've discussed my options at length, though it took ages to convince her that this ritual was necessary. But something has to change. I've tried this too many times.

She shakes her head and laughs. "It's one of those days, I tell ya." She rubs her chin as she scans the shelves in front of her. Each is packed with bottles, statues, and mystical objects I don't recognize. "Our only option is to bind it to your spirit."

"Will that work?"

She nods, and heads out the front door, the bowl of paste held firmly in her grasp. I follow her. The night is thick around us as she leads me into the woods. Her hand wraps tight around a slender candle, its light flickers in the wind. On a night this dark, we'd be lost without it. We reach a clearing in a few minutes. She sweeps away the underbrush revealing a circle with symbols inside etched into the ground.

She holds her arm out, "In the center, if-you-please."

I study the symbols etched into the ground before I step toward the circle. There isn't a single one I recognize. Though I trust her, my nerves are raw as I step toward the center. But I take a deep breath, sucking in the cool, autumn air. She walks toward me, a scoop of the paste on her finger. The breeze carries the scent as she approaches, a deep earthy smell. Carefully she draws a finger down my forehead leaving a line of paste there.

"This might," she pauses for a second to laugh at me, "hurt a little."

She stands in front of me, her eyes meet mine. Her palms stretch out in front of her, and she snaps her arms out to her sides. The moment her hands meet with the circle, the air around me shifts. A tingling feeling works its way from the soles of my feet. It pushes upward, through my veins, my bones, until it feels like there's static caught beneath my skin. Around me, the air twists like waves of heat on a hot summer day.

Her word rise, but they're lost on me. She chants as her hands connect with the circle. The symbols carved into her palms glow. All at once, it feel as though something is being pulled away from my body. The separation is agony, as though the bones are being ripped from my body one by one. A glowing shapeless ball forms in front of me. Light flows from the edges of the circle into the ball. It grows brighter, it twists, and then slams into me with a force that knocks me off my feet.

When I look up, she stands above me with her arm extended. She helps me up.

"Thank you," I whisper.

With the ritual still humming beneath my flesh, I walk back toward the city. It was a risk to leave in the middle of the night. If I want to break the cycle, this time I have to do something different.

4

AFTER

The bang of a nightstick on cell bars wakes me from my nightmare, my heart bursts to life. I swear something still lingers beneath my skin, something warm, something foreign. Rhythmic clangs echo through the cellblock as the guard hits the baton on each and every bar. My breaths are uneven as the dream claws at my mind.

It was a dream. That couldn't be real. It couldn't.

Since Olivia's death I've had strange dreams, visions I can't place. But I keep them to myself. It adds more evidence to the *Asher's off his rocker* pile

I realize the banging is from the guard, I breathe deep, and try to crush the fear prickling the back of my mind. My gaze moves to the window. It's so early, darkness envelopes the world outside, stars flicker against the black sky. The guard stands a few feet from the bars, eyeing me, like he expects me to say something. I prop myself up on my elbow; the metal frame beneath the thin mattress bites at the bones in my arm. My body is stiff, muscles tethered by sleep.

"What?" I ask, trying to stretch my night-cramped muscles. My joints pop and crack, and the slightest bit of relief rushes through me.

He can't be here to move me already, can he?

He slides a pack of cigarettes through the bars, just enough for me to see them. Though it feels like a trap, I force myself from the bed, and take them. After all, who knows the next time I'll get another one. When I flip the top open, a lighter waits for me inside. My eyes linger on it for a moment, considering. The lighter is too small though, and surrounded by cement walls and metal bars, I can't do much damage with fire here. In one fluid motion I strike the flame, inhale, slide it back into the pack. He eyes me as I set the pack on the bars.

"Thanks." Smoke trails on my words.

"Thank your father." A hint of a smile lingers on his face, his words are laced with venom. He's toying with me.

My father, of course. It'd make sense even here he'd have favors to collect on. He seems to have them everywhere. It seems strange and unlikely he'd waste a favor on me. I sit back on the edge of the mattress, just barely enough to hold myself up. My elbows rest on my knees as I savor the cig, it's the first I've had since I've been in holding.

He motions at me, his gaze rests on my hair, "They're probably going to shave your head, when you get to wherever they sends you." His jaw juts out as he laughs at me, there's a nasal quality to it that puts me on edge.

I shrug. Keeping my hair long doesn't matter anymore, it's this way because that's how Olivia liked it. The "bad boy" look, she called it. Long hair, a leather jacket, faded Chuck Taylor's with yellowing rubber, and whatever band t-shirt I'm able to find—it's the uniform Olivia loved. All those things are now piled high in a closet I'll never see again. They should have buried them with her.

"Why'd you do it?" the guard asks, he looks at me out of the corner of his eye, like he's trying to hide the curiosity on his face.

Ah, there it is. The question he's wanted to ask. I could see the question on his face each time he came in, but now it's his last chance. He must have heard they'll be shipping me off soon. This is the moment when anger used to flare up inside me, I was never sure where it came from. It doesn't do anything more than nag at me now, nothing more than frustration digging under my skin.

"I didn't." I'm not sure how many more times I'll say it. Each time I say it, I'm less sure it's the truth. Each day that passes I grow more and more bitter that my memory hasn't returned. There's nothing worse than being betrayed by your own mind.

"That's what they all say. If you're innocent, why did they find you holding the knife? Why'd they find her blood all over you?" He crosses his arms and leans against the wall. Fucking know-it-all.

I shrug. There's no point in getting angry or arguing. Instead I savor the cig. Each one lets me breathe in the memories of her. And hopefully gets me one breath closer to seeing her again.

"Don't know, don't care." The lie slips out easily. And I'm amazed how convincing it sounds, even to me.

I do care. Every part of me aches to know what happened that night, to know what I did or didn't do. Burying myself beneath lies has become an easy defense mechanism. I figure one day, if I tell the lies enough, eventually they'll become true.

An uncomfortable laugh pours out of him, the kind born deep down. He turns, and walks away, spinning his night stick. I sigh with relief as his beige uniform disappears. There's a certain kind of relief that comes when someone gives up on you.

~

The same guard leads me to a room, it looks like it's normally used for interrogations. Solid concrete walls, small metal table, and a barred window the size of a shoebox. The only difference between this and a normal interrogation room is the cart standing beside the table. Several stacked glasses and an ice bucket sit in the center. If I didn't hear my mother's sobs outside in the hall and feel the eyes of the guard behind me, I'd spend longer considering the damage I could do with the glass.

My mother's sniffles echo inside the room, they slip easily through the thick, metal door before she comes in. It's hard to even look at her. Her eyes are pink, rubbed raw. Bright red skin puckers around her nose and above her lips. The way she looks at me, it's like she thinks I'm going to kill her, too, or maybe she thinks she's never going to see me again. The weight of her gaze makes me slump against the chair. She cowers from me, clutching her purse in her lap. Her beehive is disheveled, stray hairs flying off in every direction. Maybe she slept on it and didn't bother to check the mirror before she left.

My dad doesn't look at me, or in my direction. He walks across the room to the cart. After all, it must be here for his benefit. Ice cubes clink loudly as he drops each one in. An amber liquid streams from a flask he removes from his blazer pocket. He sits down like he hasn't a care in the world, especially me. I'm not sure he realizes I'm here.

Mom tries to smooth her hair. It doesn't work. She doesn't look at me when she says, "I can't believe they're sending you to that...place." She blots her eyes with a soggy tissue; it's limp, lifeless in her hand.

Did she already forget he's sending me there?

I know she won't take the issue up with him. He's infallible. In her mind, this will never be his fault. It's probably better if she doesn't bring it up, I won't be at home to intervene on her behalf anymore.

"It's going to be fine, Mom." Though I try to reassure her, I'm not sure myself. I'm so uneasy, unsure, I'm surprised my voice is even. I press my handcuffed arms down on my legs to keep them from bouncing.

"They're just stories, Barb," my dad finally says, giving the slightest wave of dismissal. "They've done investigations for years. He's better off there than prison. He can go to class, work. They've even got team sports. In winter they set up those nice Christmas displays folks can drive through."

The way he talks about it, like he thinks it's summer camp. A surge of fire flickers through me. I cut him off and glower at him. "So outside of the guns and torture, it's just like a regular high school?" Sarcasm and anger are thick on every single word, I spit them at him.

"Exactly," he says as he shrugs and takes a drink. I clench my teeth. I hate when he acts like we're on the same team.

"I can't believe my little boy is a murderer. Asher, you've got to be good. I don't know if my heart can take you going to prison." The tears pour from her eyes. Black rivers form on her cheeks.

"I'm *not* a murderer." I slam my hand on the table. My palm stings, and regret hits me before I even close my mouth. My heart sinks, I don't want to yell at my mother. More, I don't want her to believe I'm a monster. Her eyes go wide, and she looks at me like she doesn't even know me. It's a knife to the gut.

After the slightest jump, she faces the door. I hear her whimper, and I know she's started crying again. Her purse has fallen to the floor, but she won't pick it up. Instead, she sobs quietly, body shaking with emotion.

I breathe in slowly. "Mom, look at me." My voice is forceful, but calm.

Her watery eyes peer at me through her lashes. She's still not quite looking at me. It's the look of a scolded child.

"I did not kill Olivia. I swear to you. You know me, you know I loved her." I stop and correct myself. "I *love* her, more than anyone, anything. I'd die a thousand times if it'd bring her back." My love for her didn't stop because she died. It's still as real as if she stood here beside me.

"I want to believe you," she says, her lips quiver, and she blots her eyes.

She wants to, but she doesn't. The words sting and I look away.

"Believe me, then, you know me. I couldn't even kill quail, deer, hogs. Every time he took me hunting. How could I kill *her*?" My dad took me on so many failed hunting trips I can't even keep count. No matter how trivial he thought the animals were that he put in front of me, I couldn't kill them. There's no way I could make that leap to a person, especially not her. There isn't a violent bone in my body.

If I were a murderer, wouldn't I know?

She shakes her head. After a long moment she asks, "So, what happened, then?"

I shift, and lean against the table. "I told you, I don't remember. I don't know." The words come out a growl through my gritted teeth. I've said the words 'I don't remember' more in the past few months than I ever thought possible. Anger rises again, hot and thick, it burns my throat, and blots out my thoughts. I don't want to be in the same room with her. If she stays, I'll just end up yelling.

"Mom, Dad, I love you, but can you please send Eden in? I really need to talk to her."

A tight-lipped little nod from my mother follows. Neither of them say they love me back. I swallow the pain. They don't even say goodbye. But I hear my mother's sobs when the door closes. My stomach knots. *What if I never see her again?* I might have ruined my only chance to convince her I'm not a killer.

Eden flashes me a half smile when she comes in. Her long black hair covers most of her face and falls onto her shoulders. For a moment, she peeks at me through her hair, and I see her face is deathly pale, red halos hang around her brown eyes, too. I shake it off. She can't have been crying, Eden *never* cries. A golden necklace with several planets and a star hangs loose from her throat. It's a trinket I stole for her form the Kennedy Space Center when we were thirteen. She distracted Mom and Dad while I pocketed it. As far as I know, she hasn't taken it off once. Eden says she's going to be the first woman on the moon. Funny how it turned out for us, she wants to leave the planet, all I want is to get the hell out of Florida.

For a moment, she makes me forget everything else. There's never been even a flicker of fear in her eyes when she looks at me. I shouldn't be surprised. She's always been on my side—no matter what. Guess that's what happens when you share a womb.

She rests her arms on the table and looks at me for a moment. When her head falls and rests on her arms, it feels like my heart is breaking. Being apart from her all this time, it makes the situation so much worse. I reach out and take her hand. She looks at me again, her eyes flooded with tears. She chews her lip, and the tip of her nose turns red.

"I hate this," she says as she sniffles. Her honesty startles me. Eden has a habit of acting tough in front of everyone. I always see right through it, but seeing her like this, so broken, it kills me.

I nod. "I can't say it's my favorite thing."

"Not even in your top ten?"

I almost grin at that. "How's life on the outside?"

She shrugs. "Weird. Mom barely leaves her room. Dad barely leaves work. Things are so quiet at the house, it feels like we live in a graveyard."

I look down as frustration prickles inside me. I don't like that I'm stuck in here while she's going through this. But I push past it, there's something more pressing.

"I need your help," I plead. I've never been one to plead with Eden, it feels strange. Spending eighteen years with someone will teach you when you need to jump directly to pleading. This is one of those times.

"What?" She asks, her eyebrows pull together. And I know she's taken off guard by the request.

I look down at my handcuffed hands. The weight of the situation, the guilt, overwhelms me, and my words sink to the bottom of my mind. I hate to ask her for help. This can't have been easy on her. She lost someone, too. And here I am, wanting favors, needing her help. I swallow the guilt when desperation wins out. This isn't something I can do myself, and there's no one else I can ask. "I need you to keep looking. We have to find out who really did this."

"I've *been* looking. I haven't found anything." She looks down, but it's not sadness on her face. It's frustration. She likes to puzzle her way through things. It kills her when she can't solve a mystery.

While I was in the hospital, she gathered articles from the newspaper, and tried to figure out what possibly could have happened that night. We haven't found a single clue, not so much as a rumor someone else might have done it—someone who isn't me. There are only two things left—the mansion and the police report. No part of me wants her to go to the mansion, especially not alone.

"Can you try to get the police report? There might be something in there." I know it's a stretch, it's asking too much. But we have to try. There has to be something.

"I'll try, but I don't know if it's possible. Thanks to everything that's happened, we're now the most well-known family in Ocala. And it doesn't help that Olivia's dad works at the police station. He'll kick me out the second I come through the doors." The way she sits back in the chair and crosses her legs, I can tell she's debating the challenge. She *wants* the challenge.

Maybe it's a stupid idea. I don't want her getting in trouble for me. Who knows what they'd do to her if they find her snooping around a police station.

"Look, one of the guys at school, his dad works at the station, too. I'll talk to him, see what I can do," she offers.

"Thank you," I say, as I sit back in the chair, and she glances toward the window. "How's school?"

Her eyebrow perks up as she looks at me in disbelief. "You didn't even care about school enough to go. Why do you care now?"

I shrug. Really, it's just a distraction. Something to fill the time before they drag me away to Dozier. I'd rather think about anything else.

"Did Mom say something to you?" she asks as her eyes flash toward the door.

I shift in my seat and lean forward. "No. What's going on?"

She laces her fingers together and avoids looking at me.

"What's going on, Eden?"

She shrugs and chews on her lip. "Nothing." She clears her throat, and turns slightly toward the door. "I've just missed a few classes is all."

"You never miss class, ever. You gave me a twenty-minute lecture when I got a D in gym because I never went," I remind her, as I shake my head.

"It's not a big deal." She leans back and crosses her arms.

"It wouldn't be a big deal if it was me. If you're not going to class, there's obviously something going on. How has Dad not grounded you for life?"

She looks away again. "Mom is covering for me."

"Ah, the new favorite," I joke.

"Yeah, it only took being the last kid left in the house," she says with a half-smile.

"Right. So...why are you skipping?" I ask.

"It doesn't matter."

I lean across the table, and hold my hands out toward her. "It does matter."

For a long moment, she doesn't take my hands. She just look at them. Her hesitation isn't lost on me.

"I don't want you to worry."

"Too late," I say as I tap the table.

She finally gives me one of her hands. Her fingers are ice cold. "Dominic has been following me. Well, I think he has," she shakes her head. "I might be crazy, imagining it. But he wouldn't stop following me to class. Then, I swear, I saw him standing in the tree line outside the house." She shudders.

"Why would he do that?" I ask, careful of my tone. I don't want Eden to think that I don't believe her. Eden's always hated Dominic, but I can't let that fact overshadow what she's telling me. Every other time she's complained about Dom, I've shrugged it off. But this time, something feels different.

"I don't know, I don't want to talk about it." She looks away.

"Amma is back," she says to change the subject. My guts twist. A wave of homesickness crashes into me. She was the best part of being home. Amma is our housekeeper, and she was our nanny when we were younger. I miss her fiercely. "She wanted me to tell you that she doesn't think that you did this, not for a second. She knows you couldn't kill Olivia." She continues, and my eyes burn with tears. I blink them, and look at the wall for a minute, breathing through my nose to calm myself.

"Are you holding up okay?" I ask, hoping that changing the subject will dry up the tears in my eyes. I don't ask her if she's okay often enough, it's hard to remember sometimes that she lost Olivia, too. It's even harder to remember that her whole life has changed.

"I'll survive." She rolls her eyes at me. But I see the sadness there, no matter how she tries to hide it. I know she's just putting on a brave face to be strong. I wish I could be more like her—stronger.

There's one thing I know that she's going to have to do to survive. "Eden, now that I won't be there anymore, you can't protect Mom."

Eden's eyes go wide for just long enough for me to notice, she presses her lips together into a thin line. I know what she's thinking when she won't look at me. She's going to take her place in the food chain. She's going to take my place in the beatings.

"Eden," I say, my voice firmer, nearly scolding her. "You can't intervene. Dad could do a lot of damage. He could kill you."

I don't want my mother to get hurt. But I'm not willing to sacrifice Eden for her. My mom chose Dad, she'll choose him every time over the two of us.

"Fine," she relents. But she still won't look at me. I know she's lying.

There's no use in arguing with her. I don't have time anyway, a guard bangs against the metal door. She pulls herself from the seat and gives me a hard hug. I press my eyes closed as she squeezes me. Eden *never* hugs me anymore. I savor it, it may be the last one I'll get. I pat her shoulder with my shackled hands. When she leaves the room, my head swims like all the air rushed out of the room at once. Part of me left with her.

5

AFTER

I'm awake before they come for me. My tired eyes burn. I try to blink, but it feels like I'm dragging sandpaper across my eyeballs. Last night, though I lay on the thin mattress waiting for sleep to come, I watched the sun sink below the horizon, then the moon rise. Every time my eyes began to droop, my heart would skip into a gallop, and my thoughts would swarm. I replayed my conversations with my Mother and Eden so many times I have them memorized. After that, I tried to run through any scenario I could think of for when I get to Dozier. But I kept coming up with blanks. I don't know what to expect.

"You ready?" A short guard, with buzzed brown hair asks from the cell door.

I'm not. It doesn't matter, though.

The old rusted springs creak when I shift on the mattress, I slide from the bed. I won't miss this place. After I sit up, I have to force myself to breathe. Anxiety has wound itself so tightly around my chest, I feel like I'm bound with ropes.

I've been the only inmate on this cell block the whole month and a half I've been here. You'd think I'd have a better rapport with the guards, but I still don't know any of their names. I'm shitty when it comes to people.

"Cheer up," the guard says to me. "It won't be so bad."

I feel like the words haunt me and dig at me. As though he threw knives at me. *What does this guard know about bad?* Things will never be *good* again. No matter what happens. Olivia's still gone, I'm still here. She should have lived, I should have died. No matter what else happens, there will always be a void in the world where she should be.

We weave through what seems like miles of identical looking cinderblock-lined hallways, they file me out the back door and onto an empty bus with "Florida Department of Offender Rehabilitation" painted on the side. It's obviously an old school bus, converted for their needs. Painted white, bars added to the windows.

The soft leather of the seats reminds me of school, home. But I distract myself, and stare out the windows, before I allow it to remind me of her. There's one good thing about being shipped off to a reform school, I won't have to go home where everything will remind me of Olivia. If I had to live with that, I'd off myself in a month.

As the old diesel engine roars to life, one of the guards takes a seat in front of me. He's surprisingly young for a guard at a jail. So young in fact, I'm not sure he's out of high school. His face is smooth, there's not even a hint he's ever had to shave. I've noticed a common theme amongst the guards, all of them have their hair shaved nearly down to their skulls.

I try to swallow the unease digging at the back of my mind. Not knowing exactly what's waiting for me at Dozier is setting me on edge. I press my elbows into my knees, leaning on them, to keep my legs from bouncing. When I can't distract myself, I decide to talk to the guard.

"I'm kind of flattered," I say to him, making small talk.

"Oh?" He's not quite interested.

"This whole bus, for little ol' me."

"Don't worry, it's not star treatment. Maybe if you'd gone a little more cannibal on the girl. Dozier is getting a fresh shipment of *several* bodies today." He smiles at me, and I notice he's missing several teeth. The few he has don't look in good shape. "You're going in with a few other newbies, lucky really, all the heat won't be on you."

I look out the window and chew on my thumbnail. I've never been to a new school. I've never even moved. I went to a high school so small, I'd grown up with every single student since kindergarten. The guards may not be the only ones who are dangerous at Dozier, the kids might be just as bad, or worse.

"Not sure it will do you much good." He eyes me. "Long pretty hair like that." His tongue flits across his remaining teeth, and he reaches out, like he's going to touch me. I recoil. "They're gonna eat you up." He drags out the words like he's telling me a ghost story.

I hope it's all talk to scare me. But I can't shake the feeling that he's being honest.

A nervous laugh slips through my tightened jaw. The bus jolts forward, I stiffen, and the guard's attention moves to the front as we drive. First, we travel west, picking up three other inmates. After, we course north-west, picking up two others in Gainesville. Every mile we rumble along, anticipation is thick in my blood. Thoughts clot in my mind each one tainted with anxiety, and all I can do is try to distract myself with miles upon miles of swamp land.

After one of our stops, I look up when someone sits across the aisle from me. His black hair is only a few inches shorter than mine. Dark eyes glisten as they inspect me. His skin is a deep warm shade of brown. He has a wide build, but he's skinny, like he doesn't get enough to eat. Stubble clings to his hollow cheeks, and forms a neat square around his wide mouth. His arms are muscular, but the rest of him is straight lines and sharp bones. I nod my head at him, he nods back.

"Sayid," he says introducing himself, glancing at me for just a moment.

"Asher."

This is the part where we'd shake hands if we weren't handcuffed. He raises an eyebrow as he inspects me. The incredulous look leads me to believe he doesn't think I should be here. I see him start to speak a few times, my guess, he's trying to pin down what exactly I did.

"What'd you do? Steal a motorcycle?" he asks. The way he clamps his lips shut, and his cheeks brighten after he asks, I think he's trying not to laugh.

If only.

"Murder." The word slips from my lips too easily. I've gotten too accustomed to saying it, it doesn't burn my throat and bring me to tears anymore. This time, only a few knots form in my stomach, and after a deep breath they come loose.

The way his eyes go wide, and his mouth hangs slack, I regret saying it. Maybe I should come up with a lie. I can't spend the next five years of Dozier with people looking at me like *that*.

"You?" I ask, though by the look on his face, I'm not sure he'll ever talk to me again. I don't blame him. Would I react any differently if I was in his situation? *Not likely.*

"Running away. Third time I'll be back at Dozier." He settles into his seat. I notice he's moved a few inches away from me. His bound hands are pressed against the back of the seat in front of him, like he's ready to use it to run from me.

"To punish you for running away, they send you away?"

"Fucking stupid, ain't it?" He laughs, and if I didn't know better, I'd say he's happy about his return to Dozier. His apprehension seems to float away on his laughter.

I nod. The stories I've heard rush into my mind. He's experienced, he'd know. "How bad is it really?"

"Eh, depends whose bad side you get on. Any of the guards hate you, you're gonna wish you were dead." He squints, like if he looks at me close enough, he might be able to tell what I'm really in for. "You really killed someone? How long did they give you for that?"

"Just because they sent me here doesn't mean I'm guilty," I clarify, maybe, just maybe, I can convince him I didn't do it. "They gave me five years."

His eyes bug, and his mouth drops open. With his mouth this wide, I can see he's missing a couple teeth in the back. "Five years? Longest stretch I've ever heard of was three. You're going to be there 'til the cutoff?"

"The cutoff?"

"Once you're twenty-two, that's the cutoff. Then it's either prison or the real world," Sayid explains.

Something tells me I won't be there for five years. Though I'm not sure what my future holds, I can't see Dozier being a part of it. I'm not sure I'll even make it another year if I don't figure out what happened with Olivia.

"How long you got?" I ask trying to fill the silence. I'm not sure if he's as uncomfortable as I am, if he is, he doesn't show it.

"A year," Sayid says. "I'll get out when I'm nineteen."

"That's not bad."

How many more times after that will he be back?

He scoots closer to me, on the edge of his seat. Dark hair covers the left half of his face. But I can still see his dark brown eyes are wide, hungry. "Who'd you kill?"

As much as I don't want to talk about it, I know how curiosity works. The more I avoid it, the more he'll want to know. Then stories will start to circulate, things far worse than the truth. And that's how I'll end up with 400 people asking me questions instead of just one. That's the way the lies spiraled out of control at my old school. That's how I went from the bad kid who skipped class, to the bad kid who supposedly robbed liquor stores while I was supposed to be in biology. I might have rarely gone to biology, but I never robbed a goddamn liquor store, or any store for that matter.

"My best friend." The words sting, not only because I may have killed my best friend, but because she was never more than that. It feels wrong even calling her my best friend. There's no way those words will ever convey how close we were.

He leans back against the seat, not looking at me.

Is this how it's going to be? Am I at the top of the criminal food chain now?

It will be a lonely five years if everyone avoids me, fearing they'll end up my next victim. Then again, maybe that's safer. Maybe, it's for the best if I'm on my own. It's not safe for anyone to be around me.

Finally he asks, "How'd you get into Dozier with that on your record? Hearing about a murderer there, it's rare. I mean, some people become murderers *while* they're at Dozier. Hardly anyone ever comes there that way, though. And if they do, they're locked away with the crazies. By the looks of it, since you get to ride in on the bus, you're not one of the crazies."

"My dad's a judge." I'm not sure if it's the money or his judgeship that got me into Dozier, or a combination of the two, at the end of the day, I don't really care. But I do know if it hadn't been for my father,

I'd be on my way to prison.

The light inside the bus dims, I look out the window. Outside, the trees huddle around the road. Spanish moss waves, and hangs low from the branches. The trunks grow so close together, it starts to stamp out the sun. At the edges of the road, light gleams on the water. Swamp creeps onto the road, green water laps at the pavement. I watch the trees pass, and for a moment I swear I catch a glimpse of something red slipping between the trees.

"We're getting close," he says looking out the window. "The sign is coming up here soon."

The bus starts to slow, a large brick sign says, "Arthur G. Dozier School for Boys," in white letters.

We follow a long winding road. The trees crowding around the road seem to weep. A groaning gurgle comes from the bus engine as we lurch to a stop. The driver leans out the window, making small talk with someone at a guard station. I try to tune in to hear what they're saying, but it's impossible over the rattling and sputtering. Finally, the gate lifts and we roll forward again.

My eyes are glued to the window. What the hell is this school doing smack dab in the middle of nothing? It's sandwiched between Alabama and the gulf. We're so far into the sticks of the Florida panhandle, I'm sure no one bothers to try to escape.

"If someone tried to escape, where would they go?"

Sayid lets out a little laugh. "Marianna, somewhere else in Florida. It takes time, but it's not impossible. I've done it."

The trees scatter, the forest opens to large expanses. We pass cornfields, barns, grazing cattle, and come up on what looks like a small town. Above everything, a large white water tower looms. In its shadow colonial houses stand. We pass several modern buildings, a playground, a football field, a pool. I make out words like dormitory and dining hall. And take notice of a small white building at the center of it all.

"What's that?" I ask Sayid when I see it, there's no sign.

He fidgets and chews on his lip before he says, "The white house."

His words leave me even more confused. I start to ask, but he continues.

His voice drops, I can barely hear him over the engine. "That's where they take you if you break the rules." All the life seems to drain out of his face, and his body stiffens. "Beatings, torture, those are the best things that happen there. You don't want to end up there."

Then I see the white crosses growing from the stretch of greenery beside the white house. There has to be fifty of them. Some are newer, bright white, standing straight up. The older crosses, the ones in the back, they're yellowed, and falling over. Dozier has its own graveyard.

He motions toward it, tapping his finger on the window. "That right there's the worst. Don't break the rules, or be careful if you do. This isn't like school where you break the rules and get detention. The guards lose control sometimes, kids die. Kids just like us die. If you see Melvin, you go the other direction. Stay away from him. He's as bad as it gets." His eyes are wide when he looks back at me. "Unless you're one of the privileged few, you've got to be careful. If you get on the wrong guard's bad side, you could end up in there for practically nothing."

A lump forms in my throat, I try to swallow it. My veins run cold, and goose bumps prickle my neck. "Privileged few?"

"The kids who can buy their way out of the white house."

"Then how'd they end up here in the first place?" I ask. Seems if your family can buy you out of the white house, they should be able to buy you a one-way ticket to somewhere more accommodating.

"High profile cases, those kids have to go somewhere. At least for a little while. Believe me, their life at Dozier is nothing compared to ours."

I swallow hard, and look back at the white house. "Why would you do anything that might get you sent back here again, then?" I ask. If it's so bad, if there's a risk that great, why would anyone come back? If I ever get out of this place, I'm sure as hell never coming back.

He shrugs. "I'm good at making bad choices. That's what everyone says, anyway. Here though, I don't do anything to get me put in *there*." He pauses for a moment, then adds. "Well, I don't get caught." A sly smile creeps across his face.

My mouth goes dry when I ask, "Ever been in there?"

He shakes his head. "But one of my old roommates in the dorm, he got welts so bad he couldn't sit for days. Didn't learn his lesson. The next time they beat him so badly he had internal bleeding. He was in the Dozier hospital for months."

"Dozier has its own hospital?"

"Of course. If they didn't, they wouldn't be able to hide all the shit they pull." He looks at the cemetery. "There's no way that's all the bodies. There's probably bones under every inch of this place. The gravel on the roads, the pebbles in the flower beds, bet those are ground up kids too. Sometimes, I wonder if they're in the food."

A creeping feeling slithers up my spine. My palms are slick with sweat, I wipe them on my pants. I won't let it show how much it scares me. After all, they may just be stories to frighten the new kid. At least, I can hope. After all, they've done countless investigations.

Otherwise they would have shut this place down, wouldn't they?

"How does no one notice so many people going missing?" I ask.

Sayid shrugs. "There are no walls around this place. It could be as simple as saying they ran away. Mark my words, one day people will realize what really went on here. One day they'll find all the kids who disappeared."

The bus stops. When the engine dies I realize how numb my ass is from the vibrations. My ears still hum, waiting for the sound to return. Several guards come onto the bus. It looks like we'll each get our own guard. *Joy.*

Students line up outside, their hungry eyes watch as we file off the bus. Several kids wave hello to Sayid as we pass. We're ushered into a modern building, if this had been anywhere else, this building would be a welcome center. Here, though, it's an administrative building. Inside there are several threadbare cells, along the left hand side. Along the right side, desks are scattered without rhyme or reason. Each has its own personality. Ugly knickknacks, family pictures, and greeting cards cover each one.

We're led into a back room, one at a time. After two boys come out uneasy, white as a Camarillo Stallion, I know what's coming. Though thanks to county lockup I've now had to strip, crouch, and cough in front of more people than I'd like to admit. It feels stupid now only six months ago, I hoped the first person to see me naked would be Olivia.

"Asher," a gruff guard with a few remaining tufts of gray hair, calls from a clipboard. He laughs and murmurs, "Pretty boy" as I walk past. Then he looks closer at the paperwork. It's obvious when he reads what I'm in for. He stiffens, statue-still as he observes me. His eyes narrow, he looks at me like I'm about to kill him, I'm a bomb with less than an inch of fuse left. If I were in his position, I'm not sure I'd act much differently.

The guard waves me into the back room, he looks relieved to be rid of me. Inside I find two more guards. It's like an ant colony. They exchange a look, sharing a private joke. One guard is short with a face that reminds me of a bird. Pointed nose, beady black eyes, line of a mouth pokes out like a beak. The other man looks more like a lion. Flat nose, long sandy blonde hair, a long beard that seems to grow from his neck. He removes my handcuffs, and I rub my wrists.

"Strip," the bird guard squawks at me. His eyes are hungry like this is his favorite part of the day.

I pull my shirt off, followed by my county issued sweat pants; the cord sewn in so I can't hang myself with it, not that I checked. The socks are so small I have to peel them off. Then I slide off my underwear. No shame, no embarrassment. These guys get paid to look at dicks all day long, and I feel sorry for them.

"Move your legs apart, crouch, and cough three times," the lion guard growls.

I follow his instructions. It's sad I've gotten so good at naked crouching. My balance is perfect. Six months ago, I'd have fallen over.

"Good, stand, turn around, and do it again," the bird guard titters.

I do as I'm bid. The guard says *good* again, like I've earned a gold star. They allow me to put my clothes back on, after they've thoroughly checked them. I face them, waiting to be dismissed, waiting for something.

I join the other inmates. When Sayid is done with his strip search, I'm happy to see he seems as unfazed by the ordeal as I am. I'm even happier they don't shave my head. It'd be a dead giveaway how new I am. Though I want to ask him what happens next, since everyone else is as silent as a vigil, I do the same. Anything to keep myself out of trouble, out of the white house.

Once they've verified none of us have brought in any contraband, we walk along one of the streets to the auditorium. I'm surprised by the size, large enough to hold at least three hundred people. The walls are stark white plaster. An ancient black curtain hangs at the back, flanked by the American flag on one side, and the Florida state flag on the other. There's a podium in the center of the stage.

I take my seat next to Sayid. We've already broken off into little groups. Sayid and I. Three kids, barely thirteen. And a lone kid with long black hair, staring daggers at everyone.

Sayid takes over the arm rest, and I fold my hands in my lap. I look over and catch him staring at me. For a moment, I appraise him, trying to discern the intent hidden behind his deep brown eyes. But he looks away too quickly. I swallow hard, and fix my eyes straight ahead. I sink into the seat and fold my hands in my lap.

Once we're seated on the uncomfortable dusty seats, the clicks of fine dress shoes on the tile floor draws my attention. An older man in his fifties, with a square jaw and a prominent brow strolls to the podium.

There is a lightness in his step, like he's unburdened by anything in the world around him. Even the rules of gravity don't seem to apply to him. He looks down at all of us through thin rim glasses. I notice how much longer he focuses on me, not speaking. Just staring at me, through me. His message comes across clear as a bell, he's watching me. Maybe, they're all watching me.

When I shift uncomfortably, he finally looks away. "Hello, Gentlemen." His southern drawl manages something I'd never heard before. It makes him sound refined. And somewhat terrifying. A mix of bouji and New Orleans. I'm not sure if it is his tailored suit, his pocket square, or how every hair on his head is in exactly the place it should be. Someone this perfect must have something to hide. He's probably got more secrets than the swamp.

"Welcome." He doesn't quite mean it. Finally his eyes move away from me. "Your sentences may vary in length, some of you may only see us once." He eyes linger on Sayid. "Some of you, we may see again. The same is expected of all of you, exemplary performance while you are here. As a student. As a worker. And anything else you may undertake while you are here. There are also important rules you must understand and follow. I'll go over them today, but don't worry, they are posted throughout the campus:

1) Violence will not be tolerated.

2) No sex or sex play.

3) No illicit substances.

4) No sneaking out.

5) No swearing.

6) No smoking.

7) No skipping class.

8) No skipping work detail.

9) Lights out at 10pm."

He drones on for what seems like hours, talking about rules, punishments. I can't focus, his voice is too monotone. I look ahead, like I would in class. Pretending. Finally, he finishes and signals for us to stand. The guards lead us out, and we make our way across the campus. We pass a few buildings that look like they're decaying, others that look brand new, perfectly cut lawns, and boys playing basketball. Finally, we come to a stop.

"These are the cottages, Washington." He points to a large colonial house a few minutes' walk from us. "This is Madison. Sayid, Asher, come with me."

When he says my name, my stomach jumps. It takes a few moments to realize I haven't done anything wrong. There's a strange comfort from Sayid being at my side, like the warmth of an old familiar blanket. I've never been comfortable with strangers, the only people I've spent much time around are people I've known my whole life. There's only been one exception to that: Dominic. We follow our guard, the four remaining kids follow the other guards.

"You'll both be bunking here," he explains. "We're low on residents at the moment, so you two will have a room all to yourselves." He laughs at a joke we aren't privy to. "That is, until one of the other kids tries to shank you for your bed."

It takes a lot of effort to keep my face stoic, while the fear drags its cold fingers along my spine. But I manage. I have to be strong.

The guard leads us up the ancient steps, across a groaning porch, and into a foyer. Ahead of us, a steep narrow staircase disappears into the darkness. To the right is a room filled with couches. Every inch of wall space is taken up by them. Only one small bit of the room escapes the couch occupation, here the smallest TV I've ever seen sits. Ugly green wallpaper with a flower pattern coats the walls.

To the left there's another room scattered with floral seating options. Everything here is dirty and worn, as beaten as the boys in the white house. They've been sat in so many times there's holes straight down to the fiber. Streams of light pour in the moth-eaten curtains. At the back of the house, there's a pool table, foosball table, and a shell of a kitchen. Well, a kitchen minus all the appliances. Really, it looks like it's just for water.

The guard leads us up the stairs, and I realize he's been talking the entire time. But I haven't heard any of it. Upstairs there are five rooms and a small bathroom with just a toilet across from the stairs. Each of the rooms holds rows of bunk beds, and sparse furniture. Every room looks well lived in, clothes strewn across beds, posters taped behind bunks.

When I walk into our room the fear from the guard's words dissolves. There isn't much chance of anyone coming after us for these beds, or this room. It's unused, untouched, stale. Our room holds three barren sets of metal bunk beds. One on the left, one on the right, and one smack dab in the middle of a window, a dresser at the end of each. This room isn't quite as worn as the living room. It smells vaguely of dust, a thin film coats everything. The curtains are a patchwork of what looks like old dress shirts. There's no life in this room like there is the others.

"Sayid, there." He points to the left. "Asher, there." He points to the right.

Relief washes over me when I realize that I'll be sharing a room with Sayid. Something tells me I'm not going to have to watch my back around him. I notice a stack of sheets atop a thin pillow. A few pairs of jeans, some more suicide-proof sweatpants, several white t-shirts, underwear, and socks are folded, sitting on the striped mattress. Despite standing a few feet from the mattress, I can see the stains marring the surface. Old war wounds. Amma could get those stains out in five minutes flat.

"Welcome home, boys," the guard says as he leaves, but not before smacking his hand on the door frame hard enough to make me jump. His laugh trails after him.

Sayid takes his stack of clothes and linens and throws them onto the top bunk. He falls back onto the mattress, it groans and squeaks beneath his weight. I take my provided clothing and place it in the dresser at the end of the bed. I pull the sheets over my mattress, smooth out the top sheet, blanket, then slide my pillow into the case. I throw the pillow onto the scratchy sheets. It's not much, but my guess is it will be more comfortable than the bed I had at the jail. I miss my bed back home, I took for granted how soft it was, the way it'd fold around my body.

"Dinner should be soon." Sayid watches me as I make my bed.

I try to sit on the lower bunk, but I'm too tall. The back of my head touches the metal framing of the upper bunk. Awkwardly I lean forward, elbows on my knees. The afternoon light pours in through the window, the white walls seem to glow. Outside an orange grove grows, it reminds me of home, of her. It's too familiar a sight outside my window. Then again, it's a familiar sight in nearly every part of Florida. Sometimes, I think of Florida as a patchwork of nothing but alternating orange groves and swamp.

"Not really hungry." It's the truth, at least part of it. Anxiety and stress fight for space inside me, snuffing out any desire I might have to eat. I'm also not in the mood to be stared at by hundreds of strangers' eyes. I'm not good with new people, or in fact, any people.

"Want me to bring you back something?"

His offer surprises me, but I decline. I'm not going to get into the habit of asking favors. "Thanks, but I'll survive." There's a growing nervousness in the pit of my stomach. "If anyone has a cig, I'd kill for one." As soon as I say it, I regret my choice of words.

"No smoking on campus." He winks at me, another joke I don't get. "I'll see what I can do. If you want to keep it up, you're going to have to make friends with a guard, and learn where to hide."

The way he says 'friends' I'm sure it's not what he means. He disappears without another word. The house is silent and still around me. I relish the solitude. It's the first time I've really felt alone since... before. Even by myself in the cellblock, I never felt it. It always seemed there was someone watching.

I walk to the window, and peek out beyond the bunk bed, past the frayed curtain. Beneath the window, the shingles stretch over a back porch. Clinging to the dirty gutters are several abandoned birds' nests. Even the birds didn't want to stay. Beyond the porch, a manicured green lawn that must be at least a hundred yards. The lawn is freckled with large oak trees. Behind that, the orchard. I watch the wind whip through the rows, and I swear for a moment I see a white dress and blonde curls disappear into the trees.

6

BEFORE
Date Unknown

The best time to walk through the city is early in the morning, long before the sun rises and the stars are burned away. But tonight isn't the same peaceful city I normally know. The sounds of jazz may have died, but something else fills the streets. Though I can't pinpoint what it is, I can feel *something*.

Magic still hums beneath my skin, my body alive, on edge, after the ritual. I weave the long way through the French Quarter. I know it's unlikely that he's following me, that anyone is following me, but something tells me I'm not alone. My eyes travel down every dark alleyway as I search for him. Something tugs at the back of my mind.

He's getting close.

I turn down Bourbon Street, just as a few stragglers stumble out of a bar. My breath catches in my throat when I see startling red hair. The man turns, and I'm met with the face of a stranger. A haggard breath of relief bristles through me.

As I course my way through the city, my thoughts are scattered and frayed, I'm not sure if it's the ritual, or something else. The gas lamps cast a shimmering glow on the cobblestones. The address I seek was listed in my journal, the one that's taking me longer and longer to find each time I die. Though my memories have begun to unravel, I know the man inside has answers. Something tells me he may know more about myself than I do. More importantly, some part of me knows the dagger will be safe with him.

When I knock on the door, a small uniformed man with a hunched back answers. He looks at me with a tired, uninterested stare. Yellow rings encircle his brown irises, his mouth is creased into a deep perpetual frown.

"I'm here to see Alaric," I say as the man glances over my shoulder to the alleyway behind me.

His eyes narrow at the name, and suspicion clouds his eyes. The way he looks at me, I'm not sure if using Alaric's name was a mistake.

Another man saunters down the hall, a red velvet jacket hugging his gaunt frame. He looks different from the remnants of my broken memories, but not enough to turn me away. This is Alaric. His pace slows as he approaches the door. He cocks his head to the side and waves me into the house.

"Really Abner, where are your manners?" he says as he sweeps the doorman to the side. He grabs my shoulder and kisses me on both cheeks. "Devet, I've felt your presence for months, what kept you?" An accent bleeds onto his words, but I can't place it.

My brows furrow. "Devet?"

He cocks his head and flashes me an apologetic smile. "Devet is a joke, you used to think it was hilarious. I guess that part of your memory has failed you."

I nod. The journal mentioned Alaric, but I didn't realize he and I were close enough to share jokes. What else did we share? How much information has he given me that has been discarded by my broken mind?

He shakes his head and looks at his feet. "Shame," he says as he grabs my arm and pulls me inside.

The walls are lined with intricate burgundy and gold floral coverings. Paintings of people that are almost familiar hang on the walls. The living room is filled with ornately carved wooden furniture, bold curtains, and ancient dusty knickknacks. A painting of a tree with seven branches stretches along the longest wall, golden apples hang from the branches. I'm drawn to the painting for so long, Alaric walks over and faces me.

He brushes my arms, and grips them, holding them out. "Let me get a good look at you." He cocks his head as his dark eyes travel my body. When he lets me go, I sit on his couch.

"I liked the last one better," he says with a chuckle.

"Maybe the next one will suit me more," I say with an edge to my voice.

He shakes his head. "You never have even an ounce of optimism."

I lean closer to him, resting my elbows on my knees. "Would *you*?"

"Touché," he says, and his accent bleeds through. A flash of déjà vu hits me so hard, it nearly knocks the wind out of me. It's a sign this is where I should be. I should have come sooner.

"You look different than I remember," I say.

"I'm surprised you remember at all." He looks down. "Sometimes, it seems your memories are crystal clear. Others, it's like they're held together with thread. Every time you disappear, I expect it will be the last time." His voice trails off, and his eyes darken.

"Me too."

He rolls his eyes at me. "So, what do you need?"

"Getting down to business so quick?" I say as I rest my arm on the back of the couch.

"Always." He takes a slow sip of amber liquid from a crystal glass.

"I may have all the time in the world, but you sure don't."

I swallow my pride, I've never liked asking anyone for favors. "The dagger, I need to keep it here."

His eyes narrow, and his lips twist. "I don't want that *thing* in my house."

"It's not like it can bring any harm to you," I argue. Everyone I've shown the dagger to treats it like it's far more deadly than it is. But no one will tell me the truth about it. If you ask me, the biggest danger is having it end up in Dominic's hands again. Alaric is immortal, even if I stabbed him through the heart with this right now, it wouldn't do a damn thing to him. Or, at least I don't think it will.

"A curse is a curse. I have staff, I won't risk it. I won't cast life aside as easily as you."

A curse? I clench my jaw. My normal hiding places aren't going to cut it, not anymore. It's too much of a danger. I need to be sure that next time I come here first. Alaric has answers I'll need. Eventually, he might tell me everything. Or maybe he already has, but the memories are lost to me.

"You owe me," I challenge him.

He laughs and leans back against the armchair. "I owe you nothing."

"Once I'm gone, she's gone, you know you'll be next. You'll be at risk. And if he gets this dagger back, it might end us all," I explain. Alaric and everyone left like him, they'll always have a target on them.

He looks away and frowns. The silence between us grows, but I know not to push it any further. "Fine," he relents. "I'll have to hide it somewhere safe."

"Thank you," I say. "There's one more thing."

"There always is."

"I need to know how to break the connection. It's taking too long to rid myself of her influence. No matter what happens, we always end up finding one another."

He shakes his head. "There's no fix for that. And the longer this goes on, the worse it will be."

"So what do you suggest?"

"Add another piece to the puzzle." He smiles. "After you do, bring the dagger here."

I say my goodbyes to Alaric, knowing the next time I see him I'll have no time for pleasantries. When I leave, the sun is breaking the horizon. I've been gone too long. Because of my meandering path, it takes me nearly half an hour to make it home. She waits for me, her attention on a book. Though her long, black hair shrouds her face, something tells me she's not actually reading. She's got her knees pulled up to her chest, a fire at her back. Something about her feels familiar. But I can't quite place what it is. A prickle at the back of my mind tells me I know her, but the void in my mind puts me on edge.

"Where have you been?" she asks without looking up.

The lie is bitter in my mouth before I tell it. She'll know it's a lie. But I can't tell her the truth. "I had some things to attend to."

She looks up from the book, her dark eyes flashing, and her eyebrow perks up. Her mouth twists as she stares through me as if she can see the truth etched on my soul. "You need to be more careful. You could lead him back here."

I nod, because there's nothing else I can say to her. Instead, I head to the back room to retrieve my journal. There's something I need to figure out before he comes for us. The earliest entries give us clues, but it's not everything. There are hundreds of years—hundreds of entries— missing. It's lost knowledge we may never get back.

I run my hand across the cover, energy hums from it. I flip to the final page where I scrawled, "Don't trust her." My eyes follow the curves of the letters again.

7

AFTER

"Wake up, Asher, we've gotta get breakfast before class," Sayid says, kicking my bunk.

I peel my eyelids apart and groan. My heart is heavy, strange dreams haunt me. Dreams so real I can smell the strange scents of cities I've never visited. The thoughts prickle at the back of my mind. They always leave me feeling disconnected, like I woke up somewhere I don't belong. Before Olivia died, I never had strange dreams. I barely dreamt at all. Eden was the dreamer.

"Are you coming?" he asks, and looks back at me from the doorway. He sweeps his long black hair back, and it nearly reaches the collar of his white t-shirt. Sayid's eyes travel down my chest, and my cheeks burn. I rub my bleary eyes, and I swear I see a hint of a smile curve his lips.

"Yeah." I nod and take a couple seconds to put on my shirt and jeans, the uniform. I follow him, even though the thought of going into the dining hall makes my hands tremble. A cold sweat coats my neck, and I tug on my collar. It's been so long since I've eaten, my stomach is eating itself. After weighing the possibility of awkwardness in the cafeteria with the new kids, against feeling like my stomach is dissolving all day, I'll take the awkwardness.

"Sleep okay?" Sayid asks.

"Yeah," I lie. Since Olivia died, I haven't slept well. Most nights I'm thankful if I don't see her corpse in my dreams. But I don't feel like explaining. It frightens me lately, lies have become so much easier than the truth. None of the guilt I expect follows. I don't know this new me, and I'm not sure I want to.

We trace through Madison cottage, down the stairs and across the rubbery boards of the porch. I'm thankful I've got Sayid, otherwise I'd probably hide in my room and starve to death, rather than face the school alone.

"We'll eat, then go get our schedules. Are you going to sign up for any sports?" he asks as we cross the lawn toward the dining hall.

I shrug. "Wasn't planning on it. Not really good at any sports." Gym has always been pretty much the most embarrassing hour of my day.

"Me neither," he commiserates.

"How does this all work?" I ask as I watch several groups of boys run across the campus to the dining hall. There always seems to be so much going on. I can't help but notice how few guards there are. Those who are around don't seem concerned at all about the boys who dart across the fields. A few hundred feet from us, two boys disappear into the trees. I'm the only one who sees them apparently, or the only one who cares.

"It's a lot like a regular school, for the younger kids. There are teams, extracurriculars, the usual stuff. If you're over sixteen you'll be assigned full time work detail unless you need training for the job you pick," Sayid explains as we walk. "The kids who are in classes only go for half a day, the rest of the time, they're in work detail, too."

"What are the options for work detail?" I imagine five years with my face in a toilet, nose dyed blue from urinal cakes.

"Depends on what's available. Jobs come and go as we do. Typically, the younger kids get more of the grunt work. Cleaning, that shit. There should be a short list to choose from," Sayid says as we walk. "Usually, there's farm work, laundry, kitchen, electrical, library, or clerical. If you hate the options, you can convince a young'un to switch with you."

"Do we get paid?" It's probably a stupid question, but I can hope. After all, there isn't exactly a steady stream coming from home anymore. Even if my parents tried to give me money, I'd refuse it.

"Technically, no. Working gives you commissary credits though."

"Commissary?" I ask. I'm thankful even though I've asked a thousand questions, he doesn't talk to me like I'm an idiot. Embarrassment at my naivety twists inside me.

"It's like a general store. Shampoo, soap, toothpaste, magazines, candy, that sort of stuff. If your parents haven't disowned you they can also load your account with cash," he says. "However, if you want to skip the commissary all together, I offer most of the same items, and others. I take trades, in lieu of cash, if you don't have any," he says with a hint of a grin on his face.

I'm not really sure where I stand with my parents. But I'm not about to write home and ask for money. There isn't anything I need, or will need, that bad.

"What do you take in trade?" I ask, though there really isn't anything I have to offer. Not yet, anyway.

"It depends on what you need. Usually cigarettes, magazines, comic books, that sort of thing. You can also help me out in the laundry, if you don't have anything to trade," he says, nudging me.

I'm never going to have anything to offer, but I nod anyway. I'll learn to live without. After crossing the street, Sayid leads us toward a long, narrow building. The windows are caked with dirt, some of the shutters lie amongst the dead plants lining the flowerbeds. The Florida sun has boiled the paint around the windows and roof, it bubbles and peels away.

When we get inside I'm surprised how big the building is. There must be enough room to feed five hundred. Today it's barely half full. Along the back of the room is a line, and a cafeteria-style setup. Sneeze guards, chrome plating, only where the lunch ladies should be, there are boys in hairnets.

Rows of wooden tables fill the room. Each table has an uninterested guard standing watch. I'm surprised when the door groans and slams shut behind us no one even looks our direction. If a new student walked into lunch at my old school, everyone would have noticed. Then the new kid would be pelted with about five thousands questions. My shoulders fall, and I let out a shuddering breath, relief.

I follow Sayid, and pick up a tray after he does. I'm handed plastic plates covered in pancakes, sausage, eggs and toast. Amazingly it's an even bigger spread than Amma used to give me. I grab a large glass of orange juice, trying to balance it with my tray full of food. I'm relieved when Sayid picks a table close, it'd be just my luck to drop all this on the floor. Though I'm not quite as relieved when I'm sitting amidst eight people I don't know.

"Sayid! Thank God you're back. I've needed a cig for weeks. Never thought they'd get merch moving again." A squirrely kid says. His auburn hair is stuck up in a thousand different directions, like he stuck his finger in a socket. By the looks of it, he didn't do it on purpose. His face is narrow, and pointed, his brow low. He has a dopey smile that reminds me of my friend Dominic.

"Good to see you too, Gord. Don't worry, I should have my

channels open again in a day or two. Prices will be high until I get back to full supply. I'm sure you understand." His words are smoother than a Lucky Strike. He's like some kind of reform school diplomat or something.

"Gordon." He points to squirrely kid who greeted him. "This is Asher."

He then points to the rest of the guys at the table, introducing them one at a time: Chris, Westly, Brandon, Josue, Alex, Cameron, Luis and Hunter.

There's no way I'll ever learn all their names. Not today, anyway. They all blur together, a sea of names and features I don't want to remember. I'm not planning to be here long enough to make friends.

When I look up from my tray, Sayid is staring at me. What is he looking at? My eyes move around the room as I shift in my seat. My glance drifts toward Sayid again, and I swear his eyes dart away just as a smirk creeps across his face.

Gord starts talking to Sayid again. "What'd you do this time?" His eyes are wide, hungry. Scrambled eggs nearly fall out of his mouth when he talks.

"Same." Sayid grins. If I didn't know better, the way he puffs out his chest and grins, I'd say he's proud.

"Ever gonna learn your lesson?" Gord laughs, spraying his tray with half-chewed eggs.

Sayid folds a pancake and shoves it in his mouth. He chews twice, but doesn't swallow before he says, "Probably not." Half chewed pancake squishes around his teeth when he smiles. "You ever leave?"

Gord shakes his head.

"I thought you were supposed to get out right after I did." Sayid's brows furrow and leans into the table on his elbows, waiting to hear the reason.

"Was, I got in a fight with Tory. That and my parents don't want me back." A smug look creeps across his face, he crosses his arms, and leans toward Sayid. "Good fucking riddance, right?"

"Fuck them." Sayid says, but not loud enough for the guard a few feet away to hear.

I pick at my breakfast while they talk back and forth, for what feels like forever. Once I've finally gotten down to my last bite of sausage, a bell rings. I look toward Sayid as the rest of the boys scatter. The sounds of shuffling, clinking, and a rush of voices fills the dining hall. In thirty seconds flat, only Sayid and I are left.

We walk from the dining hall to a small administrative building. A few older women sit at the desks, they only glance at us when we walk in, then immediately return their attention to their work. Toward the back of the room is a corkboard covered in flyers for boxing, football, basketball, and all the other sports offered at Dozier. On the desk beneath the board sits a pile of schedules and a list of jobs with spaces beneath them for names. I look over the work detail options and spot the job I want immediately.

"Ugh, really?" Sayid asks as he watches me write my name on the list.

"Yeah?" I'm not sure why he seems upset with my choice, it's my dream job. I put my name next to Stables/Vet Assistant.

"You're going to shovel shit all day," he explains, as if I wasn't aware. Then his face falls, like he's about to tell me something horrible. "And you're going to have to be around *horses*."

"So?" I still can't understand why he cares what job I'll be doing.

"You're really okay with that?" he asks, baffled. "That's a job for the kids."

"I like being around animals," I say as I shrug, "even if it's just shoveling shit, better than cleaning it up with my hands."

"Suit yourself." He shrugs and puts his name next to 'Laundry'.

"Laundry?" I ask. That seems like just as much work as the stables.

He nudges me and says, "That's how I get things in." He raises his finger to his lips. Guess it's our secret now.

After I've got my name on the work detail list, I find my schedule on the desk. I look it over.

Monday to Saturday

6am - 7am - Breakfast

7:30am - 11am - Work Detail

11:30am - 12:30pm - Lunch

1pm - 5pm - Work Detail

5:30pm - 6:30pm - Dr. Lennox

7pm - 8pm - Dinner

Sunday

6am - 7am - Breakfast

7:30am - 9:30am - Worship

10am - 11am - Work Detail

11:30am - 12:30pm - Lunch

1pm - 5pm - Work Detail

5:30pm - 6:30pm - Dr. Lennox

7pm - 8pm - Dinner

"Who's Dr. Lennox?" I ask, noticing he appears on my schedule every day.

"Shrink."

I nod, unsurprised. Maybe it'd help to see a shrink after all, there has to be something he can do to help me get my memories back.

"So, this is it?" I say, holding up the slip of paper. This is the next five years of my life lined up on this thin piece of paper. It hits me then, I'll never get more than a eleventh grade education. Hell, I'll never even graduate.

"Unless you try out for sports, then you get less work detail. If you're really good at sports, you don't have to do any work detail at all." He explains. "There are bells that ring out over campus for breakfast, lunch, and dinner. Since it's your first day, work detail is technically optional. My work isn't optional, I've got to start getting resources in the doors. Otherwise, I might end up with some really unhappy customers." He claps his hand on my arm, and heads out the door. At the last moment, he turns around. "Whatever you do, don't duck that appointment with Lennox."

"I won't. Thanks," I say as I wave at him.

Sayid doesn't leave, instead he hovers, his hand on the knob. "You going to be okay?" he asks, his eyes survey my face. I can tell by the look on his face, he's torn. He doesn't think I can handle this place by myself. He's probably right.

It's strange to have someone care. I don't want him to worry about me. "Yeah, I'll be fine." I say, though I'm unsure.

He doesn't move, but studies my face for another moment, lips pressed together, like he doesn't necessarily believe me. Finally he nods and says, "See you later," before disappearing outside.

I head out of the administrative building and take a long look around the campus. Now that the bell for class has rung, there aren't any students lingering. I don't want to head to the stables just yet, the horses will be able to sense I'm uneasy. It will be better to introduce myself to them tomorrow, once I'm more settled. I wind my way to the library, check out a book and disappear until it's time to meet with the shrink.

8

AFTER

Dr. Lennox has a small office outside the hospital. The large brick building is two stories tall and nearly a hundred and fifty feet long, and a circular porch sticks out from the front doors lined with white columns. I find it frightening the hospital looks more than big enough to room every student in Dozier.

Why do they need a hospital this big?

I walk toward the small building, a lump forms in my throat as I pass a group of guards. They're laughing and smoking, they don't even give me a second glance. I'm starting to wonder if the guards ever do anything.

I turn the handle, and find myself in a small waiting room. A haze of cigarette smoke hangs in the air. An ugly shade of light blue carpet lines the floor, the walls look like they were white once, but are now a sickly brownish-yellow from smoke stains. A few cracked plastic chairs line the walls. At the back of the room there's a small desk with a receptionist behind it. It appears to be a work assignment, because it's a boy behind the desk. He has shaggy hair hiding his face, until he looks up.

"Asher?" the receptionist asks.

I nod.

"Head on back, he's expecting you," he says, completely uninterested. He waves his hand toward the hall, but doesn't bother to show me back himself. As soon as I start to walk back his attention snaps to a magazine.

Down a narrow hallway, lined with pictures and diplomas, I find a large office. The door peeks open into the room, where a thick cloud of cigarette smoke hangs in the center. It's so thick, I'm tempted to ask him to open a window, but I don't. Everything I'd expect to find in a shrink's office is here. Couch, chairs, ornate wooden desk with a large typewriter. When I push the door open I see a husky hunchbacked, gray-haired older man watering the plants crowded in tiny pots on the windowsill. He doesn't look up at first. Though I'm ten feet away, I can see the milky quality of his eyes behind his glasses. His skin seems to sag, like someone let the air out of him.

"Hello, Mr. Flemming," he says as he sets the watering can on his desk, and squints at me.

"Nice to meet you." I extend my hand to shake his, I'm surprised how thin and cold his skin is. His grip is light, his hand feels brittle beneath mine. I pull my hand back faster than I mean to. I shift as he stares at me. I feel like he can see what's wrong with me just by looking.

"Take a seat wherever you like." He extends his shaking hand to show me toward the couch and one of the sitting chairs.

I plop down on an ugly green arm chair, a cloud of smoke and dust escapes the cushion. The scratchy fabric bites at my exposed arms. I cross one leg over the other in an attempt to keep myself from fidgeting, or to keep my legs from shaking. It doesn't work. He grabs a notebook and a pen before sitting down in the chair across from me.

"So," he says as a warm smile creeps across his face, "why do you think you're here today?" His voice is friendly, but waivers slightly as he speaks.

"Here in this room, or at this school?" I ask as I lean into the chair arm and prop my head up on my hand.

"Either, both. Whatever you prefer to tell me," he says ardently, and folds his hands across the notepad in his lap.

In the brief moment before I speak, after he finishes speaking, he starts to write on the paper. His hand trembles as he writes. Though I try to look at the notepad, from where I sit all I can see are scribbles. He takes a slow drag from his cigarette, and the smoke wafts toward me. I watch him as lifts the cigarette to his lips, then rests it on the ash tray. There's an urge growing inside me, I need a cigarette. My eyes fall to the paper again.

Is he writing down how long it takes me to answer?

I pause, uncertainty twists my thoughts into a tangle. I've never been the kind of person to share my secrets with strangers. Even if I did want to tell him anything about myself, I wouldn't know where to start. So, instead I look out the window as I chew on the inside of my cheek.

"I know how difficult this must be," he finally says when the silence between us becomes palpable. "You don't have to tell me anything. We can sit here if you like, and you don't have to say a single thing," he offers.

My eyebrow perks up. "And I won't get in any trouble?"

He shakes his head. "You won't get in any trouble for anything you say in this room." He clears his throat. "That is, unless you threaten to harm another student here. That's where I have to step in."

"Okay," I say as I turn my attention back to the window.

He lights another cigarette and eyes me as he smokes it. I can feel his eyes burn against my flesh. "Where are you from?" he asks.

"Ocala," I say simply.

"Did you like it there?"

I shrug. "Before—" I catch myself and swallow the truth before it tumbles out of me. "Before I was sent here, yeah. It was okay."

"Do you have any siblings?"

"A sister," I pause. "Twin sister," I correct myself. "And an older brother, but he's in 'nam."

"That's brave, honorable."

I eye him, unsure if it's a jab at me. Brave, honorable brother, and here I am, murderer. He smiles kindly, and I shrug off the comment.

"What's your favorite color?"

My eyebrow perks up. It's a strange question. "White," I guess.

"Why white?"

"Because that's the color she always wore," I almost say, but I catch myself. I take a deep breath and clear my mind. "It just is."

I don't want to tell this guy anything about myself. But I realize, if I don't try, I'll never get better. I'll never figure out what happened. As much as I don't want to, as much as I don't trust him, it may be the only way to uncover the truth.

I press my lips together as a question bubbles to the surface. "Have you helped anyone else like me?"

His lips twist, and he looks down for a moment, his brows drawn together. "With your specific set of circumstances, no." He clears his throat. "But lost memories are something I have helped other students with. It's a lot of work, it's a big undertaking. Memory is not something to mess with lightly…"

"But you can help? You have done it?" I interrupt him.

He nods slowly.

I take a deep breath and try to remember where we'd been in

the conversation. *Why are you here?* "I'm here at Dozier because the police think I killed my best friend, Olivia," I explain, shifting uncomfortably in the chair as I talk. "I imagine I'm in this room because I don't *remember* killing her." I expect my response to get stuck in my throat, but it doesn't. The words fall out of my mouth easier than usual.

Is it possible I'm finally numbing to their grip on me?

"I see," he says as he takes notes. "How old are you?"

"Eighteen. I was seventeen when it happened." I'm not sure if that detail matters, but I add it just in case.

There was no ceremony around my birthday. Not that I remember, anyway. I turned eighteen in the cellblock six weeks after Olivia died. Even if I survive this place, I will never celebrate another birthday. It won't feel right. Prior to eighteen, every single birthday was celebrated with Eden and Olivia. Though Eden and I are twins, she was born before midnight, I was born an hour after. Olivia and I have closer birthdays than Eden and I do. Olivia was fifteen minutes younger than me. Our mothers met in the hospital and became best friends.

"Have you ever suffered memory loss before?" He doesn't look up from the paper when he asks, he barely stops writing at all. His hand shakes so much, it looks like the paper is covered in a series of scribbles. I'm not sure how he can read what he's writing.

"Along with not remembering when she died, I also don't remember most of the month after. I was in the hospital, they said I was mostly catatonic. Other than that, no." I try not to pry, but I can't help but stare at that piece of paper.

What could he possibly have to say about me?

"Do you have a history of violence, fights, threats? Anything like that?" He stops writing to take a sip of water, and looks at me over his thin glasses.

"No, never." I shake my head. It's much easier to talk to Dr. Lennox than I imagined. The last time I tried to talk to a shrink at the hospital, tears pricked at my eyes and my throat went so dry, I thought it might crack and bleed. Here though, I feel like I can breathe, and I can talk to him.

"Have you ever had a head injury or a concussion?" he asks, lifting his shaking hand to light a cigarette.

Though a few times, breaking up fights between my parents I did get hit in the head, I doubt that ever caused a concussion. So I say, "No."

He hunches his shoulder forward, his glasses slipping toward the end of his nose, as he takes a long drag from his cigarette. It's torture sitting so near, while not being able to have one myself. A long knobby finger reaches up, pushing the glasses up.

"How would you describe your relationship with Olivia?" He waits for me to answer, the pen hovering in the air above the paper.

"Great, I mean, we've been best friends since we were little. Our moms are—were—best friends. So we grew up together. We were even born on the same day." When the words are out, my eyes fall to the floor. Talking about her like this, about my history with her, rather than about the night she died, warmth floods my chest. The cold fingers of guilt squash it nearly as quickly as it came.

I don't deserve to be happy.

"Did you ever wish that there was more to this friendship?"

I consider lying, because of how embarrassing it is. But if I lie, he may not be able to help me remember. "I hoped it would become more, that maybe eventually she'd be my girlfriend. I've told her I love her about a thousand times." It takes me a moment to find the words to go on. Explaining our history makes me feel like an idiot.

I spent so many years loving someone who didn't love me back. But I wouldn't change any of it, I wouldn't take anything back—except the night she died. I'd spend every day of my life loving her, getting nothing in return, if it'd mean I'd get her back.

"I stopped saying I loved her for a while. It hurt to keep saying it, since she never said it back. I'd been planning to try again, tell her I still loved her." I look down at my feet. The tears sting my eyes, knowing I missed my opportunity, the reality of it crushes me. I'll never be able to tell her again how much I love her—loved her. Even though she's been dead for almost four months now, it doesn't feel like she's gone to me. I swear, sometimes I can still feel her.

"I see. How long had you been romantically attracted to Olivia?" he asks after taking another note. He sets the cigarette down on the ashtray next to him.

"As long as I can remember." I shrug. Trying to calculate how long I've loved her would be like trying to figure out how many breaths I've taken, or how many heart beats have passed. It's impossible.

"Can you tell me what you remember of that night?" He starts to write again.

My mind jumps back instantly, replaying the few details I remember.

While I lay in bed, staring up at the ceiling is the only thing I can do. The clock ticks down the minutes, but it's still not ten o'clock. Eventually, when I'm sick of counting the knots in the wood on the ceiling, I sit up. With a few minutes to go, I creep to my door. My footfalls are silent as I pad down the hallway.

Careful not to bump into the pictures lining the wall, I stand a few feet from my parents door. Their snores echo inside their room. Hopefully, my dad won't wake up when I start his car. I turn around, my heart pounding. My hand claps over my mouth, holding in a scream.

Eden's wide brown eyes are inches from mine. We look so much alike, it's like I nearly bumped into a mirror. When we were little, people always thought we were identical twins. Never mind she wore pink and I wore blue.

"What are you doing, Asher?" Her voice is smooth as silk, but too loud.

I roll my eyes and grip the wall to settle myself. She knows, of course she knows. Olivia would have told her. After all, Olivia tells her everything. I try to swallow my jealousy.

"Like you don't know," I whisper, creeping around her, away from our parents room. If they wake up, I'm dead, and it will crush Olivia. She's been looking forward to this night nearly our entire lives.

Her arms cross ceremoniously across her chest. "Humor me," she says as she leans against the wall. "I want to know what you think you're doing." Eden has always been overprotective of Olivia, probably because she's her only friend. This is why I usually don't bother to bring Eden along when I sneak out.

"Olivia and I." My words are sharp. I want to be sure Eden knows she's not invited. "We're going to the Howey mansion."

"You're going to get caught, that old woman calls the cops anytime a flood light so much as flickers," she warns, a serious look on her face. Her brows are so low, it looks like they're tangled in her eyelashes.

"Not anymore." I retreat to my room. Once inside, I dig at the back of my dresser, behind my underwear, only pulling back once I have my cigs in my hand.

Eden follows, curious as a cat. Eyes wide. "What do you mean, not anymore?"

Several flicks of my lighter later and I inhale slowly. I push the pack of cigarettes into my pocket. Eden must know everything. The power of knowing something she doesn't thrills me. All the years of her lording information over me fades away. This one's mine. I open my mouth, like I'm going to tell her, then I smile and clamp my lips closed.

"You're such an asshole. Just tell me."

I fall back onto my navy blue comforter. The smoke rings I blow grow as they float toward the ceiling. I cross one leg over the other, and shift so I prop myself up on my elbow. My chin rests on my hand.

"Ugh, fine. I don't want to know anyway." She turns with fury toward the door. Sometimes, I swear, the only emotion Eden feels is anger. She's got a temper worse than a feral cat.

"Fine," I say before she disappears, "I'll tell you."

When she turns, I can see how hungry her eyes are. That makes me want to withhold the information even more. To mess with her like she always messes with me. But I know if I don't tell her now, she'll probably go wake up Mom just to spite me.

"She's in Leesburg now, at a home. The place is all but abandoned, it's been empty for almost a week," I explain.

"When did this happen? And how did you find out?" Her eyebrow arches.

"Last week, and it's none of your business how I found out."

Her lips purse, and I know she wants to pry. But she must have something more pressing, because she says, "Well, you two have fun. Please bring Olivia back in one piece, I need her opinion on some dresses tomorrow." She waves at me as she walks out. I'm surprised at how easily she drops it. Normally Eden would grill me.

"Yeah, yeah. Sounds thrilling."

Propping up on my elbows I look over at the clock. "Shit!" Thanks to Eden, I'm now running ten minutes late.

I pull on my favorite jacket, the leather is soft and worn, from years of abuse. The air is still warm when I step out onto the roof of our *porch. When I get to the end, I bound off and land on my feet. There's no time to waste climbing down the lattice.*

Closing the distance between our houses, I reach Olivia's in a few strides. I look in her window, but she's not there. Nerves clench my stomach, I hope she doesn't think I forgot.

Turning the corner, I head to her backyard. Moonlight spills across the grass, dew glistens. A soft warm breeze kicks up the sweet smell of the orange blossoms. Beneath the blanket of the stars, in the distance, lightning flickers. The storm is so far off, I doubt we'll see much rain tonight. That's when I notice her. Sitting beneath an oak tree with a book and a flashlight. Her blonde curls dance in the wind. She looks up at me, smiling, as she closes her book.

I explain it all in detail for him, every second I remember, maybe some of it will help.

"I'd planned to take my dad's car and drive her out to Howey-In-The-Hills. That's all I remember though, just getting to her house. All I can remember after that is waking up in the hospital a month after everything happened." I look at him, waiting, like he has some cure, some way to turn those few memories into an entire night.

"How did you get to the hospital, did they tell you?" he asks.

"They found me next to her, covered in blood, the cops did. After they found me, I was out of it, they brought an ambulance to bring me to the hospital." I sigh and look toward the window. "For the next month, I was catatonic. Then I slowly started to come around." I remember the look on Eden's face the first day I spoke to her in the hospital. She'd been at my bedside waiting, no one else wanted to be near me. When I spoke to her, she broke down and left the room. She looked so angry, so raw. Two days passed before she came back and finally talked to me. At the time, I didn't know what I had done, why she was so mad at me. I was confused, scared, handcuffed to a hospital bed. The first words I heard about Olivia's death came from the cops who questioned me within an hour.

"Can you think of any reason you would have hurt her?" His voice is calm, and even. Not even the smallest hint of accusation lingers on his words.

I look back at him. "No, I'd never hurt her, for any reason. All I ever wanted was to be around her, to make her happy. Even if she never wanted me, if she loved someone else, married someone else, I could live with it. As long as she was happy." The truth of it aches. I would give anything for her, I'd trade my life for hers right now.

"Have you ever gotten so angry you've blacked out before?" he asks.

"Never." I shake my head. *Then again, if I'd gotten so angry I blacked out, would I remember?* I hardly ever get angry, though.

"Is there any history of mental illness in your family? Has anyone ever been hospitalized for being mentally unwell? Been placed in an asylum for any length of time?" He scratches something out on the notepad.

"Not that I know of." My family isn't the type to discuss things like that. No one in my family has ever seemed anything but sane. If anything, I'd say they try to be too buttoned up, too normal.

"How would you say you feel now?" he asks looking at me now, instead of at the paper.

"Sad, nervous, anxious. Pretty much all the time. Some days I think I see her. It's all just really strange. A lot of the time I feel like I'm far off watching myself go through the motions. It doesn't feel like this is my life anymore. All the people I care about, I can't even see them anymore. No one believes anything I say. And the way people look at me now, that's the worst." I can't look at him when I admit it.

My cheeks flush. I shouldn't care what he thinks of me. My eyes burn, I look away, there's something thick caught in my throat. I don't like people to see me cry. This isn't my life anymore. Before all this happened, I *never* cried. The tears come so easy now, I feel broken. There's something seriously wrong with me.

Without skipping a beat, he asks, "How do they look at you?"

"It's hard to explain. It's like a mix of anger and disgust, I'm the worst thing they can imagine," I pause for a minute, and take a deep breath, as I try to wish away the tears in my eyes. "Now, most of the time, I wish I'd died with her."

"Have you thought about killing yourself?" he asks, setting the pen down.

"In passing, I've considered it. No serious plans." I shrug. It's a half truth. I've more than considered it. Sometimes, it all becomes too much. Everything weighs on me, I feel like I can't get out from under it. Maybe it's not worth getting out from under it. *The wrong person died that night, is it so wrong that I want to correct it?* I'm a coward, I can't kill myself any more than I could kill someone else.

"If I prescribed you something I thought would help, would you take it?" His milky eyes are wide as he looks at me, it feels like they're boring into me, searching for the truth.

I shrink beneath the heat of his gaze. "If it will make me stop feeling like this. I want to feel normal again. I don't want to feel hollow anymore. I don't want my mind so crowded." I chew on my thumbnail and stop talking. I've reached the limit of how far I'm willing to dig today. Though I want to feel normal, I know I don't deserve to.

"It can help with that," he assures me. "But there can be side effects. If anything strange happens, if you feel off, please let me know so that we can adjust your dosage."

"What kind of side effects?"

"Dizziness, headaches, normally. There are a few cases of more severe reactions, but they're so rare, you needn't worry about it," he says with a kind smile.

"What can you do to help me remember?" I ask him, though I'm not sure I'm ready to remember. The fear I'm wrong, that I actually did kill her, crushes the part of me that is so sure I didn't do it. I just hope that one day I'll wake up knowing with absolute certainty that I didn't kill her. That hope is the thing keeping me alive right now. The thing keeping me going. I can't die without knowing for sure.

He looks at me over the rim of his glasses, his eyes are blue with a white haze in the middle. His lips are pressed together for a long moment before he replies. "Are you sure you want to remember?"

I nod automatically. But I'm still torn. If finding out means I'll know for sure I killed her, that's not something I could live with. My breath catches in my throat. Then I have to start convincing myself all over again I didn't do it, I couldn't have.

"Sometimes the mind protects us from things for a reason. There might be something that happened that night that you're not ready to deal with. We can try hypnosis. It's not terribly effective. That's really the only option. And unfortunately we don't have time for that today. I'll let the hospital know that you'll need to start some medication tomorrow. They'll give it to you with your breakfast." He smiles, and stands up, extending his hand to shake mine. "It was good to meet you."

"You too, thank you."

9

After

After dinner, Sayid and I walk together back to Madison. Dinner manages to be no more awkward than breakfast, thankfully. While we walk back, Sayid gives me the general rundown of what's involved for him to get supplies, and I tell him all about the book I'd intended to read but didn't.

I slump down on the back porch, belly aching, too full of mashed potatoes and meatloaf. The buzzing of mosquitoes and horseflies fills the air. Automatically, I lean back on my elbows, closing my eyes as my head lulls back. Sayid sits down beside me, and I feel his eyes on me. But when I glance at him, he looks away. With Sayid at my side, I feel the anxiety balled up inside me slowly unravel. A breath slips out of me, it's heavy, like it's been trapped in my lungs all day.

"It's a good thing I've got stuff stashed everywhere. It doesn't seem like anyone found my caches since the last time I was here," he rambles as he looks off toward the orange trees. "It's probably going to take two weeks until I start getting a good flow coming again. I've got to work something out with a new guard. The guy I used last time, Scott, he doesn't work here anymore, apparently." He sighs.

"How exactly do you, uh, work things out with the guards?"

He gives me a sideways glance, like he's waiting for me to understand something. "What?" I ask.

He laughs at me and shakes his head. "Ah, to be young again."

I roll my eyes at him. "What's the deal with the showers here?" I ask, trying to change the subject, and diffuse the heat rushing to my cheeks. Since we got here, I haven't seen any showers, and I'm starting to think my stink could gag a pig.

"The showers for us are downstairs. I'll warn you though, never shower alone. If you do, you're just asking for it. You'll end up..." He pauses, for what I guess to be dramatic effect, "Let's just say you'll end up getting something I'm pretty sure you won't like."

It feels awkward to ask, but it's not like I've got anyone else that's going to volunteer to help me. "Do you mind keeping watch while I shower?" I ask.

He shrugs, "Sure."

After I've gathered my things, Sayid shows me where the downstairs bathroom is. It's nearly the size of the bedroom we share upstairs. It's dirty and has a musty mold smell to it. Black sticks between the tiles, making the beige seem a lighter color than it is. On the right side of the room there are six half walls separating showerheads. To our left, there are three urinals, and three toilets hidden behind stalls.

I throw my clean clothes over the edge of the sink, which reminds me of a pig trough. My bare feet stick to the tiles, and the film on them makes me wish I'd brought my shoes. I flip on the water, and wait for the steam to come. Sayid leans against the wall, and I look back toward him.

"Does it ever get warm?" I ask after what feels like ages, the cold streams tickle my fingertips.

"Nope." It looks like he's trying not to laugh at me. "The warmest water you're going to get here is if you go stand in the rain."

I jump when the cold water hits me. The flow pouring from the showerhead smells off. Everything here seems to have its own strange odor. When it finally manages to get to a tepid temperature, I lose myself beneath it. With my eyes closed, the water trickling over my body, I forget the hell around me entirely.

The door squeaks open. Since I know Sayid has the lookout, I don't bother to turn. I trust him. Footsteps echo through the bathroom.

"Well, well, well, now this is the kind of scenery I wouldn't mind seeing every single day," a deep voice says, a southern drawl thick on the words.

I turn to find a large boy with a wide stance in the middle of the bathroom. His hands firmly on his hips, or where his hips would be if he had them. He's heavyset, built like a linebacker, or maybe a sumo wrestler. He's got long black hair slicked back against his square head. His large brow droops down over his eyes.

"Oh, and it can get better," he says, as his eyes travel up and down my body.

"Come on, Becks, don't scare him. This isn't even your cottage," Sayid says, trying to diffuse the situation, he manages to keep up his usual diplomatic tone.

"I am well aware. I heard about the new meat though, and I had to come see it for myself. It's just as delicious as I heard." He runs his tongue along his top lip. "I will be sure to see you later." He winks at me.

Though I know his intentions are to scare the new kid, I'm more bothered by the water growing cool again. Even if Becks did bother me, I know well enough to not show it. Sayid holds the door open for him, and waves him out. I stand watch for Sayid while he takes his shower. While he's lost beneath the water, I start to wonder, *why does he want to be friends with me at all?* He shouldn't trust me. I don't even trust me. For all he knows, he could be next.

10

AFTER

Long after Sayid is asleep my mind still buzzes from the day. I want to tell Eden about it, share some of what's going on in here with her. Without her, I don't feel like myself. Eden was my sounding board. I told her everything—well not everything. But more than I told anyone else. I slip from my lower bunk, the springs whining in protest as I stand. Snores from the other bedrooms flow into the hallway, as usual, I'm the only one awake. Even at home I had trouble sleeping. When I couldn't sleep, I'd sneak down to the stables and spend time with Lady, my favorite horse.

I sneak down the stairs, and search for a sheet of paper to write to Eden. Every drawer I open comes up empty. A few old odds and ends, an abandoned comb, a toy car with no wheels, a book with yellowed pages.

There's a school here, there must be paper somewhere.

Finally, in a bottom drawer folded up inside a textbook I find two unused sheets of paper. And I realize how good my luck is when I also find a pencil. I sit down at one of the metal desks and stare at the white paper in the dark. I've never written her a letter, and now that I have the tools to, my mind is as empty as my growling gut.

Eden,

Do you remember that time Mom tried to take us to Miami to visit her sister? She was so mad at Dad that she took us in the middle of the night. We didn't even have a map, and she had no idea where we were going. I'd never been so scared in my life as I was when the car broke down. She'd gone the wrong way, and we were in the middle of Alligator Alley. We walked ten miles together behind William, while Mom stayed in the car and cried. I can still remember the way the moon reflected off the pools of swamp, and in the darkness, we'd hear the hissing of the gators.

There have been two more times that I've been that scared. The day I finally came to in the hospital after Olivia died. And today.

Asher

I fold the letter carefully. As I stand to head back up the stairs, I feel someone watching me. Though I check the room, I'm alone. I head toward the stairs, movement outside catches my attention. My heart stops as Olivia's face comes into focus just outside the window. The look she gives me, it tugs at me. A memory I can't quite grasp lingers at the back of my mind. Her milky eyes stare through me, haunting me. My insides twist, and I turn away. I clench my eyes closed and my heart pounds. A haggard breath works its way out of me.

It's not real. It's not real.

When I open my eyes, she's gone.

I climb the stairs to my room, my throat thick with emotion. I hide Eden's letter. I'll have to figure out in the morning how to get it to her. I collapse back onto the bed and try to blink away the tears stinging my eyes. She's haunting me, she's punishing me. Guilt coils inside me. Sleep finally claims me, but the face of Olivia's corpse is still fresh in my mind.

11

The warmth of humidity embraces me. My head rests against my hand as I lean on the table in front of me. Cluttered walls of a well-lived-in shotgun house seem to stretch on forever, until the darkness swallows them. In the orange glow of the candlelight, I can see a girl across from me. Though she doesn't look over twenty, the lines on her face, the darkness in her eyes, tells me there's more to her than what's on the surface. The table is scattered with maps, open books, and several daggers, carvings etched into their handles.

"He's getting close," she says. Her face is shrouded, eyes focused on the table, not on me. She's gotten so strong now, she shares a closer connection with him. I hate her for that. I spent nearly a hundred years with him, and I can barely feel him. She's never spent more than five minutes in the same room with him.

A tight lump forms in my throat. "I know." The words come from my mouth, but my voice is unfamiliar, it's deeper, rougher. Even my body feels foreign. My hands are larger, jagged and calloused. Supple leather winds its way around my chest, a vest that fits me so well, it's nearly a second skin. Coarse linen pants hang limp off my legs.

She slides forward on her elbows and a flicker of light catches her face. The woman before me isn't someone I know, not physically anyway, she's a stranger. But I feel a connection to her. She's someone I've known before. Maybe I know her now. A familiar twinkle lingers in her eyes. The connection that binds us stretches across the table and pulls at me.

"How are we going to hide it this time?" she asks as she sweeps her long black hair away from her dark eyes.

"I've created other journals, he won't be able to tell the difference. You hide one of the fakes. I'm going to hide a couple, too. But that leaves what to do with the real one..." The lie slips out easily. When you tell a lie over and over, it becomes much easier to tell. It's so easy now, it almost feels like the truth.

She grimaces and looks uneasy. "You know the risk we're taking if he finds it." Her words aren't a question, they're a warning.

"It's the same risk we've taken every other time." I explain. Sometimes, I'm not sure if it'd be worse if he found the journal, or if she did.

"If he finds it, if he figures it out though, that will be the end of us." Her words are so low, it's like she thinks saying it out loud may make it happen.

"Will it though? The best we have are guesses. We don't know if any of them—"

She holds up her hand as she cocks her head. Her eyes tighten, and she clenches her fists atop the table. "We don't know that they won't work, either." She shakes her head. "And we would lose so much if he knew everything."

"I know you can feel it. We aren't meant to kill him this time."

Though I'm not sure how it will feel when we *are* supposed to kill him, I know this isn't the time. We will get one step closer, we will prepare, and maybe, just maybe, we'll be able to kill him next time.

12

The letter for Eden is heavy in my pocket, where it's been for nearly two weeks. When I went to the office to mail it, the women working in the building laughed at me. I know there's only one hope to get the letter to Eden, and he's sitting across from me. Sayid shovels his breakfast into his mouth like he may never eat again. The question I've been wanting to ask him for days has formed a hard lump in my throat, even if I swallow a million times it won't go away.

I don't want to ask him for help, I hate asking anyone for anything. Every single cigarette he gives me has guilt heavy on the smoke. Everything is another favor I won't be able to pay back. He's unreasonably nice to me, and I haven't figured out if it's because he's too stupid to realize how dangerous I really am, or if it's that very danger keeping me in his good graces. But no matter how much I try to build up the wall between us, Sayid manages to break it back down. There's something between us, but I don't understand what it is yet.

You could be next. I've almost said to him a hundred times. *You should stay away from me. You shouldn't be my friend.* I don't want his blood on my hands, or anyone else's. But especially not his. Every time I swallow the words down, because deep down, I don't want him to stay away.

The words bubble to the surface again, and this time, they come out even through my clenched teeth. "I need your help," I say. I know part of me should feel relieved that I finally said the words, all I can feel is the weight of his stare, and the silence building between us.

He studies me, his left eyebrow droops. The speed of his chewing slows. But he doesn't speak for so long that I shift uncomfortably. "You need help?" The words seep out of him slow, almost forced, like he's testing his knowledge of a foreign language. "You've been here two weeks and haven't asked for a single thing, color me impressed it took you this long." He jokes, but laughter only comes from his side of the table.

"I need to get a letter to my sister." I pull the wrinkled letter from my pocket and slide it across the table to him, after I'm sure the guards aren't looking—they never are.

He snatches it up before I'm even able to blink. "Really, this is it? Just a letter?" He eyes it, like he was expecting something more scandalous. If I didn't know better, I'd think he was disappointed.

I shrug, and let my eyes fall to my plate. "What do I owe you?" There's no way for me to pay him, I have nothing of value. All I could offer is taking shifts for him at the laundry.

He laughs again, and pokes my tray so it bumps into my arm. When our eyes meet, he says, "Cheer up, it's on me."

I can't even get a breath in to argue, a loud voice cuts across the cafeteria like thunder on a silent afternoon.

"Gather 'round boys," a lumbering hulk of a boy says as soon as his tray hits the table. I recognize him right away from my lovely shower, Becks. He's so big, he looks out of place here. A kid this tall, this big, it can't be possible. I'm pretty sure he could break the table in half, if he had a mind to. His eyes are wide, playful, he's chewing on a thin breadstick like it's a piece of straw. Though he's got a playful air to his tone, his presence makes a bad feeling snake its way under my skin.

"What's the lesson plan today?" Sayid asks. I listen to his voice for an edge, for any hint that this kid is the bad news I think he is, but there is none. Sayid actually looks interested in what Becks has to say.

Becks thumbs his bulbous nose and looks up at Sayid through the bushy eyebrows drooping over his eyes. "Hotwiring, never know when it will come in handy." He blinks a few times, and I think his eyelashes may have gotten tangled in his brows.

Sayid rolls his eyes, "You've already told us how to do that."

Becks cocks his head to the side and glares at Sayid, challenging him with his eyes. All six foot, six inches and 300 pounds of him is crouched, like he's ready to jump across the table at him. "You eva' actually stole a car?"

A lump forms in my throat. But Sayid just shakes his head, completely unfazed by Becks brooding stare. *How is Sayid not scared of him? Becks could rip him in half.*

"You planning to get straight after you leave here? I mean considerin' this ain't your first rodeo, I'm guessing not." Becks words snap, each one hits Sayid so sharply, I expect him to flinch, he doesn't.

Sayid doesn't answer, instead he stares at his food. I try to catch his gaze, but he doesn't look at me. Instead of piling the food into his mouth quickly, now he takes slow, calculated bites. I think he's avoiding looking at Becks.

I'm not sure how or why Becks ever got into grand theft auto, he looks like he's from a rich family. You can still tell by the way he slicks his hair back with pomade. Though I came from a well-off family, and I know my fair share of other people who come from money,

Becks oozes wealth. His t-shirt is pressed, not wrinkled like the rest of ours. Even his jeans have a seam ironed in them. And I'd guess if I looked under the table, his shoes would shine.

"Depending on the type of car, there are two easy ways to hotwire. Both ways you'll need a screwdriver. Remove the panel beneath the steering column, pull down the wires, you'll want to cross the red and black ones. Or, remove the ignition switch, slide the screw driver inside, turn it, and tah-dah, new ride." He smiles, and something dark flashes across his face. "Time to pay tribute, boys." He holds his hands out, urging everyone to fill them.

A collective sigh comes from the table. The boys start to pass things to Becks, bacon, toast, whatever they have left. One boy pushes his entire tray toward him. But I don't.

"Newbie?" he finally says to me over a tray brimming with food.

I say nothing, though my hand almost shakes, I hold it steady. My jaw is locked, I keep my eyes on the tray in front of me.

"He deaf?" Becks asks Sayid, there's levity in his voice, like it'd all be a hilarious misunderstanding if I were deaf.

Sayid looks panic-stricken. His mouth drops open, but words don't come out. I won't make him choose who he betrays here.

My eyes meet Becks' for the first time. Despite my desire to defy him, to be the one to tell him no, I slide my tray across the table.

"Good boy," Becks says as he snatches the fork from my hands.

Anger twists inside me like a knife in my gut. I wish there was something I could do to stand up to him. But Becks is nearly three times my size. I'm not sure I *could* do anything to him.

"Next time I'd hand over the food a 'lil faster," Sayid warns.

I nod. But deep down, I'm hoping there won't be a next time.

13

AFTER

The second the smell of straw, horse shit, and old pine hits my nostrils, I feel like I'm home. I breathe deep, like it's the first breath I've taken in hours. It feels like coming up for air after swimming underwater. Wood covered in peeling paint stretches high above me. Bent, rusted nails curl, like overgrown fingernails, from the old splintered beams. There's no one in the stables to greet me, just the way I like it.

Though I've made a dent in the work to be done in the stables since I came to Dozier, this place has needed love for a while. My attention has mainly been focused on the horses. Cleaning their hooves, washing them, brushing them. And, more importantly, making sure they don't fight the saddle.

From the stacks of molded hay, buckets filled with as much feed as water, and air thick with flies—it still drives me crazy to see this place in shambles. The clipboard hangs from a rusty nail on one of the supporting posts. My tasks are neatly written out on a dirty scrap of paper, the same tasks that have been there for two weeks. The same tasks that have probably been there since the beginning of time.

Shovel Stalls

Replace hay - New bales in loft
Replace water
Brush horses
Clean hooves

The stables aren't large, there are twelve stalls in all, less than a quarter of the stalls we had at home. Each stall is about twelve-by-twelve, with four stalls on each side. A long hallway about eight feet wide runs along the middle, separating the rows of stalls. With the state these are in, cleaning them will definitely take all day. I'll be lucky to get it done. I search the small tool closet for a shovel, but there isn't one. I walk from stall to stall, hoping no one was dumb enough to leave a shovel in with one of the horses.

As I search the last one, there's shuffling behind me. I turn to find Becks and two cronies. Both of the cronies look similar enough to be brothers, white dirty skin, tangled mounds of brown hair, and dark eyes. Becks holds the shovel across his body with his right hand, resting it on his left shoulder.

"Looking for this?" he asks in a tone that makes me want to punch him. The shovel dangles from his hand in front of me, and taunts me.

"Nope," I lie. I'm sure I can find something else to use, in fact, I'd rather use my hands. I don't know why he's come here to mess with me. I gave him my breakfast, and now my stomach is suffering the consequences. White-hot anger flares up inside me, but I refuse to let it show on my face. I don't want to spend the next five years with this kid making my life hell.

I head out of the stall and walk around him, without so much as looking in his general direction. Becks wants me to fight. My father has made me well aware of the signs someone is looking for a fight.

He snorts so loud, I almost mistake it for one of the horses. "You know, Asher," he says my name like I'm lucky he knows it. "This morning I gave you a chance out of the kindness of my heart." One of his cronies snickers beside him. Becks shoots him a look that's laced with venom. "I go out of my way to educate you all, and all I ask is for you to pay tribute. And this morning, you took way too long."

"I'm sorry," the lie tumbles out, the words bitter in my mouth. This kid is never going to be anything to me other than a menace. I could sense that from the moment I saw him. And I know what will come of these interactions, he'll probably pound my face into the concrete. I wish he'd get it over with so I could get back to my work.

"You don't sound very sorry," Becks says as he takes a step toward me.

Though his size terrifies me, I keep my attention on my work. I force my face into a stoic mask. He may scare the shit out of me, but I won't give him the pleasure of seeing that.

I stop sweeping to look at him. "Well, I am."

I cross my arms, leaning against a stall wall and wait for them to leave. Every cell in my body aches to run. *Get as far away from here as you can.* But I don't move. I don't listen to the voice in the back of my mind. Giving in to the fear will only make it worse next time.

Becks and his cronies walk toward me. I think they're going to walk past me, slink away in defeat. I've never been that lucky. The two cronies grab me, each taking one arm. They pull me back, and slam me into a support post. My teeth clink together, and my head thuds against the wood. A sharp pain radiates from my teeth all the way through my skull. My shoulder blades ache as the wood digs into them; it's hard enough to know I'll bruise.

Becks cocks his head to the side, and smiles when I wince. He looks down at his right hand as he steps closer. Then he backhands me with his palm open. My face burns in response. Every breath breathes fury through me. But I steady myself. *Stay calm*. This isn't my first fight, it won't be my last. If there's anything I can do, it's make it through a beating.

His knuckles bite into my cheek, teeth. The force of the impact disperses through my entire face. I force myself to keep quiet. I won't moan, I won't cry, I won't show any weakness to this asshole. In fact, after he steps back, I smile at him.

His eye twitches. The veins in his neck rise to heights I never knew possible, like a pulsing snake trapped beneath the taut skin. The flesh on his face glows red. He pulls his lips tight. His massive brow nearly swallows his eyes. I tug, and try to free myself from his cronies, but I can't get free. The more I struggle, the tighter they grip me. Blood pours from my arms where their nails dig into my flesh. Becks lumbers closer, towering above me. I decide to stop fighting. Instead I slump, looking off into the distance. If I can't fight back, I will make him as angry as possible. Maybe he'll give himself a heart attack.

"Look at me." Spit hits my face as he throws his words at me. The words are a monstrous growl.

Ignoring him, making him scream at me, it gives me a sick pleasure. It's the first time I've actually been happy since Olivia. When I realize it, a fist of guilt twists inside me. It hurts worse than my swelling face. Warm blood pours from my eyebrow, down my cheek.

He doesn't speak again, instead he drives a fist into my jaw. It aches, and throbs, but he clearly doesn't have much experience with his left hand. I look at him, almost smiling, daring him to hit me again.

"Can't you do any better than that?" I challenge. "I'm pretty sure my sister could punch me harder."

He snorts, knuckles split my lip.

Come on, hit me.

"Are we done here?" I ask, trying to sound like this is nothing but an inconvenience. The swelling has the benefit of making it easy to keep my face straight. Or maybe it's my experience taking a beating that makes it easier.

Knuckles burst my forehead open, blood drips into my eye. Another punch. I taste more blood. A laugh slips from my lips, but it's so foreign, so deep, it doesn't sound like it's mine. At the sound of laughter, Becks snorts like a raging bull. He's a shade of red I've only seen on tomatoes.

He hits me again and again, until my head hangs slack and his knuckles are swollen and purple. Over and over, until I finally black out.

14

AFTER

When my eyes finally open, I swear I hear trumpets and smell the scent of something sweet on the wind. The sun bears down on the stables. It's so hot, the air burns away in waves. My face aches, I pull myself up from the floor, and dust the straw from my shirt. A hunk of horse shit clings to my pants. I feel my face, it's swollen, but not as badly as I expect. Blood clings to my hand, I wipe it on my jeans, and pick up the shovel.

The flies buzz loudly around me. In the distance, I can hear the laughs and the screams from the pool. Sweat has soaked through my shirt, it clings to me like a sticky second skin. As nice as it'd be to fall face first into that pool, I've got work to do.

I move from stall to stall to check on each of the horses. Nothing has ever made me feel as good as being around horses, it makes the persistent throb from my face fade into the background. This was always my escape, how I healed after fights with my dad. They're skinnier than the horses my family breeds, but that will change once I start feeding them. On each stall door there are names scratched, my favorite of the horses is Ginger. She's a sweet, rust colored Arabian. She reminds me of Lady, my favorite horse from home.

Halfway through cleaning, the sun dips toward the horizon. Sayid leans up against the stall and watches me for a few minutes, but doesn't say anything. He holds out a pack of cigarettes, I take one. I wince as I slip the cigarette between my lips, the filter brushes up against a cut.

"Who happened to your face?" he finally asks, his eyes appraising me, like he might be able to tell who did it, if only he stares long enough.

"Becks and his cronies," I say as I shrug.

He shakes his head and looks down, "Seriously? He's such an asshole. One of those dogs that has to piss on everything to prove it's his. I'm not surprised, though, after how long you took this morning."

"Yeah," I say, the scrape of my shovel hitting the ground cuts the air. "You could have warned me."

"You going to be alright?" He takes a step closer to look at my wounds and touches my arm. His warmth seems to meld into my own, my arm tingles in response. My eyes linger on his lips.

"I'll live," I shrug. It's not that bad, I wave him away. I'm not about to go to see the nurse over something as trivial as a fat lip and a couple black eyes. Though the wounds pulse every few minutes to remind me of their existence, my dad has put me in far worse states.

"You should probably steer clear of him," he warns, he crosses his arms as he talks. "Becks can do a lot worse than this, rumor is, he has." His face is flat, the color drained. I'm not sure how he manages to keep up appearances around him, if he's this scared.

"How does that kid not end up in the white house for his handiwork?" I ask. Last I checked, fighting was firmly in the *against the rules* category.

"Know how I told you about those privileged few?" he asks and takes a drag from his cigarette.

I nod.

"Well, if the others are privileged, Becks would be their king."

I shake my head. "Of course." It doesn't surprise me in the least.

"I'm pretty sure his father's money lines the pockets of every single guard in this place," Sayid says as his eyes scan the trees.

"Any idea what his dad does?" I ask.

"Something about rifles, or some kind of guns," he shrugs. "I've heard someone mention it, but I didn't really pay attention."

Hopefully he hasn't smuggled guns into Dozier. Keeping yourself out of the white house is one thing. Guns would be much, *much* worse.

Sayid flicks his cigarette to the ground, he digs in his pockets for another. The lull in the conversation reminds me of the favor I wanted to ask. If I don't want to lose my nerve, I'll have to ask fast.

I stop shoveling for a moment to look at him.

"I need another favor." The words are easier to get out this time, all the adrenaline in my blood makes it hard to feel anything other than the buzzing.

"My, my. Another? Already? I haven't even gotten the letter in the mail." His tone makes it obvious that he's joking, but I don't laugh.

I'm going to owe him big for this one, I know it. And the price is going to be far too high for me to ever pay. But whatever the cost is to see Eden, it will be worth it. "I need you to arrange a meeting with my sister."

His eyes nearly bug out of his head. He crosses his arms, and I see a familiar look on his face. I know it well, I've seen it on Eden's face many times: determination. This isn't a normal request, because of that I think he might be more likely to help me. Hopefully, he likes a challenge.

"That's going to be a tough one." He starts to pace, his eyes tightened in thought.

"Is it even possible?" I ask.

"Anything is possible." He stops pacing to smile at me. "It's going to take a few days to coordinate, but I think I can make it happen."

I swallow hard, "And what will I owe you?"

He shrugs. "I don't know, I'll think about it. Want to get dinner?"

I prop my arms up on the handle of the shovel. Becks must have knocked me out for a while if I missed lunch, even the bell hadn't woken me up. But I'm not hungry.

"I'll pass." Even if I was hungry, I'd probably still avoid the cafeteria. I don't want to explain my face, and I don't want to see Becks. It occurs to me, if it's nearly time for dinner, that means I need to hurry to see Dr. Lennox.

"Suit yourself," Sayid says and shrugs before walking away.

I turn and notice he left a pack of cigarettes sitting on the stable wall. For a moment I stare at them. I can't keep them, as much as I might want to. He's almost out of the stables. I grab them and run after him.

I hold them up and call out, "Hey, you forgot something."

He looks back long enough to say, "No, I didn't."

15

AFTER

I rush from the stables to see Dr. Lennox. I'm late, but I hope that
he'll still see me. When I burst through the door, the receptionist
doesn't bother to look at me, instead he waves me back, nose buried
in a magazine. The clock on the wall tells me that I'm only fifteen
minutes late. That should still be long enough for a session, and not
so long that I can't talk my way out of it.

"I'm sorry I'm late," I say as I open the door.

Dr. Lennox waits for me, sitting in one of the arm chairs with a
notepad in his lap. He's wearing a gray suit with a light plaid pattern
on it. Beside him on the small glass table, is a glass filled with an
amber liquid.

He nods, but doesn't say anything. Instead he eyes my face, and
I'm not sure if he's staring at my wounds from the fight, or if his
cloudy eyes can even see them from this distance.

We exchange small talk before he finally asks, "How are you
doing today?"

"Not so good," I admit.

"Oh?" he asks, but he doesn't bother to grab his notepad.

"I need some answers, and I think there's only one way to get them," I say, my voice far more sure and steady than I expect it to be. Deep down, I *need* to know what happened that night. But the thought also terrifies me. It haunts me. Whatever thoughts my mind has locked down so deep could tell me that I'm a killer, that I did it. And that would mean that I'm capable of doing it again.

"Are you sure you're ready to try regression therapy?" he asks.

I've toyed with the idea for a couple weeks now. In our meetings we've discussed my home life, the friends I had, my relationship with Olivia—but none of that is going to give me answers. Those are the things I already know.

"Yes." My stomach leaps as the word slips out of me. My nerves nag at me, and I can't help but wonder if I will be able to handle the truth hidden in my mind.

"You understand that sometimes the visions may not be completely accurate, but may instead have some symbolic meaning?" he says. This is at least the tenth time he's told me this. "What you could see might end up being worse than nightmares. It could also cause other memories to return, or resurface."

"I understand," I say again. It's not like my brain could really get much worse.

He hesitates, and narrows his eyes. I can tell by the way he's looking at me, he doesn't think it's a good idea.

"Please," I plead. I have to know, I have to try.

"I'll need you to lie on the couch," he relents.

I lean back on the couch, the leather is cold against my skin.

"Close your eyes," he instructs. "Count back from ten slowly, at ten, your arms and legs will begin to relax."

"Ten," I whisper, but I feel nothing.

"Nine, your thoughts will become lighter."

"Nine," I whisper, and something prickles at the back of my mind.

"Eight, slowly the rest of your body will become lighter, weightless."

"Eight," I say as my eyelids flutter. It feels like I'm slipping away.

"Seven, all the tension, all the tethers to this world will begin to fade away," he whispers.

After seven, my mind blurs. His instructions seem to drift away, mingled within my fuzzy mind. The next thing I remember is him telling me to imagine a bridge with mist on the other side. Slowly, he instructs me to cross the bridge, and beyond it I'll find the memories I'm searching for. I cross the misty bridge, and then slowly, I begin to descend into darkness.

The engine of the car rumbles, sputters, and vibrates until my left foot falls asleep. Droplets of rain bomb the hood of my dad's brand new Cadillac. Olivia is cuddled up against me, sitting on the small hump of a seat in the middle. My dad will kill me if he finds out I took his car tonight, but her smile makes it worth it. No matter what my punishment, at least I'll have my memories.

"What do you think our lives will be like after we're out of school?" She tilts her head slightly when she asks, but she's still pressed against my side. Her warmth spreads through me.

"I'm not sure." I have countless fantasies about how I'd like our lives to play out, in all of which she's my wife, but I'm not about to tell her that and embarrass myself. "What do you want life to be like?"

She sits up, her face stern, she's thinking about it. For the briefest of moments, I look at her, hanging onto the silence. In that moment, there's enough time for me to imagine every word I'd like her to say. She chews her lip so hard, I can almost hear it. The moonlight hitting the raindrops on the windshield casts a glow on her face; the way it twists, it's a dance.

My eyes dart back to the road. The headlights flood the street, but there's a dark figure. Someone standing in the middle of the road. My body moves instinctively, jerking the wheel. While I was looking away, we'd started to cross the Sharpe's ferry bridge on my route from Ocala to Howey-in-the-hills.

Rain collects on the bridge, I'm going too fast. I can't pull the car out of the spin. We spin over and over, bouncing off the metal railing until a portion gives way. We hit the water, and Olivia hits the dashboard face first. Metal groans and aches, the water hisses as it pours into the gaps in the frame. I reach out, grabbing onto Olivia as I release my seat belt. She's limp, lifeless as a ragdoll, blood pours down her face. Most of her blonde hair looks red.

As the water pours in, I pull her toward the open window. The car lurches forward as it starts to sink. I wedge my foot against the dash to steady myself as the water rushes over the windshield, I push the door open. My mouth fills with the taste of the swamp. I breathe in the water, and darkness takes me.

I'm gulping the air when my eyes open. Tears burn my eyes, even though I know it wasn't real. I know it was a false vision like Dr. Lennox spoke about. But it doesn't make the pain of watching her die fade. Dr. Lennox waits for me to sit up. His face is heavy, he's as disappointed as I am. *Why can't my mind just cooperate?*

"That can't be what happened," I finally say.

"Like I said, your mind may not give us the truth easily. You still aren't ready to deal with what really happened that night. Your mind might slowly release parts of the truth, eventually you'll be able to piece together what happened," he says, in a comforting voice. "We'll try again in a few days."

16

After

For three days, I've been walking around like a zombie. Counting down the hours, minutes, seconds until I get to see Eden. Every part of me wants to go running into the woods until I find her. But I know she won't be there yet. Though I try to shovel the stalls, and take care of the horses, a slug with a sprained ankle would have been able to do a better job than I have today. My eyes have spent more time searching the tree line than focused on my work.

The afternoon sunlight streams into the stables, and I swear when it starts to set, I can feel it. Excitement and anticipation bubbles up inside me in a nauseating mix. Ginger snorts at me again. She's at least a welcome distraction. I lean the shovel against the stall wall, and scratch her beneath her jaw. Her skin twitches happily, and she closes her eyes. Sayid jogs up behind me, and I can hear the disgust seep out of him in a sigh. It's obvious the way he looks at horses, he hates them, he looks at them like most people would look at rats.

"As soon as the dinner bell rings, we're going to head into the woods," he says as he leans against one of the support posts, taking slow drags from a cigarette. "They're meeting us near the edge of the property, close to Marianna."

I nod, and give Ginger a final scratch before leaning against the stall wall. She rests her head on my shoulder and watches Sayid. It feels familiar, like being stuck between parents that aren't getting along.

"Are we going to be able to make it out there in time?" Dozier has a lot of acreage, it seems like a lot of land to cover in one night.

He shrugs. "I've done it before, once a week actually," he smirks.

I look at him questioningly, then remember it must be part of how he gets things into the school.

Sayid drops his cigarette to the ground and extinguishes it with the toe of his shoe. "You know, we could run." He says like he's not really sure it's a good idea. I'm not sure why he'd want to run, he just keeps coming back.

Every thought in my mind screeches to a halt. We *could* run. But I'm surprised that I don't want to. There's still work I have to do with Dr. Lennox to get my memories back, and I can't leave until I know for sure. Deep down I know what will happen though. If I find out I killed her, I'll leave here in a body bag. If I didn't kill her, I'll have to find who did.

"I can't, not until I'm done with my sessions with Dr. Lennox," I say. The very idea that there's an end in sight, a day that isn't five years away, it makes me feel lighter. One day we'll run. But I have to know what happened to Olivia first.

"One day," I promise.

He looks at me surprised, he probably thought I'd flat out refuse to leave. Sayid opens his mouth to speak, but the bell rings across the campus. Behind us, the sun seeps toward the horizon. I pat Ginger, and follow Sayid behind the stables toward the tree line. The way Sayid stomps through the woods I'm thankful that everyone else is having dinner. Otherwise, people a hundred yards away would probably hear us. As the final slivers of light are snuffed out by the darkness, his footsteps lighten.

"You want a cigarette?" he asks as he thrusts the pack toward me. "You look tense."

I *am* tense, and nervous, and excited. There's so much going on inside me all I can really feel is the prickle at the bottom of my stomach and the sweat growing on my neck. I've got so much energy bound up inside me, I want to sprint off into the woods as fast as I can. Without Eden I feel perpetually disoriented. Every day of my life has had her in it. It's hard to exist without her around. But tonight, knowing I'll see her—it's like getting a lost piece of myself back.

"Yeah, sure, thanks man," I say as I take one from him. He lights it for me, and smiles. It's obvious that he's waiting for me to smile back, I don't; instead I keep walking.

"How old is Eden?" Sayid finally asks.

"Same age as me, eighteen," I explain. "She's technically a day older though."

"Twins born on different days?" he asks confused. But I'm not thrown off by the confusion, Eden and I have dealt with it our whole lives. It's not often you hear of twins at all, let alone twins born on different days.

"Yeah, she was born right before midnight. I was born after, little more than an hour between us. We even have different astrological signs," I say as I weave between the tree trunks. A cool breeze slips between the trees, it's a breathy rush, like the forest sighs.

He doesn't say anything, occasionally he takes a slow drag from his cigarette, and the wind carries the smoke into my face. The ember at the end bobs along with each step he takes, like a lantern caught in the sea.

"Do you have any brothers or sisters?" I ask when I'm sick of hearing the thrumming of my heart in my ears.

"Nope," he says quickly, his word as sharp as a dagger.

I know better than to ask, or pry any further. Instead, I follow along silently. Sayid has never offered up much information about himself. He locks everything inside, and I'm not the kind of person to pry. Secrets don't bother me, silence is much easier to swallow. No one ever got hurt keeping their mouths shut.

Ahead of us, between the trees, I see flutters of white. The memory digs at me. In my peripheral vision I see Olivia running, only to disappear the second I turn my head to look at her. My breath catches each time she appears, and then escapes the second she's gone.

If I had to guess, I'd say it took us forty hours of walking to make it to the clearing right outside Marianna. It's probably more like a three-hour walk, but the way my feet ache, it might as well have been clear across the country. If Sayid wasn't so spooked by horses, I'd have ridden Ginger out here.

"How will they know to find us here?" I ask as he takes a seat at the base of a large tree. I use my t-shirt to mop the sweat off my brow, neck. Dew clings to the strands of Spanish moss, when the moonlight catches them, it looks like they're wet with blood.

"Gave them some landmarks, a house a couple blocks away, the huge willow tree right out there. Really, we're watching for them, they won't be able to see us in the trees," he says as he points to the enormous willow tree that looms over the field beyond the tree line.

My blood buzzes as I watch the field. In the distance, I see headlights glow against the empty road. The lights die, a door shuts, but I don't see her until she's under the tree. Her long black hair blows in the wind, she pulls a jacket tight around her as she looks around for us.

"There she is," I say, but it feels impossible. It can't be Eden, she can't be so close.

We emerge from the tree line, and she starts to walk toward us. My pace quickens. She starts to jog. We careen into each other in a hug that makes my chest ache. I wish I could have really hugged her at the jail, but it's hard to manage when you're handcuffed.

"I missed you," she says as she squeezes me.

"Of course you did," I say, and a laugh pours out of me. It feels so foreign, so strange to laugh. It's been so long, it almost feels wrong. The second the happiness bubbles up inside me, guilt follows.

You don't deserve to be happy.

She pulls away and looks me over, like she's expecting to find broken bones. When she finally nods with approval, someone saunters up behind her. It's a kid I've seen at our old school, but I have no idea who he is. He's got long blond hair, a Jimi Hendrix t-shirt, and he absolutely reeks of weed. I can smell him from ten feet away. This is the kind of kid my dad would look at and grumble *burnout* beneath his breath. The way he did before William went off to Vietnam. To me, this is the kind of kid I could be friends with.

"Who's this?" I ask her.

She rolls her eyes, she doesn't want to tell me. I push past her, and offer the kid a cigarette. "Asher," I say.

"Blake," he says as he takes the cigarette, and nods a thank you.

"How do you two know each other?" I ask him, I know she's not going to offer the information willingly. I've never actually seen her hang around with a boy—not that I'd care if she did. She's always acted like boys were beneath her. Like, she'd never be bothered.

He eyes her, searching her face. I'd guess, for how much he's allowed to tell me. She glowers at him, a look that could sour milk.

Blake doesn't shrink beneath her glare like I expect him to, instead he smiles and winks at her. Her mouth twists and she sneers. I know I'm going to like anyone who can make my sister sneer like that.

"Can we move on to more important matters? Please?" she says, as she tries to take the attention off Blake. She thinks I'll forget all about Blake, her boyfriend, I'd guess by the way he looks at her—I won't forget, by the way.

We walk back to the tree line, Eden sits in front of me. Our legs crossed, knees touching. She slides a folder from her bag. I reach out to snatch it, but she yanks it away. Her eyes are serious, pools of amber swimming with warnings. I know the words that linger behind those eyes.

"There are pictures," she warns. But I don't need the warnings. I've already seen her body, it's all I remember from that night. It appears over and over again in every-single-one of my nightmares. I snatch the folder from her and shine my flashlight onto the contents.

It's heavy in my lap. I can feel the weight of the words about her death, about the murder, about the suspect: *me*. The papers crinkle as I open the folder, for just a moment I see her body folded up on the ground like a wilted flower. I flip the pictures over face down on the folder. But not before my dinner creeps up my throat. My head swims, and my throat burns. I close my eyes. In a few seconds, it passes.

There are pages and pages of handwritten notes so scribbled they may as well be in Hebrew. There are several diagrams, and then more pages of notes. Eden must see my confusion, she watches me scour over the pages like a hunting dog watches the ducks.

"There really isn't much in there," she finally says.

I sigh, and disappointment seeps into me slow and steady.

"One thing," she says.

My ears perk up.

"There was a third set of footprints at the scene that the police couldn't identify," she says, her voice barely above a whisper. The way she says it, she may as well be telling me a ghost story.

My stomach drops, there was someone else. It *wasn't* me. "Thank you," I say, it's the first time I've said thank you to her and *really* meant it. "How's Mom?" I ask, when she goes quiet.

She rolls her eyes. "A mess. You know how she is. She lost her favorite, and then her backup favorite. But without you and William around she has been nicer to me. Dad, though..." She shudders.

I don't particularly care about how Dad's been, but because it's bothering Eden I ask, "What about him?"

She plays with her necklace and thumbs the Saturn charm. "The day we left the jail, he issued an edict. No one in the house is allowed to say your name, as far as he's concerned, you don't exist. He's hoping you die here." She looks away from me, her jaw set in anger. Her elbows propped on her knees. "He said he rather you be dead than have a murderer in the family."

I shrug, I figured as much. A few months ago, that might have devastated me. Now it doesn't even give me pause.

"I need to tell you about something else," she says, her voice barely above a whisper. She looks to Blake and Sayid first, before she continues. They're immersed in their own conversation. "Know how I mentioned before that I thought Dominic was following me?"

"Yeah?" My mind flashes back to the first time Eden told me about it, while I was still in county lockup.

"He was following me from class to class, so I stopped going to school because he's creeping me out. He won't even talk to me, I've tried," she says, there's an edge to her voice, like it's about to crack. Eden is anything but emotional, there's only ever one emotion that she shows: anger. She's like a rabid, cornered cat. "He's been hanging around the house. At night, I see him near the woods. I don't know what he's doing out there." She wraps her arms tight around herself. "I feel like he's everywhere. Like he might even be out here," her eyes search the trees, like Dominic might be hidden in the shadows only feet away from us. "He's always watching me."

"When's the last time you saw him?" I ask.

"Yesterday." She looks down at her hands and picks at her fingernails. "I went to the Howey mansion with Blake to see if we could find anything. When we got there, I was looking through the windows while I tried to find a way in. Dominic was there, in the house, covered in blood. He saw me and chased us off." She stops talking, and I see her shiver. Her face darkens with something I never see from my sister, fear. "I think *he* did it, I think he killed Olivia. There's something off about him, Asher, something that creeps me the hell out."

It's only because of the way Eden stares at me, that I realize my mouth is hanging open. "Covered in blood?" I ask, my mind spinning wildly. There has to be an explanation.

She nods.

"What could he have been doing there?" I ask, careful that my words aren't defensive.

"I have no idea," she pauses as she scans the trees around us. "He had something to do with her death, I know it."

I don't want to believe it. No part of me wants to believe that he's following my sister, or that he killed Olivia. More importantly, *why* would he have killed her? Sometimes he seemed jealous of her, but never deadly. Never threatening. I know better than to ask Eden. Rather than her understanding that I'm trying to puzzle it out in my mind, she'll see it as a challenge. The last thing I want to do is to challenge her. She wouldn't make up something like seeing him at the Howey mansion. I swallow my questions, I know what I have to do, I have to trust my sister.

"Don't go back to that house," I beg her. It kills me that I can't protect her.

She nods. "You don't have to tell me twice."

"And I want you to stay away from Dominic."

"It's not like I'm seeking him out," she says, her eyes flashing.

"That's not what I meant." I look down as frustration pools inside me. Eden's always a bit defensive. "Just don't go anywhere alone. I don't even want you staying at the house," I explain.

"Last couple days, I've been staying at Blake's," she says, and even in the dim light, I can see her cheeks turn pink. Any other time, I'd tease her about Blake, but I know I'll risk her storming off. We've got so little time together, I don't want to waste it on a fight. I try to stifle my smile, but it doesn't work.

"Shut up," she says as she glares at me.

I hold my hands up in surrender. "I said nothing."

"Uh huh, I know what that look on your face means."

I roll my eyes at her.

Silence brews between us for long enough that I light a cigarette, and she scowls at me for it. The trees above us seem to ripple, moved by a breeze that I can't feel. In the distance, I can hear the low drill of a cicada.

"Is it really as bad in there as they say?" she asks.

I shrug. "Yes and no. Some days, it's not so bad. But there are things in there worse than the rumors say."

"If you made it all the way out here, you could run away," she says, pleading edges on her words.

I look down at my lap. The truth of it is, I'm too selfish to run away. Before I go anywhere, there are too many answers I need. Part of me knows I should leave and protect my sister, but I just can't.

"Not yet," I say. "There's someone at the school who might be to help me get my memories back."

She looks at me confused. "A shrink?"

I nod.

"Maybe you don't remember for a reason." Her eyes narrow and she presses her lips together.

I didn't give her the answer she wanted.

"What if you die in there?" she asks.

"I'm not going to die, Eden."

Sayid stands up, pulling our attention from our conversation. "We need to start heading back, or we won't get back to campus before the sun comes up."

"Our two hours is up already?" I ask.

Sayid taps on his watch and nods.

Eden and I hug, but refuse to say goodbye. She's got a pool of tears in her eyes. But every time I think she might start to cry, she sniffles and looks away to compose herself. She clings to me, like she did when we were little, before she got strong, before it was clear that she didn't need me anymore. Usually, she's as vicious and hardened as a feral cat, but today, I can see it on her face that she needs me.

"I won't be here forever," I promise her and hope it's not a lie.

She nods, and disappears beyond the woods with Blake. I watch them go, forcing myself to stay behind, and not follow them. Deep down, I know if I don't stay at Dozier, if I don't get the answers I need, I'll hate myself. Turning back into the dark woods, I convince myself it's for the best.

The moonlight filters through the trees above barely lighting our path. My eyes burn, my body aches for sleep. Sayid follows along behind me, his steps much quieter than they were on our trip out here. He stops, but it takes me a few more steps to notice. I turn, he stands looking at me, and brings his finger to his lips. I hold my arms up toward my shoulders, to ask *what?* He holds his hand up, as if to cup his ear, and points out to the woods. *Listen.*

For a long time, all I hear is the thud of my heartbeat, and my own breath. Then I hear in the distance footsteps, twigs snapping, something clunking against tree trunks. Sayid steps closer, and leaves less than a foot between us.

"We need to sneak back quietly, that might be a guard. We're close to the school." He whispers, barely loud enough for me to hear.

I sneak silently through the woods at his side. We walk so close, his arm brushes against mine. No matter how we try to distance ourselves from the sound, it seems to grow closer. *Step, step, drag, clunk.* Over, and over. Louder and louder. He reaches his hand out to stop me, and pulls me behind a tree. That's when I see a guard, dragging a kid's body through the woods. Blood trails down the face of the corpse. I don't recognize him.

I'm paralyzed, rooted to the ground with fear. My breath sounds loud to my ears, I slow my breathing, not wanting to make any noise that might alert the guard.

For nearly five minutes we wait as the guard drags the body farther into the woods. *Step, step, crack, clunk. Step, step, clunk.* Until, finally, he disappears into the darkness. But even after he's long gone, we wait, just in case the sound of our steps carry.

When I see the stables, relief washes over me. Madison stands in the distance, calling to me. I feel dead on my feet, so tired that my bones ache. I fall back onto my mattress, it creaks beneath me. My eyes close, sleep takes me. And the nightmares seep in like a dark fog spreading in my mind.

17

BEFORE
Date Unknown

Her face glows. It's so close to the candle, I don't know how it's not burning her. Maybe it is burning her, she just doesn't care. It's not like it can hurt her, not long term, anyway. Her eyes are far off, she hasn't looked at me or spoken a word in nearly an hour. She's lost in thought. All day she's argued with me without saying a word. Every glance, every glare, she can stir up a fight without a single syllable. As I watch her intently, the ghost of a memory pulls at me. She's so familiar, but I can't quite place who she is. Physically, she's a stranger. But there's something inside of her, a soul, a spirit, that I recognize. Someone I've known before, someone I'll know again.

"If it doesn't work," she finally says, her words trailing off. Her face is grim, but it's always grim. She's always been a pessimist, and always will be.

"It will work." I say firmly. I'm sure of it.

"Fine," she says with gritted teeth. "But if it doesn't. I have a theory."

I lean back against my chair, and pull away from the table far enough to cross my legs. I wave my hand at her, "Go on then." Even if I told her I didn't want to hear her theory, she'd tell me anyway.

"We need to convince him to make more of us," she says, the smallest smile curls her lips. "Better though, would be to make more of us without him ever knowing what we had."

"What?" My brows pull together.

"I think each time he makes another one like us, it makes him weaker. If he keeps doing it, we might finally be able to kill him," she explains, her face hardens and she looks away. "We're going to need his blood."

I don't want to try this. Doing it could risk everything. It could ruin our plans. She can try to get him to create as many others as she wants, but if I get his blood, I'm not using it to curse anyone else.

"Whatever we do, he can't see you. We have to be sure." Warning is heavy in my words.

She rolls her eyes at me. "Am I ever anything but careful?" She pauses, and her eyes tighten. "This is important, I think it might be our only chance."

It's a good theory, however, it's the exact opposite of mine. My fear, if we do finally kill him, all of us will die too. Then again, maybe that's for the best. We are meant to die after all.

18

It's been three weeks since I saw Eden. Without her I feel like I'm stuck behind a wall while the rest of the world keeps moving around me. Though I can hear the muffled voices, I can't break through. I go through the motions because I have to.

Sayid is off in the woods tonight getting a fresh shipment. I offered to help, but he has to warn his suppliers I'm coming before I tag along. So while the night thickens around me, I sit on the back porch and watch the orange trees. The smoke from my cigarette swirls up to the roof. Mosquitoes buzz too close to my face.

A breeze whips through the trees, and my eyes narrow as I search between the rows. I've seen her three times tonight. Her glowing face pops in and out of the trees. And I swear, each time the wind blows, I hear her laugh.

My skin warms, my cheeks burn. Someone, something, is watching me. To my left and right there's nothing. I scan the rows again. At the edge of the trees, Olivia stands watching me. A shuddering wind sweeps across the campus and the branches creak. Her white dress whips against her legs, the fabric is stained with something dark.

"Asher," she whispers my name.

It's the longest she's ever stayed, and the first time she's spoken to me. I stand and jump off the edge of the porch, never taking my eyes off the trees, off her.

I walk toward her, she cocks her head and smiles. My head is thick with static. This isn't possible. *This isn't real, is it?* As I get closer, she spins on her heel and runs into the trees. I follow, only a few feet behind her. She weaves in and out of the rows. I'm breathless as I try to follow her. As quick as a bullet she races into the next row. I follow, but find it empty. My gait slows, and I listen for her. But she's nowhere to be found.

Each of my limbs is heavy, weighted with sadness. My eyes burn. *You're fucking crazy.*

Behind me something moves, I try to turn, but arms wrap around me. Her body presses to my back. Her cheek is against my neck. She leans into me. My body recoils at her touch. Confusion and panic tethers me to the ground.

"I'm sorry. But in the end, it's for the best," she whispers. But it's not Olivia's voice. It's a voice I've heard before, but I can't place it. The words cause something to stir at the back of my mind. I shift and try to pull away, but she grips me tighter. Slowly she drags something across my throat. I hear rain. But it's not rain. It's my blood.

My legs tremble, and my knees give out. Blood covers my hands and drips down my arms. Panic rises up in my throat, it pools just beneath the wound. The world shifts around me. And I know I'm dying.

I fall backward. Black edges in on my vision, my thoughts slow and blur together. Olivia crouches beside me, her hands stroke my face.

"One day you'll understand," she says as she pets me. Her words are soft, sweet. But something's wrong.

"You have to stay away from Dominic." Her eyes scan the trees. "He can't take you. He'll try to get you to go with him willingly. Don't do it, Asher. Don't let him trick you."

The edges of my vision blur. My breaths are shallow, hollow.

"This will help," she says as she pets my face. "It's okay." She slips a dagger into my hand. "Don't let him take it. Don't even let him know you have it."

The last thing I see before I die is Olivia giving me one last kiss on the cheek.

19

BEFORE
Date unknown

"Run," She screams at me as she looks back, but the darkness hides her face. Her dress billows behind her, like a ribbon seized by a squall.

She runs fifteen feet ahead of me. It's so dark, I can barely see her. Sandwiched between stone buildings in an alley, we're so deep in the shadows I'm not sure I'll see light again. I'm lagging behind, my shoes slip on the slick cobblestone streets. The night envelopes us. As we run, the alley seems to close in. But it goes on forever. I'm not sure we'll ever reach the end.

It's the footsteps in the distance, only fifty or so feet behind me, keeping me going. My heart beats so hard, it hurts. Pain spreads to my ribs, my legs, its claws digging in. Each pump seems to propel the agony further through my body. Beneath the pain, I feel the slightest prickle of excitement—not fear, like I expect.

Ahead of me, the alley opens into the street and spits us out. The gas lamps are so bright, my eyes burn. Her eyes are wild, she's searching behind me. Her long, brown hair is tangled. The skin on her face seems to contract, like it's pulled tight. In this light, how wild she is, I barely recognize her. She thrusts something cold and metal into my hand. The footsteps grow louder behind us. They're close now, in a couple seconds, they'll be on the street with us.

"Hide it with the book," she says as she turns to run. She flashes me a look, but it's not one I recognize. Whatever she's trying to say, it's lost on me. My body turns away from her automatically. I weave around light posts; flickers of gas flames send dancing bursts of light across the wet cobblestones. Each post makes the smell of gas grow stronger, my throat tightens. Moths gather around the light, forming shifting otherworldly masses. My feet slip over the stones, and I slam into the door of a row house and it shudders under my weight. I push off, my breath caught in my throat. Cold mist stings my face as I run into it.

This city may be unfamiliar to *me*, but it's not unfamiliar to my body. Expertly, I work my way through alleys, stick to the shadows, and disappear when gathering voices grow. As the crowded streets grow sparse, I slow. On the outskirts things seem to huddle, trees, people, even the fog gathers around the light posts. As the pounding of my heart slows, the sounds of a trumpet far away sweeps through the streets. It's slow, sad, a lament.

As I walk, I stash the blade in my coat. I feel exposed, but I don't stop, even for a moment. The symbols on the hilt of the knife seem to hum with energy. I feel them, but I can't look at them, not now. He's too close. His footsteps quicken.

Beside me, a stone wall forms a perimeter around an ancient cemetery, I slip through the open gates. Marble statues and mausoleums are built so closely together here, there isn't even room for grass. There's barely room for me. The dead are as crowded as the buildings in the city. The only living thing here is me. But somehow, I know I won't be for long. Each breath I take is on borrowed time.

I weave in and out of the rows of mausoleums and finally find the one I seek. The one I've seen in my mind a thousand times. The door stands out to me. An intricate bird is woven in the wrought iron. As I reach for the door, something grabs me, and I feel cold bite my neck. I reach for the blade as the steel slices my flesh.

20

AFTER

"Asher, put down the knife," Sayid pleads, his arms are out in front of him, palms facing me.

It takes several seconds of blinking before I realize where I am. The boards of the creaky back porch bow beneath my feet. Darkness edges on my vision, his voice is impossibly loud. His pleading calls to me, calms me. A few moments ago, I was frightened, but now I can't remember why. The fear disappears like a whisper in the wind. Goose bumps trail from my neck down my arms, I shiver. My heartbeat is uneven, like I've been running, or fighting. My thoughts are thick, slow, like my mind is filled with molasses.

My hand moves to my throat, but I'm not sure why.

"Asher, please," he says, his voice slow and even. Sayid steps closer, the wood creaking beneath his feet. His brown eyes are wide, almost panicked.

Though I look at him, I still can't make sense of the situation. I have no memory of coming to the back porch. My thoughts are disjointed like they're foreign to my own mind. Darkness surrounds us, stars twinkling in the inky sky above. Fear hovers in his eyes. Sorrow wells inside me. I can't stand for him to look at me like *that*.

I can't stand for *anyone* to look at me like that.

"What's wrong?" I ask, my voice is thick, and sounds strangled.

"The knife." He points toward my left hand. After he points, his hand returns so that both his palms are out, facing me. Like he's surrendering.

I look down and find a small silver blade with what looks like runes and symbols etched in the handle, I'm so engrossed by them, I almost miss the blood dripping from the point. *Where did I get a knife?* Unaware as to why I'm holding it, I point the hilt to Sayid, and surrender it to him. A shuddering breath slips through my lips as my heart quickens. Panic tightens my throat. *Another knife. More blood. Who did I hurt this time?*

"I'm sorry," I say, my insides twist. My mouth is drier than month-old hay. I try to swallow, to clear the dread pooled in my throat, but it doesn't work.

Sayid is the only friend I've got. The last thing I want to do is scare him, to make him look at me like a rabid animal. He takes the knife from me and inspects it. A few times, he rolls the blade over in his hands, looking it over before he speaks.

"Where'd you get this?"

"I have no idea." I shrug. I wouldn't even know where to look for a knife here, even if I wanted one. If I had access to a knife, chances are, I wouldn't be standing with it on the back porch.

"You don't know where you got the knife?" His head cocks to the side as he asks.

I shake my head.

"How can you not know where you got the knife?" There's an edge to his voice, his brows are furrowed in disbelief. "You can tell me, it's okay," he says as he takes a step toward me.

Frustration flickers inside me. "I don't know where I got it. I've never seen that knife before. I don't even know how I got on the porch," I snap, and regret it immediately.

Sayid looks at me like he doesn't quite believe me, but he doesn't push it.

"Any idea whose blood this is?" he asks, shaking the last bit off the tip. He then walks closer, and inspects the small red pool next to my foot.

I shake my head, and step back. I look down, there's blood soaked through the top of my shirt around my neck. The knife's proximity makes me recoil. I never want to wake up with another knife in my hand. My pulse quickens to a frenzied gallop when I look at the blade. I reach for my neck, but there isn't so much as a scratch lingering there. It couldn't be my blood, I'm not hurt. *What if I killed someone? What if it's like last time?*

Maybe the three sets of footprints were a mistake. That would mean I really did kill her. The realization nearly knocks me over, and I grab the wall to brace myself. It crushes me. I could have done it. I could have. Guilt digs at me, slowly winding it's cold fingers around my mind. The thoughts rush in, the vision of her pale face, her blue lips.

What if I had hurt Sayid? What if he's next?

He's only been nice to me. I don't deserve his friendship.

"What's going on Asher? You can tell me," he urges.

"If there was anything to tell, anything I remembered, I'd tell you," I say, and my voice falters.

"If someone tried to hurt you, if you were just defending yourself, I'd understand. It'd be okay." There's an edge to his voice that flickers anger inside me.

Why would I lie?

When I don't speak, he says, "I'm going to hide this, if you don't mind." The way he says it, I know there'll be no arguing. Good thing I don't plan to argue. He steps off the porch, and disappears into the darkness.

My thoughts are unsettled, they swim in my mind as I walk upstairs and collapse onto my bed. I close my eyes, my mind turns the thoughts over and over again as I sink into my mattress, hoping that the next time I wake up, it will be without a knife in my hand.

21

AFTER

The tray in front of me looks like a buffet, it's stacked so high with bacon and pancakes, I'm not sure where to start. The food is stacked so precariously, I'm afraid if I take a bite, it might come crashing down onto the table. Sayid is friends with every single kid who works in the kitchen. Since we go through the line together, that means I get enough food to feed three of me. Luckily, they've also started giving me the cast-off vegetables and fruits. I'm always well stocked on treats for the horses.

"So, I still haven't heard back from Eden about the next meetup," Sayid says as he chews a bit of his breakfast.

"What do you mean?" I ask, confused. Why would I want to meet up with Eden again so soon? I didn't want her to come again for another few weeks. It's too risky of a venture more often.

"We agreed that I'd try to coordinate with Eden and Blake for them to come back. It's been almost three weeks since the last meeting, so I figure now would be about right," he says, his brows furrowed. "It might take a week to figure out the timing."

The words get stuck in my mind, it takes a long time for me to process them. "What do you mean it's been *three weeks*? We met with them last night."

"It's definitely been about three weeks."

I shake my head. "That's not possible."

He stops chewing, and sets down his fork. It takes him a long time to speak again, "What do you think today's date is?" he asks.

I shrug, I'm not certain. I guess, "April 6th?" I haven't exactly been keeping my eyes on a calendar.

He shakes his head, "It's April 27th."

I may not have been watching the calendar closely, but there's no way it's almost May. That just isn't possible. That would mean that I'd been at Dozier almost two months.

I rack my brain for the memories I know must be there. Last night I saw Eden, I know it. Then there are pieces of a memory, something with Olivia. But that couldn't be real. I remember her, and a knife.

No. That wasn't real.

I feel like I'm coming apart at the seams. My mind churns, every thought clogging my mind feels frayed, broken, damaged.

What's wrong with me?

Frustration strangles the questions that rise up in my throat. What else did I miss? There's so much that could have happened in three weeks. I could have hurt someone else.

"There's no way, why can't I remember the last few weeks?" I ask.

"What's the last thing you remember?"

The knife and the dream. But I don't want to tell him about the dream. I look crazy enough as it is. "Waking up on the porch with," I scan the room, and lower my voice, "the knife."

"That was last night," he confirms. "What do you remember before that?"

"Seeing Eden." My eyes drop to the table, and my mouth goes dry.

"You seriously don't remember anything else?" Sayid asks as he shifts on the seat and pulls away.

I shake my head. There's a fragment of a memory that lingers in the back of my mind. But it can't be real.

"That's really weird." He points down at the two pills on my tray, the ones prescribed by Dr. Lennox. "Could it have something to do with those?"

I shrug. I push my tray away, pills and all. My stomach is uneasy, filled with questions. I trust Sayid, but he has to be wrong. I saw Eden last night, didn't I?

What if it happened again? What if I can't remember because I hurt someone?

Out of habit, my eyes scan the room. I try to see if anyone is missing, but it's no use. I don't know the faces well enough yet.

There are a thousand questions I want to ask Sayid. And by the way he eyes me, I know he's got questions of his own. But before I can even open my mouth again, a kid from the lunch line comes over and sits across from us. He pulls off his hairnet, and hunches over the table, blue eyes locked on Sayid. The kid has a shaggy mop of startlingly blonde hair, it's nearly white. His face is serious, and he looks at Sayid like he's about to lay into him.

"I wanted to give you a heads up," he says to Sayid, while looking toward the end of the table at the guard posted there. I'm not sure why he bothers, none of the guards in the cafeteria ever pay attention to us. His voice is low but even. "They busted me with contraband yesterday."

Sayid's jaw tightens, just long enough for me to notice. He doesn't look worried though, his fork is stuck through a large clump of scrambled eggs. He pops them in his mouth before he speaks. "And why should this concern me?"

"I didn't say nothing." He presses his lips together, and shifts uncomfortably. "I swear it, I'd never rat you out."

Sayid sets his fork down, and leans against the table, eyeing the kid. "Brandon, what has you spooked? Why are you even telling me if you didn't spill?"

He looks down. "Lately, they've been taking kids to the white house for practically nothin'. They knew before you left last time that you were supplying. I think they're on to you again. You gotta to be careful. You need to find a new place to hide your stuff." He glances at me, just long enough to give me a slight smile. "They're going to move in on the laundry soon. Maybe *today*."

Sayid nods. "Thank you, I'll do that. Don't worry, I'm not going to raise my rates on you or anything. In fact, the next one is on me."

Brandon's mouth drops open, then he smiles. "Thanks man, you're the best. You're going to get a full pig's worth of bacon tomorrow, promise."

"If you keep this up, I might die of a heart attack before my next shipment," Sayid laughs.

I've barely dug my way through one of the stalls when I hear someone walk up behind me. My heart skips a beat, and my throat tightens, expecting that Becks and his cronies have returned. Instead, Sayid nods at me, sweat clinging to his brow. He carries a stack of horse blankets nearly as tall as he is. His arms shake under the weight. Sayid's eyes are narrowed in an unusual way, they flick from one stall to another, searching.

"Hey!" I call out, and prop the shovel against a wall.

His eyes go wide when one of the horses pops their head out

of the stall, I see him swallow, and the way he looks back, I can tell he's seconds away from running. I step back into the stables, brows furrowed as I wait for him. *What has him spooked?* Once he's nowhere near any of the horses, he lets me help. I'm not entirely sure why he's bringing these over, it's eighty degrees outside, none of the horses will need a blanket for another six months.

"Everything alright?" I ask.

"No, the guards are moving in on the laundry, I need to hide most of my shipment somewhere else. I had to get it out now. I'm looking for a good place to hide everything, at least for a few weeks." He drops the blankets onto the ground, and takes a deep breath as he rubs his arms. When the blankets hit the ground, I hear the muffled clink of bottles hitting one another.

"It'd depend on how much you have in there." I point to the blankets. "But you should be able to hide most of it in the hay bales up in the loft. I'm the only person who ever goes up there, if you hide the stuff in the back, no one would ever find it," I offer, trying to discern how much he actually has bound inside these blankets. *Does he have more back at the laundry?*

"I could kiss you right now," he laughs.

I press my lips together and shift uncomfortably.

"Mind helping me get it up there?" he asks after a few awkward moments.

I grab the top two blankets, and I'm surprised by how much he's managed to stash in them. There's a good fifty pounds of merchandise.

"What the hell's in here?" I ask, my arms feel like Jell-O beneath the weight.

"Cigarettes, hooch, girly magazines, junk food, the usual." He shrugs, like I should know the items he stocks. Other than the cigarettes, none of the other items concern me. It's not like I'm one of his customers.

He must have a year's worth of smokes for the entire school for it to weigh this much. It takes nearly ten trips each for us to move all the merchandise up into the loft, and he has to make two more trips to the laundry to get the rest. After we carry it all up, we go about sorting everything. All the cigarettes go into the closest hay bales, since those get used up first, and technically speaking, they're the least dangerous contraband. Magazines get rolled up in the inside the bales behind those. And the furthest, that's where we hide all the bottles. There are so many bottles of different kinds of liquor, I'm not sure how he tells them all apart.

"I owe you," he says, breathless, falling against one of the hay bales. With his shirt balled in his fists, he wipes his brow. I catch myself staring at his exposed stomach. My cheeks burn, and I look away.

"Yes, you do," I say dryly. My arms ache, and my back is stiff. I sit next to Sayid, and the straw pokes at my lower back. His arm brushes mine, it's slick with sweat. The heat coming off him tickles against my skin. Something prickles in the pit of my stomach, something I try to smother the second I feel it. It's something I haven't felt since Olivia.

"How about I let you shower first tonight?" he says.

"That's a good start."

In the loft with Sayid at my side, I sit with my legs crossed and lean on my knees. I take a drag from my cigarette as I stare off at nothing. I rub my aching arms. Questions about my missing weeks prod the back of my mind.

"Can I ask you something?" The question tumbles out of me. It's for the best, it's only a matter of time before I lose my nerve.

He shrugs and waves his hand at me. "Ask away." A sly smile creeps across his face, but I'm not sure why.

"Have I been here the last few weeks?"

His eyebrow perks up, and he nods. "Sure have. Where else would you have been?"

"Have I been weird or anything?" I ask as uncertainty nags at me. It seems a strange thing to ask, but I need to figure out what happened to me over the past few weeks. My sanity depends on it.

"Weird for here, or weird for *you*?" The way he asks, I can't tell if he's joking or not.

"Both, I guess."

"You've been a little quiet. But nothing weird." He scoots closer to me. Close enough that I look away and swallow hard.

A bit of the anxiety welled up inside me unravels as I exhale.

"It's going to be okay," he says as he pats my arm.

How can he be so sure? He found me with a knife. He knows I may have killed at least one person already.

I wish he was right, but deep down, I know he's wrong.

Sayid's snores echo through our bedroom, he sounds like a growling bear. I lean against the wall using the scant moonlight to read. Sleep doesn't come easy, fears that I'll wake up with another knife in my hand, that another few weeks of my life will disappear nearly give me a panic attack if I close my eyes on purpose. It's so late, the only thing I can hear outside is the trickle of rain and a breathy wind. The rest of Dozier is silent, deep within a slumber like Sayid.

I turn the page of my book after I've read the same sentence five times and my mind still won't process it. I'm not sure how long I've been staring at the words not really reading. Downstairs, a noise cuts through the silence, the sound of a body hitting a wall. Thanks to my father, it's a noise I've heard at least a hundred times. I wait, my ears perked. I hear the noise again, followed by a high voice I recognize.

"Help me," Olivia screams.

I run down the stairs two at a time, gripping the handrail so that my rushed steps won't send me careening into the floor. On the first floor I search for her, my heart pounds, my breaths are as sharp as razors. My chest is tight with fear.

Where is she?

Behind me, I hear banging. Another slam. I burst through the bathroom door. But it's not Olivia.

Of course it's not her, she's dead you idiot.

I see a mop of brown hair on the floor. A scrawny kid is face down, eating the tiles. Crony one sits on his lower back, and holds his head down with his palm. The other crony tugs on the kid's pants. Becks stands beside them, arms crossed, a smirk of approval creases his round face. He turns when the door claps shut behind me. His eyes trace up and down my body, the way he looks at me makes my skin crawl.

"Well, well, well," he says, each word slower than the last. "You eva' had one of those Christmas mornings where every single present you open ain't what you want, and then there's that last one, and you *know* from the moment you see it that it's exactly what you've been waiting for?" He runs his tongue across his lips.

I cross my arms, and set my feet in a wide stance. It doesn't matter that this kid makes my skin crawl, or that breaking this up, saving that fucking kid, is going to get my teeth knocked in. My face is a mask, a glare etched so deep into my features it may as well be carved. I'm frozen, fear glues me to the floor, but I'm not going to let Becks do this.

"Let him go." I keep my voice even, firm, strong. I don't let any of the fear coursing through me taint my words. My words are so loud, they echo off the tile walls.

Becks steps closer to the boy. The boy has turned his head to look at me, disgust boils up inside me, a bitter taste is so strong in my mouth that I almost gag. He can't be older than eleven.

"And why would I eva' do that?" he asks, and winks at me; like there's a fucking inside joke between us.

"You'd rather have me, wouldn't you?" I ask, I already know the answer. I take a step toward him and hold my arms out as an invitation. It's obvious in the way his eye twitches when I say it aloud.

"Fine, let him go," Becks waves his hand.

The boy scurries to his feet, like a mouse scrambling on a wet tile floor. His wide brown eyes lock on me, his pale face still contorted with fear. If he could speak, I know he'd say thank you. The door squeaks open, the boy disappears, and it slaps closed behind him. Becks saunters toward me, his cronies flank him. He closes in on me, when there's less than three feet between us, when I can smell the mix of pomade, cigarettes, and hooch on him, I rush forward and punch him hard in the nose. He laughs, a small stream of blood erupts from his nostril. Victory flares inside me. I may not be able to stop him, but making him bleed still feels like a win.

His laughter dies, Becks lumbers forward and slams into me. My head cracks against the tile wall, my teeth clack together, my vision blurs. Pain grows swift and steady from the back of my skull, with each beat of my heart, it swells until it consumes me. The world goes black for just a moment. He hits me again and red spots explode behind my eyes, my cheek throbs.

"Becks, if you leave him alone your next order is on me," Sayid says. His voice pulls me from unconsciousness.

"Next two orders," he growls.

"Fine, two," Sayid agrees quickly.

Becks and his cronies leave the room seconds after Sayid concedes to giving them free goods. After they leave, I feel like I can breathe again. There's a soft touch against my head, my face, my hair, I flinch. Sayid's hands are rough, warm. Light pours into my eyes when I open them, and I wince. Pain throbs from the back of my head and my mouth. There's a dull ache in my stomach, like I've been kicked in the gut a few times.

"You alright?" he asks, as he looks me over. His hand rests against my head. Somehow, his touch numbs the pain nagging at me.

I pull myself up from the floor and nod. "I'll live. You didn't have to do that." Sayid doesn't need to sacrifice product on my account.

He shrugs like it was nothing. But it wasn't *nothing*.

"Trying to shower alone?" he asks.

"No, there was a kid. They were attacking him," I explain, as I try to stand. Sayid wraps his arm around my waist and helps steady me. I lean on him, all my weight against his. The tethers binding my lungs seem to unravel. My pulse evens out as Sayid walks with me toward the sink. I grunt as I sag against it.

His rough hands brush my face as he appraises me. He tilts my chin up, and for a moment his eyes meet mine. My cheeks burn. I wish his hands would drift further, I want to feel his arms around me.

"Stay here," he says as he inches away. He watches me, like he expects me to fall over.

"I'm not going anywhere," I try to joke, but the levity never reaches my words. My ribs ache, and I hold my side as I wait for Sayid to return. The mirror is painfully close, and I'm tempted to look over my wounds. A golf ball seems to be forming under the skin near my cheekbone. Each time my face throbs, I swear I feel it grow.

The door groans as Sayid pushes it in. He's clutching a first aid kit.

"Where did you get that?"

He shrugs. "I've been known to find things from time to time." He grins at me.

I shake my head, and smother the smile before it forms on my lips.

The first aid kit clicks as he opens it, I stare at the tiles as he rummages around inside. His face pops into view, a few inches from mine, and his eyes narrow on my wounds. I watch him chew his bottom lip. My guess, he's trying to figure out where to start.

"What hurts the most?" he asks, his hand brushes against my jaw.

"My ribs."

I can deal with the throbbing in my face, but my ribs give me a sharp kick every time I take a breath. Sayid reaches for my shirt, and looks at me for permission before lifting it. I give him a slight nod. He sees me shower. Why would I care if he sees my ribs now?

His fingers dance across my rib cage, and goose bumps trail up my spine. "Here?"

Somehow, his touch bleeds into me, and it's not pain coursing through my veins anymore. My head swims, and I look away. Confusion blurs my thoughts.

"Sorry," he says as he pulls his hand away. "It looks like it hurts."

He takes a few cotton balls in his hands, and the air grows sharp. "This is going to sting," he warns less than a second before he presses the alcohol saturated cotton ball to my forehead.

I suck in a sharp breath as the alcohol seeps into my wound, its sting radiates through my face. Pain rips through my lungs, like claws twist inside them. My body doubles over automatically, and I grab for my side. I never want to breathe again if it means feeling pain like that.

"Sorry," he says as he presses his lips into a thin line.

"Can that be it? I'll be fine. Really," I say as I push his hand away.

"Fine, fine," he says as he waves his hand toward me. "I tried."

"Thank you," I say, as I reach out and rest my hand on his shoulder. He nods. "Anytime."

He just shakes his head at me, a sly smile on his face. Sayid helps me make my way out of the bathroom. Night still blankets the campus outside. I walk up the stairs first, he follows. I fall into bed, pain twists in my stomach as I fall. But it's the springs that groan, I manage to swallow the pain down. Sayid's bed creaks as he lies back .

"Hey, Sayid."

"Yeah?" he asks, rolling over to look at me. When he looks at me, my eyes linger on his, and something inside me shifts. The thought of his arm around me, the comfort I felt there flashes through my mind, and I'm thankful the dark conceals the heat rising to my cheeks.

"Thanks."

22

AFTER

I follow Sayid in the dining hall line. My tray scrapes across the metal bars, I'm on autopilot. Every time my mind begins to wander, I tongue my swollen lip until I taste blood. A spoon whacks against the sneeze guard in front of me, and I jump. I look up, Brandon's face is screwed up in annoyance.

"Hello, anybody home?" he asks as he waves the spoon in front of my face. Scrambled eggs fly off the spoon, showering the sneeze guard in yellow clumps.

How long has he been talking to me?

"Sorry," I stammer, and hold the tray up for him to fill.

He slides a plate of pancakes and bacon onto my tray, along with a small plate of biscuits, a pile of carrots, and two apples.

"I heard you helped a kid last night in the bathroom in Madison," he says, adding another carrot to the pile.

I shrug. "Yeah, what's it to you?" My words are harsher than I mean for them to be.

"That was my brother, so, thanks. Most kids around here wouldn't stand up to Becks. They'd just look the other way if a kid like Kevin was being beat up, or worse." He nods at me, like I've just earned his approval. I've already earned extra food because I come through with Sayid, but I guess this gives me clout of my own.

I nod. "Anytime. Thanks for the extra food."

He nods back.

Sayid and I take a seat at our usual table, smack dab in front of the dirtiest window, next to the back door. He sits across from me and I push my tray toward his automatically so he can pick what he wants off it. He eats more than three of me put together. I figure if I can't pay him for everything he does for me, the least I can do is give him first pick of the food I don't want to eat anyway.

"Still can't believe you were stupid enough to do that," he says as he takes one of my biscuits.

"Sometimes it's worth being stupid," I snap at him.

His eyes go wide, and he recoils. Guilt rises inside me and smothers my anger. I suck in a breath through my nose as I try to calm myself down.

"Sorry," I say as I look at the table.

He shrugs. "It's okay."

I lean on my elbows, and push my fork into my pile of pancakes only to watch them spring back. "I can't stand people getting hurt. I can't just stand by and watch that, especially if they didn't deserve it."

He locks eyes with me for a moment. "I don't think I've ever met anyone that deserved to be stuck in this place less than you." He laughs, but I don't.

Gord slides his tray onto the table next to Sayid and plops down. He's already got his spoon in his mouth, half chewing on it, half talking. I look down and pick at my breakfast as Gord mumbles to Sayid.

"You know of any kids here with red curly hair?" Gord asks Sayid.

Sayid shrugs. "No, why?"

"Because you know everyone," Gord says as he bites into a crisp strip of bacon.

"No, why do you want to know about a kid with red curly hair?" Sayid asks as he looks over at Gord.

"Could have sworn I saw a kid in the woods that I didn't recognize, someone who isn't an inmate. A few other kids have seen him too."

Sayid shrugs and waves his hand, as if dismissing the idea. "Ghost stories. There's always some story about weird kids in the woods."

A weird feeling settles in my guts. For some reason Dominic's face pops into my mind.

But what would Dominic be doing in the woods at Dozier?

I walk from the dining hall alone, Sayid had to head to the laundry but offered to walk me, but I shooed him away. He acts like I need a constant babysitter, especially after I pissed off Becks. But I don't. I carve my way through the orange trees, and light a cigarette as I walk to the stables.

Footsteps behind me make a smile creep across my face, Sayid must have come to walk with me after all. I turn, but my stomach bottoms out when its Melvin I find, not Sayid. The guard has about a foot on me, and even from thirty feet away, like he is right now, he's intimidating. He's built like a football player.

"What have you got there?" he asks as a sly smirk quirks his thin lips. His eyes narrow on the cigarette clutched between my fingers.

Sweat slicks the back of my neck and my guts turn to water. This is the one Sayid told me to avoid. He's known for taking kids to the white house for just looking at him wrong. My mind races as I consider my options. Do I run? Do I fight him?

I shift my hand, tucking the cigarette behind me, hoping he can't see it. There's no way I can outrun this guy, and I sure as hell can't fight him. But I won't let him take me to the white house. I've got to get out of this somehow.

"It's nothing, I just found it. I was going to put it out so it doesn't start a fire," I say, knowing there's not enough confidence behind my words for Melvin to believe me.

He lets out a dry laugh that chills my blood. "Do you think I'm a fucking idiot?" he spits the words as he stalks forward.

Thoughts rage in my mind as fear sours the air around me. Do I risk running? He's seen me. It's not like I can argue it or pretend this never happened. He's a guard. It's my word against his. As he closes the space between us, panic sets in and sweat prickles my neck. My feet are planted into the ground, as if roots have grown there, binding me.

He's so close, I can make out the white spit that's collected in the corners of his mouth. It reminds me of the horses. He grabs the cigarette from my hand, and pulls it to his lips. A steady stream of smoke pours from his nose as he glares down his crooked nose at me. Melvin raises his left hand, and it moves so quickly, the only thing that tells me that he's hit me is the pain roaring in my cheek. I fall to the ground as tears pool in my eyes, ready to fall.

Melvin thuds to the ground and rolls me onto my back. I groan as his knee connects with my ribcage, a sharp pain echoing through my injury from last night as he pins me down. Every instinct in my body tells me to throw him off, to run. But I can't. I will for my body to move, but it won't obey. Panic claws at me. What if he takes me to the white house?

"Please, I'm sorry," I beg. My voice cracks as the words come out, and shame crushes me. Tears burn my eyes, threatening to spill over. But I can't let him see me cry.

He brings the cigarette up, pulls the collar of my shirt away from my chest, and presses the cherry to my flesh. It sizzles against my skin and I yelp in pain.

"I don't ever want to catch you smoking out here again. Do you understand me?" He growls the words at me through his clenched teeth. He's panting, like a rabid dog. There's something in his eyes, a glimmer that tells me he wants to keep going. He *wants* to hurt me.

I nod and latch on to the pain to keep myself from breaking down. "I won't. I promise," I manage to choke the words out.

I expect him to hit me again. To drag me to the white house kicking and screaming. But instead, he pulls himself up, still panting from the exertion of throwing me to the ground, and stalks back into the trees.

It takes me a few minutes to haul myself out of the dirt. The wound throbs as I stand, dusting off my britches. My head spins as I orient myself. I amble toward the stables, my mind still roaring with fear. Every creak of a branch makes me nearly jump out of my skin. When I finally find reprieve in the shade of the stables, I climb up the stairs and collapse into the hayloft. I sob as the adrenaline still pooling in my blood dissipates.

I have to be more careful.

I'm not proud of how long it took me to shake the incident with Melvin. Every time I calmed myself a little, the burn would throb and remind me of how close I was to ending up in the white house. Finally, when I calm down, I spend most of my day grooming and bathing the horses. By the time the bell rings signaling time for my appointment with Lennox, my arms are raw from the constant high pressured spray from the hose. My skin tingles as the heat bites at my tender flesh. A bruise budding on my cheek makes me wince.

"Asher, it's good to see you," Dr. Lennox says as soon as I push the half-open door in.

His happiness fills the room, but it's lost on me. Our last session was a failure, what is there to be happy about? I hope my mind is cooperative today. Deep down, I know it's not likely. My mind is a dark place where nightmares dwell. It hasn't given up a single memory. I don't want to get my hopes up that it will offer up others.

"Do you have anything you'd like to discuss before we get started?" he asks.

I shake my head. I don't want to discuss the weeks I'm missing, or Sayid and I sneaking off campus to meet with Eden. Or when I woke up with the knife. I'm not here to talk, or to be cured. I'm here for answers. I slip into the hypnosis easier this time, like pulling on a pair of worn boots.

Olivia's laugh, soft, high, cuts across the night. It's so beautiful, even the crickets stop singing long enough to listen. My eyes dart to the street, though we're hidden in the shadow of the mansion, I still feel the crawl of eyes on my skin. The entire neighborhood keeps watch on the Howey Mansion, if there's so much as a mouse fart out here they call the cops.

"Olivia, please, someone will hear us." I whisper, my voice is rushed, but I try not to let the panic seep into my words. We took my dad's car to get here, and that's already turned me into a bundle of raw nerves.

The trees rustle as the breath of a cold wind blows. The night is such an inky black the circles of light from the streetlights seem to be strangled by the darkness. It's far too cold for Florida, there's a crisp chill in the air that doesn't belong anywhere south of the Carolinas. I turn back from the street and see Olivia leaning against the wall, eyeing me. Her blonde curls rise and fall with the breeze. Her white dress laps at her legs.

"Asher, calm down. You're wound tighter than a Slinky," she says with a warm smile as I walk past her.

At the mouth of the backyard, I'm barely able to sit still. The wind whips around me, and chills me to the bone. But I don't make it another step. I don't even get to take another breath before I hear Olivia gasp.

"Mr. Flemming?" she says, her voice trembles.

At the sound of my father's name, my heart leaps into my throat. I whip around so quickly my head swims. My father glowers at us. He's unsteady on his feet, with his metal flask clamped in his right hand. In his other hand, he's got a cigarette trapped between his fingers.

"What the fuck do you two think you're doing?" he spits.

How the fuck did he make it here? This is drunker than I usually see him. The drive from Ocala to the mansion takes nearly two hours, I'm not sure how he managed to make it here, he can barely walk.

His anger seeps through the air, it mixes with the sour scent of alcohol and forms a toxic cloud around us. Instinctively I grab Olivia and pull her behind me. She grips my hand, her skin ice cold. Her eyes are wide, and her hand shakes in mine.

"It's going to be okay," I whisper back to her.

My dad moves closer, and I stiffen. This won't be the first time he's hit me, and I know it won't be the last. Every few weeks I intervene on my mother's behalf, taking the beating that he's meant for her. This time though, I know it will be different. This time, the beating will be meant for me from the beginning. His jaw tightens, and he shoves the flask into his pocket.

"I said, what the fuck do you two think you're doing?" He spits the words at me, with every one I feel Olivia flinch behind me. "You took my fucking car, you drove all the way here. What are you doing?"

"I was surprising Olivia. It's not her fault, she didn't want to take *your car," I say as I try to diffuse him, and most of all, try to steer the anger toward myself. I give Olivia a nudge, she could run into the backyard, she could get far away from him. But she's just wasting time. My gut tightens, I know she won't leave me. She should leave me.*

"You're useless. You're spoiled. You're a blight on the Flemming name, just like your brother. I'm going to kill you, just like I killed him." He growls the words through his gritted teeth as he throws his cigarette to the ground.

He lunges, and I turn to shove Olivia out of the way. I need to protect her, keep her safe. But the impact I'm expecting doesn't come. Wind rushes past my face as his fist flies past me, and it hits with a hollow thud into the side of Olivia's head. Her eyes go wide, and she calls out. Her body recoils from the punch. She slams her head into the side of the house. The stucco crumbles as she hits.

"Olivia!" I scream as I rush to her side. Her head is bloody, her breaths shallow. Quakes shake her body as blood pours from her head wound, then a wound opens from her neck. Small stab wounds bloom from her chest. I look up, and the last thing I see is a flash of red before the world goes dark.

When I come out of the vision, I feel like I've been thrown into a pool of cold water. My eyes burst open, and I gasp for air. The smoke in the room burns my eyes. It takes a long time for my mind to unravel from the vision, the memory.

"Are you alright?" he asks.

I nod slowly, and he hands me a glass of water.

"Is there any reason you would believe that your father would kill Olivia?"

The question catches me off guard, I haven't mentioned anything about my father. I start to ask, but the words get caught in my throat.

"While you were going through the vision, you were telling me what happened as you saw it," he explains. He must have seen the confusion on my face.

"I was?" I ask.

"Yes, that's how regression therapy works. You'll slip into the vision, and I will talk you through it, asking you questions, guiding you, pulling you out if you get too upset." He holds out his hand, offering me a glass of water.

I take it, realizing how dry my throat is. I sip it slowly before I speak again.

"You look tired, maybe you should go have some dinner and get some rest," he says.

I nod, and stand. My legs shake beneath me, so unsteady they feel hollow. When I get to Madison, I feel like I've ran a marathon. I collapse into the bed, hungry, empty. The sleep that finds me is as restless as my mind.

23

AFTER

A choir of crickets pulls me from the depths of my subconscious. Beads of rain tickle my skin, the trees creak in the cool breeze. I blink furiously, my eyes try to focus. Above me, the blur of the full moon is the only thing I can see. For a few minutes I stare at it, without realizing I shouldn't be looking at the moon, I shouldn't even be outside. The twisted, crooked branches of the ancient trees are slick with dew, knobbed like the fingers of a wicked witch.

I pull myself up and it registers. I was asleep on the ground behind the stables. The weather-beaten wood stands beside me. Panic tightens my chest. The throb of my heartbeat pounds in my ears. My arms are sticky, caked in mud.

How long have I been here? Did I sleepwalk?

When I don't hear the bark of bloodhounds, I'm relieved, that means no one has realized I'm gone yet. I stick to the shadows until I make it back to my cottage, the downstairs bathroom is gloriously abandoned when I enter.

I toss my muddy clothes into the hamper and turn on the shower in the furthest stall, ignoring Sayid's warning about showering alone. *I can't wake him for this. He can't see me like this.* When I look in the mirror, I realize it's not just mud covering me, mixed with the dirt is deep red blood. Every inch of my skin that wasn't covered by clothing, is stained.

Whose blood is this?

Though the shower is unusually warm, I'm covered in goosebumps. As the water mixes with the mud, the air fills with the scent of copper. Shivers quake across my body. Too many questions swim in my mind, questions I may never find answers for. The most important, *who did I hurt this time?*

At breakfast, I'm barely able to eat, my stomach is already full. Thankfully the wound on my neck is covered, so no one can see it, and the bruise on my cheek is barely visible. An uneasy feeling has expanded inside me since I woke up behind the stables last night. Again, I scan the tables searching to see if anyone is missing. There doesn't seem to be a single student out of place. And when I see Becks lumber in, my hopes are crushed that I killed the one person here who's worth killing. I'm relieved it doesn't appear I killed anyone, but I still can't bring myself to touch my breakfast. Sayid sits down and eyes me.

"Not gonna eat that?" His fork is already raised, he's ready to pounce on my breakfast.

I push it toward him without a word. He shoves ham steaks, bacon, and eggs into his face. He hardly chews. *What am I missing?*

"What are you doing during worship today?" Sayid asks.

Since I've been here, Sayid and I have spent Sundays together, ducking whatever worship services they offer to the inmates. Sayid manages to be even less religious than I am. While the rest of the campus is quiet, reflecting, he and I hide out in the hay loft and talk. It's the *best* part of my week. With no one else around, no work detail to attend to, there are no distractions. It's the only time things really feel normal. Or I guess as normal as they can feel in Dozier. But he has to be confused. Today isn't Sunday.

"Worship isn't today, it's Wednesday," I argue.

He raises an eyebrow and looks at me like I'm crazy. "No, it's definitely Sunday."

"What's the date?" I ask, as I try to get my bearings. Sayid is normally better with dates than I am, after all, he has to keep track of shipments. I don't. My mouth goes dry, I take a sip of my orange juice, but it doesn't help.

"The ninth, I think." He shrugs.

It can't be the ninth. Yesterday was the twenty-sixth. *Wasn't it?* I've felt strange, off, since I started taking Dr. Lennox's pills. But since the one episode waking up on the back porch with a knife, I haven't missed any other time. *Or have I?* My mind puzzles through the dates, the three weeks I lost last time, two weeks this time—it doesn't seem any other days are missing.

A lump fills my throat for the rest of breakfast. Though words try to bubble to the surface a few times, they get stuck behind the lump. I swallow them, and keep my eyes on my plate. After Sayid is done eating I follow him outside.

"Can we take a walk? Need a smoke," I say to Sayid. It's a lie, I'm just trying to make an excuse that I know will mean I can have a few minutes alone with him. No one smokes in groups here, not groups larger than two anyway.

"Sure." He grins.

We walk from the dining hall, once the trees swallow us, I light up and turn to Sayid. "Do you have any idea where I might have gone last night?" I consider what to tell him. I don't want to scare him, especially after the knife incident. The more time I spend with Sayid, the more I like him. There's something growing between us, it's like nothing I've ever felt before. The last thing I want is to frighten him, to make him want to stay away from me. Needles prick the pit of my stomach, and I shift on my feet.

He cocks his head to the side, raising his eyebrow slightly. "What do you mean?"

It's difficult to know where to start. There's a fine line where I'll start crossing into crazy. I'm pretty sure I passed into crazy a while ago. As much as it creeps me out, I can only imagine how nuts I'll sound to him. I know I can trust Sayid. At this point, I know we're friends—and I don't want to lose him.

"Last night, I woke up covered in mud behind the stables. The last thing I remember, it was two weeks ago." After the knife incident, I leave out the blood. I don't want anyone to know about that. I swallow that secret down.

"You've been around the last two weeks, just like last time. And I never saw you leave last night." He gives me the side eye as he smokes his cig. "Are you alright?"

I don't answer, because I don't know if I am. It occurs to me I could have hallucinated waking up behind the stables, or it could have been a dream. But it was so real neither of those seem possible. That still wouldn't explain why I don't remember the last couple weeks.

"For the last two weeks, have I acted strange or anything?" I ask.

He shrugs, "No, not really. You actually seemed less depressed. You smiled a few times."

My face tightens. "You make it sound like I never smile."

"You *don't* ever smile. I can count the number of times you've smiled on this hand," he raises his left hand and wiggles his fingers exaggeratedly.

I roll my eyes and flick my cig to the ground. "Maybe I should ask Lennox for some different meds."

He laughs. "I seriously doubt they're going to waste any of their precious budget on meds for you. They're probably giving you aspirin." He looks down and brushes the hair out of his face. "But you do need to talk to someone. I'm worried about you."

"Thanks. I've got to try something. I can't keep living like this. Waking up in strange places, covered in..." My resolve hardens and seems to push me forward. It digs at me, pulls me. I start to walk through the trees toward Dr. Lennox's office, knowing that he's likely the only person who can give me answers. He's the only person who might be able to help me.

"Asher, wait," Sayid calls after me.

"Yeah?" I stop and turn to look at him.

"Be careful what you tell him. The seriously mental kids are locked in rooms barely the size of a closet with only a bucket to piss in," he warns.

"That can't be true." I glower as I look at my feet. If I try to get help I risk *that* as my punishment.

"If you don't believe me, I'll show you tonight," he offers.

"Okay, show me." I say as I start to walk toward Lennox's office.

"There's something else I need you for tonight, too," he says before I'm out of earshot, but I don't have time to ask what it is.

On my way to Lennox's office I measure the truth. I consider each part of what I remember carefully to see how crazy it sounds. The blood, I will definitely leave out. I'm also afraid if I admit I was out of the cottage after lights out he'll ship me off to the white house. My hand trembles when I knock on his door. After I knock, I regret it.

"Come in," he calls, his voice slightly muffled by the door.

I walk in and find him watering his plants with a cigarette hanging out of his mouth. His blue-gray suit seems to glow in the light.

"Mr. Flemming, good to see you," he says barely looking at me. "What brings you here this morning?"

The sessions I remember having with him are pretty mundane. Paranoia nags at me, what have I been telling him for the past two weeks? Have I been coming at all?

"I need to talk some more. Some strange things have happened," The words seep out of me slow, like they're buried so far in my mind it's difficult to dig them out. The rational part of me wants to sit down and talk through my problems, but there's a voice at the back of my mind telling me to run. I push back against the voice, I won't let control me.

I edge toward a chair and take a seat before he can tell me no. The scent of the dusty chair envelopes me. I press my palms into my knees, to keep my legs from twitching, and to hold my shaking hands steady. My body, has a life of its own now, it seems. Moving in ways I don't understand, taking me places I don't want to go. I have to take control back, or it could cost people their lives.

His eyebrow perks up, and his milky eyes settle on me. "Oh?" He sets down the watering can and fishes out a pad of paper from his desk. His hands shake as he shuffles to the chair across from me. The pen settles on his knobby fingers, and he looks at me, waiting for me to speak.

When he looks at me, I shift uncomfortably. I'm at a loss. *What do I say? How do I explain what's happened?* Sayid's warning is heavy in my mind. I wipe my sweaty palms on my shirt, and take a deep breath to calm my racing heart.

Something in the back of my mind warns me not to tell him, not to trust him. If he locked away those other kids for being *too* crazy, he could do the same to me. Part of me wants to bury the truth, to never step foot back in this room. But I can't do that. He's the only chance I have at getting answers. This is the only way to keep it from happening again.

Every time I wake up somewhere I shouldn't be, every time even a day goes missing, that's another chance I could hurt Sayid.

I won't take that chance.

I can't lose him.

"I'm missing two weeks of time. I guess I came out of it yesterday evening." I fidget in my chair, but it's the omitted truth I'm trying to get comfortable with, not the chair.

"What do you mean?" His head tilts as he asks, his glasses slip down the bridge of his nose.

"I don't remember anything for the last two weeks. This morning, I thought it was Wednesday. Then I find out it's actually Sunday." The words sound unsteady, and unsure as they come out of me. My voice waivers in an unfamiliar way, I clear my throat.

"This is the kind of place where it's easy to lose time," he explains, and rubs his chin, "But when you *came out of it* where were you?"

I look at my feet, I don't want to end up in the white house. All I can hear is the throbbing of my heart loud in my ears, and the longer he looks at me, the faster the thuds grow. The white house may not be the worst place, I could end up with the crazy kids. If I was locked away, I wouldn't be able to hurt anyone else. Maybe, it'd be for the best.

"It's alright," he urges, his kind eyes shimmer with curiosity.

"I sort of, woke up, in the middle of the night behind the stables. This morning when I asked the date, last I remembered, it was the twenty-sixth, now it's the ninth." I don't look up from my trembling hands as I explain.

"How many times would you say this has happened to you?" he asks as he writes on his notepad.

It's not something I've kept track of and for all I know it's happened hundreds of times. Maybe I just don't realize it. "There's a few big instances that it's happened, but it could happen more often, and I just don't realize."

In the end, Lennox doesn't seem all that surprised, or concerned. He tells me that I'll take three of the little white pills instead of two. If I miss two weeks while taking two pills, what will happen if I take three?

I decide to stop taking them.

~

I sit on the back porch burning mosquitoes with the end of my cigarette. I've been staring out at the orange trees for hours, waiting. Every once in a while, the moonlight will catch the dew heavy leaves, and it gives me a glimpse of the past. Each time, my heart skips a beat, then it aches, but I still can't force myself to stop looking.

"You get any sleep?" Sayid asks, stretching as he walks out the back door. He's a few feet behind me, still in his pajamas, black sweatpants and a loose white t-shirt. His long curly black hair isn't smoothed like usual, instead it's tussled, like he's had his head hanging out a car window.

He startles me, he's able to move silently, even on this old brittle porch. It gives away my secrets, but keeps his. Maybe that's just how this place is.

"Nah, haven't tried though. Been out here since an hour after sunset." I admit.

"Do you ever sleep?" He asks in a way that makes me wonder if it's a joke or not.

"Not really." Since Olivia died, I've had a hell of a time sleeping. Anytime I close my eyes I have the weirdest dreams. If they're not nightmares about her, they're about places I've never been, people I don't recognize.

"Let's get going, need to get over to the crazy house before the sun comes up," he jumps off the porch and waits for me to follow. I notice then his feet are bare, when he begins wiggling his toes against the grass.

"Do we need to worry about guards?" I ask, looking toward the front office, where they sometimes congregate.

"Nope, there haven't been any guards on night watch for a while. And unless there's another fire, don't suppose there will be." He smiles and shoves his hands in his pockets.

I stand up and follow him while asking, "*Another* fire?"

"A while ago, there was a fire at night that killed six students or so. If that happened again, I suppose they'd increase staff, they'd have to, but for now, my guess is, it's cheaper to let us be at night. The only guards out here at night aren't on duty. They're here to beat someone, or rape someone." Though his face is flat, stoic, the words chill me to the bone.

We walk across the neatly manicured lawns, and though Sayid claims there are no guards, I can't help but notice he routes our path away from the streetlights. We're never within thirty feet of the white house, but I can still hear screams over the sound of an old rickety fan. They haunt the night. I walk on the side of Sayid that keeps me furthest from the white house. Maybe if he's protected himself from ending up in there, he can protect me. He slows as we get close to the hospital.

"The guards tend to hang out here during the day, so avoid it if you're dodging work detail." He points toward the area in front of the building where I saw the guards talking before meeting with Dr. Lennox the first time.

Behind the building, lights scatter on the ground, broken by the bars on the windows. For a moment, a creeping feeling works up my spine.

Someone is watching us.

I pause for a moment, listening for footsteps, anything. It must have been my imagination. The only sounds are the trees rustling with a soft breeze, and Sayid's breaths as he takes drags off his cigarette. He's stopped at the first window, hugging the edge as he peers in.

I move to the other side to see what he's looking at. A naked, emaciated boy huddles in the corner. Though I can only see the side of his face, I can see how sharp his cheekbone is. His skin looks hollow, pale, like he's been sick for a long time. He's rocking, his head hitting the wall. Along his protruding spine are bruises, gashes, and scars long since healed. Each bone in his body pokes out so far, I could count them. He looks as brittle as a sheet resting over a sack of bones.

The cement cell he's held in is barren. There's nothing but a bucket. He doesn't get a blanket, bed, or by the looks of it, food. He starts to rock harder, slamming his head so hard against the wall we can hear it outside. Each hollow thud, makes my stomach lurch. When I notice the red pool growing, I turn away. I can't watch this boy turn his head into a bloody pulp.

"Isn't there anything we can do?" I ask, keeping my voice to a whisper.

He shakes his head, confirming my suspicions.

Sayid is transfixed, I move wordlessly to the next window, hoping they can't all be this bad. I almost miss the next room because there's no light, like there was in the last room. I'm barley able to make out the boy inside. If it weren't for the glow creeping under the door of his cell, I wouldn't be able to see him at all.

He's sitting on the floor in dirty pajamas. His head shaven clean down to his scalp. Dark circles linger beneath his eyes. It looks like he hasn't slept in days. I see the reflection of something in his hand, and on the floor in front of him. The crunch of glass cuts the silent night.

The boy picks over the shards of a broken light bulb. A terrible crunching, the grinding of teeth against glass sets my jaw on edge. He chews piece after piece, devouring the light bulb. Each time he chews, the sound is so grating, it makes *my* teeth hurt. His fingers roll the metal diffuser over and over. He brings the sharp metal to the flesh of his forearm and slices, over and over.

Footsteps draw my attention away. Sayid stands behind me. He places his arm on my shoulder, I'm guessing it's supposed to be a comforting gesture. I don't pull away.

"Are they all like this?" I ask him, my voice as quiet as I can manage.

He nods. "That's why you need to be careful about what you say. If they think you're too crazy, or dangerous, you end up here." He pauses for a moment, and sighs. "And, I'd really rather you didn't end up here."

Before I can ask why, I jump, wide eyed, when a bloody hand slaps against the window, inches from my face. His wild eyes search our faces. Nostrils flared, he exposes his red teeth, and glass shredded gums. I take a step back.

"This is worse than the white house." I say, still in shock.

"No, here at least you control the pain, the torture you endure. In the end, killing yourself gives you some control over your fate. The white house, they torture you until you're dead or they're done." His voice is flat.

"How has everyone here not killed themselves already?" I ask, I can't find a single redeeming thing about this place.

"For some of us, this is as good as it gets. If that tells you anything. There are kids here who lived lives worse than this," he points toward the barred windows. He speaks like that's the kind of life he had. "This place is an escape for them." The way he says them, he catches himself, I think he almost said 'us'.

24

AFTER

I'm still reeling from seeing the *crazy house*, so I follow Sayid aimlessly. Sayid works his way behind the hospital, toward the tree line behind the building. I've never been into this stretch of woods. I trust Sayid completely, but venturing into the unknown in the black of night still makes me anxious. A few feet into the woods, and the Spanish moss has eclipsed the moonlight completely.

"Where are we going?" I ask after we're so far in that I can't see the lights of the school behind us.

"There's a drop point up here for my shipments. I'm going to need your help carrying them back," he says, and smoke trails from his words. "Once or twice a week, depending on how fast product is moving, one of the guards brings in items from a list I give him. He drops them off in an old shed in the woods."

"How do you pay for them?" I ask. While I know they have some kind of arrangement, there has to be some money changing hands. Otherwise I don't see why the guard would keep it up.

"It depends. Any actual money I get, from kids like Becks, the guard gets half. Everything else, well..."

I hold up my hand, "You don't need to give me any more detail."

Though I have an idea what goes on, I don't want details. If he doesn't tell me what happens, it's easier to pretend it doesn't.

Helping Sayid with his black-market business is the least I can do for all the stuff he gives me for free. I've offered to take his shifts in the laundry a thousand times, but he's always told me no. His pace slows, and I catch up to him. We walk side by side, his arm brushes against me, and goosebumps rise on my arms.

I look at him at him as the silence brews between us. It's not an uncomfortable silence, but I want to talk to him about something, *anything.*

"Is it true that Gord asked the judge to be sent here?" The question tumbles out of me. It's a rumor I heard weeks ago, one that's probably not remotely true. But it's the best conversation starter I have.

He looks at me out of the corner of his eye with a tight-lipped smirk. Before he says anything, he offers me a cigarette, and I take it. "That's true," he finally says.

"Why would anyone *want* to come here?" I ask. It seems crazy that anyone would choose to come to Dozier, that anyone would ask for this.

"This place had things that he didn't have at home. Food for one."

Guilt pools inside me. I shouldn't have brought it up.

"He made the best choice he could based on the options he had. He went before the judge, and he asked to be sent here. No judge is going to argue that. You want to go to Dozier, you get a one way ticket. For him, this is better than any life he could have on the outside." There's an edge to his voice.

"Is that why you're here again?" I don't want to pry, but I really need to understand why he'd come back here. Why anyone would, really.

He sighs, then seems to consider telling me. His eyes narrow. I guess while he's the go-to-guy for anything you could want here, he's not used to handing out information as freely as cigarettes.

"The only homes I've had are those the state gave me. I've managed to hit the abusive foster home jackpot. At least here, I've never been held down in the middle of the night and raped by an old drunk asshole. I've never been beaten because I was so hungry, I ate toothpaste. I've never had someone hold my face to a stove burner for fun." He looks off, into the trees. It takes a long time before he looks at me again.

"I'm sorry." I say, because I'm not sure what else to say.

"I don't tell anyone because I don't want anyone to feel sorry for me. So don't you dare pity me." It sounds forced, but I can tell he means it. "And don't you dare tell any of them."

I won't share his secrets. But I think he knows that already. It's only fair, he's kept mine.

I grab his arm to stop him. He turns, but doesn't quite meet my eyes. I consider brushing his cheek to see what his face feels like. But I don't. I know I shouldn't. Instead I swallow my feelings and grip his arm. "I won't tell anyone," I say, even though I know I don't need to.

He looks at me with a kind smile. "I know you won't." He steps closer to me, and for a second, I swear I can see the longing in his eyes mirroring my own. The distance between us narrows. Anticipation traps my breath in my throat, and my heart bursts into a gallop. My fingers twitch, wanting to touch him, to feel his palm against mine. Deep in the forest, something moves. It's loud enough to break up whatever was brewing between us.

Stop being stupid. It was nothing. He doesn't think about you like that.

"We better get moving," I say as I take a step away from him.

Sayid sighs, and nods.

"While we're out here, we might run into the guard I've been working with," Sayid says as he scans the trees.

"Is it going to be a problem that I'm out here with you?"

"Nah," he says as he lights a new cigarette. "I've told him that there are a few people who help me from time to time."

Jealousy burns inside me. *Who else is helping him?*

Ahead of us, I can make out the sharp lines of a building. A small shack, it looks barely big enough for both of us to fit inside. It's so small, I'm not sure what Dozier could possibly use it for. Sayid digs around the base of it, and in a few seconds he finds a key. He opens the door, and peeks inside.

"Love it when a plan comes together perfectly," he purrs. He tosses out three large duffle bags, two of which clink when they hit the ground.

"This is just for a week?" I ask as I survey the bags.

"This will probably be a two-shipment-week, actually," he says as he slings one bag over each of his shoulders.

I grab the other bag and follow him. The bag is heavy, it sloshes as I walk. "Is this all booze?" I ask. With my luck some of those bottles broke and I'm going to reek by the time we get back to Madison.

"Nah, they wrap each of the bottles in a playboy. Usually keeps them from breaking, and we don't waste any of the space."

"Inventive. Who thought to do that?"

"That was my idea," he beams.

By the time we get back to the laundry, my back aches. I fling the bag onto one of the large tables that should normally be used for folding. But tonight, these tables are for sorting contraband. I help Sayid sort through everything, I stack all the bottles together, arrange the playboys, and stack the cartons of cigarettes into a neat tower. I'm desperate to find a letter, something from my sister. But there's nothing. Once we're done, he starts to squirrel all the goods away.

"This really all goes in a week?" I ask as I watch him move around the room hiding everything.

"Those playboys will all be gone *tomorrow*." A laugh slips out as he says it.

"And, I didn't see any letters. Still nothing from Eden? No letters?" I ask. Not knowing where she is, how she is, it's getting to me. There's a constant nagging in the back of my mind, waiting, wondering why she isn't answering me.

"No, I'm sorry."

His body is close, too close. And I hate that I want him closer. He bounces his shoulder against mine, and smiles at me.

"What's wrong?"

I shrug. "Nothing," I lie.

"You sure? You know you can talk to me," he offers.

I know I can talk to Sayid about pretty much anything, anything but this. Anything but the feelings stirring inside me. He ignites something inside me that's frustrating, overwhelming, and wonderful all at the same time. But every look, every whisper, every thought I have about Sayid, it's a betrayal.

Sayid takes a step closer to me. He's so close, I can see the flecks of gold in his deep brown eyes. His eyelashes are so long, they nearly get tangled in his eyebrows. I wet my lips, and breathe deep to settle my racing heart. There's a long pause, a heavy silence brews between us. His breath mingles with mine as a smile parts his lips. My heart pounds so loud, I'm sure he can hear it. And all I want is for him to close the gap between us, because I'll never be brave enough.

The front door of the laundry creaks open. My heart hammers when the young guard saunters in, but when Sayid smiles at the guard, it diffuses my fear. I take a step back, and come to my senses.

"Everything there?" The guard asks.

"Sure is," Sayid says as he takes a step closer to the guard. "Let's go outside for a minute."

A smile curves the guard's lips.

Sayid grabs the guard's arm and intertwines it with his own. They walk out the front door together. Jealousy claws at the back of my mind. My head throbs as I watch the door. I wish it was my arm wrapped around his, that he looked at me the same way.

Stop it. You're being stupid.

I keep my steps quiet as I walk to the open door. They stand a few feet away. Sayid is pressed against the guard, his mouth near the guard's neck. I swallow hard and look away when his hand moves to the guard's waist.

The only thing to keep me occupied, to keep my mind of the growing anger, is sorting the remaining merchandise. As I sort through the magazines, I slap each one down.

How could I have been so stupid? I thought he saw me the same way. I must have been imagining it.

By the time Sayid returns, at least fifteen minutes later, I feel like the biggest idiot in the world. Part of me knows he's just doing it for trade. But the louder, angry, bitter part of me thinks he's doing it for the fun, for the thrill. Sayid says nothing, and instead stashes the contraband around the laundry. While he does that, I walk outside for some air.

I light a cigarette as I try to unwind the anger that's bound itself around me. By the time Sayid comes out, I light another, and take a slow drag. He's so close, his arm rests against mine. His skin is slick with sweat. I feel his eyes lingering on me. All I want is to move away.

"Ready to head back to Madison?" he asks.

"Sure," I say as I flick my cigarette to the ground.

Sayid turns toward me, appraising me. His eyebrows draw together. "Everything alright?"

"Yep," I say, a little too quickly.

He cocks his head to the side, "Come on, spill it."

"Let's go. There's nothing wrong." My words are rushed as I push off from the wall. The last thing I want to do is to bring up my jealousy. Nothing has happened between us, I have no right to be jealous. I have no right to question anything he does, or doesn't do with anyone else.

Sayid grabs my arm. "Asher," he says.

"Sayid?"

"Is this about the guard?"

"Nope," I say as I avoid looking at him.

Sayid steps closer, forcing me to look at him. "Are you judging me? Or are you jealous?"

I shake my head. "Neither. You're just doing what you've got to do, right?" My question is a little too pointed.

He nods. "Yes, it's just an exchange. It's not the same as..." he looks down. "It's not the same as how I feel about you."

I want to focus on the words, how nice it is to hear him finally say them, to know that it wasn't all in my head. But my mind has the image of him and the guard burned into it. I shake my head and clench my eyes as I try to wish away the vision. "Let's just go back to Madison."

"Really? You're just going to walk away and leave things like this?"

"I can't deal with this right now," I say as I rip my arm out of his grip.

"After everything I've helped you with? After how tolerant I've been with you, this is *your* breaking point? You're pissed about what

I have to do to get your cigarettes?" His words rise, and he hurls each one at me like a dagger.

"I never asked you for the cigarettes. The only thing I ever asked you for is help with Eden. You give the cigarettes to me. Don't make yourself into a martyr here. You do this, you work with the guards because you want to, because you like it. So don't act like you're doing everyone some huge favor."

He presses his lips together, but doesn't say anything.

"Yeah, that's what I thought," I say as I turn away from him. I walk toward the stables, I can't stomach the idea of sleeping in the same room as him.

As I walk through the stables, Ginger pops her head out. I stop, long enough for her to nuzzle me. I wrap my arms around her neck and hug her. It isn't until she snorts at me that I let her go.

In the loft, I collapse next to the window. I pull my legs to my chest and rest my head on my knees. The anger that boiled inside me only a few minutes ago is now shrouded in sadness. The night started with Sayid almost kissing me, and now I'm sure he'll never talk to me again.

~

I wake up to the smell of bacon. My bleary eyes open, and I look at the worn, weathered boards of the stables. It takes me a second to sort it out, to realize if I'm in the stables, I shouldn't be able to smell bacon. I'm too far from the dining hall. My body aches as I push myself off the floor.

When I turn around, my heart nearly leaps out of my chest, my breath catches.

"Sorry, I didn't mean to scare you," Sayid says, he sits next to me with his legs crossed. Two plates of food sit on the floor in front of him.

"It's fine," I say as I take a deep breath in hopes of easing my fear.

"I thought we could have breakfast up here, and you know, talk," he says as his eyes drop to the floor. I'm surprised to see his food looks entirely untouched.

Though anger still nags at the back of my mind, I regret fighting with him. I shouldn't have said what I did, I had no right to be jealous.

"But we're not supposed to have food out of the dining hall," I say as I point toward the plates.

"I pulled some strings."

My guts knot. *What did he have to do to pull* those *strings?* I look away and swallow hard.

"Nothing like that," he says defensively. "Though now I'm going to have to find Brandon like, seven comic books that are nearly impossible to get a hold of."

I know I should feel better, but I don't. I grab a piece of bacon, hoping it will distract me.

He reaches out, and rests his hand on mine. I inhale sharply, and my pulse quickens at his touch. My eyes meet his, though I know I want him, and he wants me, deep down I know it'd be easier if I didn't. My mind is consumed by guilt. Six months ago, I'd been so sure I loved Olivia.

There's an intensity behind my desire for Sayid that scares me, something I've never felt before. More than that, I'm scared of what it might mean for him. All I'm going to do is hurt him. *What if the next body I wake up beside is his?*

A warning is caught in my throat. My mouth hangs open, the words just won't come. "Sayid, I'm a killer," I say, as I force the w out.

He looks down, and presses his lips together. "I don't care, I know you won't hurt me."

I look up at him, my face turned down. "I bet Olivia thought the same thing."

He chuckles once. But I'm not joking.

I pull my hand away and grab my fork.

"Are you okay?" he asks as I pick at my eggs.

"Yeah, just processing everything that happened last night." The anger, the harsh words between us, him with the guard, it's all still too fresh in my mind.

"I'm sorry," he says as he rests his hand on my knee.

"Me too," I say.

He looks away. "I wasn't sure you liked me back. Or that you were *ready* to like me back. So I didn't think the thing with the guard would bother you." He looks at me. "It was stupid, and I shouldn't have done it. Especially not with you right there. I wasn't trying to flaunt it or anything."

"I know you're just doing what you have to do to survive here. It shouldn't bother me. I never thought I'd be the jealous type."

He smiles wide. "So, you do like me back then?"

I roll my eyes at him. He leans closer, and I hold my breath. The blood rushes to my head. I pull back, and my cheeks flush.

"I'm not sure we should..." I say, but my words lack conviction. If we get any closer, I don't know what will happen to him. All I know is I can't lose him. His lips are inches away. For a moment, his breath melds with mine. Soft finger tips brush against my jaw, settling on my chin.

"I'm sure," he says as his lips finally meet mine.

25

AFTER

To my surprise when I get to the stables, I find Sayid leaning against the worn wood walls of the hayloft, smoking a cigarette. He's got two bundles of newspaper folded up in front of him. Sayid's eyes linger on my face as I approach him.

"Hey," I say, though I try to keep my voice even, the surprise lifts my words.

He nods and smiles.

"What's that?" I ask as I point toward the bundles of newspaper in front of him.

"I thought you might want to have lunch up here," he says as he unfolds the paper to show me the sandwiches hidden inside.

For a moment, I just stare at him, bewildered. I'm struck stupid by the nice gesture. My heartbeat is so uneven, it seems to flip-flop.

I take a seat next to Sayid, and sag against the wall. Thoughts swarm inside my mind, it still seems impossible what they do to *students* here, what they could do to me. I feel like the world has tilted around me.

He rests his hand on my arm. The tightness in my chest eases. "You okay?" he asks.

I nod. "I'll be fine." It's a lie, I'm saying it for his benefit. He doesn't need to worry about me.

He picks up half of a sandwich and offers it to me. I'm not hungry, but I take it. I bite through the white bread, turkey, and a thick layer of mayo. Sayid picks up another half, and rips off a chunk.

Sayid looks down at his sandwich, silence brewing between us. He nudges me, and offers me a smile. But I don't return it. I can't.

"What was the best day of your life?" he asks.

My mind is a blur as I try to grasp a memory. It's hard to narrow down the best one. One good enough that I'd call it the best day of my life. Sayid looks at me after I consider for a few minutes.

"I'm thinking," I say as I take another bite of my sandwich. "Probably my tenth birthday," I admit. My cheeks burn with embarrassment.

He turns his head, and I can tell by the way that he looks at me that he's trying to suppress a smile. "Why your tenth birthday?"

"Eden, Olivia and I all celebrated together. Our moms took us to the springs, we spent all day swimming. We got to see the manatees." I look down, realizing that he might think it's stupid. "I don't know. It was nice. We spent the next week together nursing sunburns. Amma made Eden and I a cake with so much chocolate, it made my teeth hurt." Laughter almost slips out, and a smile curves my lips. "Eden got yelled at by one of the park rangers because she hugged one of the baby manatees. They threatened to kick us out."

"I bet it's hard being away from her," he says, it's almost a question.

I nod. "I wasn't sure I could live without her to be honest." A breathy laugh slips from my lips. I'd give anything to go back to that day, to spend a day at the springs with Eden again. I take another bite of my sandwich to keep my hands busy. "Have you heard from her?" I hate to ask again and again, but I can't help but wonder about my sister. Where is she? Why isn't she answering? It feels like every time I talk about her I'm slowly sinking.

He shakes his head. "Nothing yet, I keep trying."

"What about you, what was the best day of your life?" I ask him, because I can't stand to talk about Eden anymore.

He shrugs. "I don't know. Don't really have one," he says as he brushes off the question.

"You've got to have something," I press. His life couldn't have been all bad. There has to be at least one happy memory.

"This right here," he says as he pats my knee. "This is about as good as it gets."

My cheeks burn, and I swallow hard.

"I need to check something in the laundry. I'll see you later tonight," he says as he pops up from the floor. Before I can even wave goodbye he disappears.

Why'd he leave in such a rush?

I climb up to the hayloft and pull out a cigarette. Since I got caught smoking by Melvin, I've been more careful to make sure that he doesn't see me. So many of the others here at Dozier aren't careful. They run around the grounds with lit cigarettes. I don't know how they don't get dragged off to the white house. Maybe Melvin just hates *me*.

When I climb back down, the sun is edging toward the horizon. The sky nearest the clouds is blood red, dotted with patches of clouds that are nearly black. I cut toward the forest and take the long way back to Madison. My mind wanders to Sayid as I walk. As the sky darkens, I'm swallowed by the stretching shadows the trees cast. Ahead of me, boys dart through the trees of the orange grove.

"What are you doing out here, Flemming?" A man's voice booms from the trees.

I nearly jump out of my skin as I scan the darkness. The voice is familiar and makes my blood run cold. Melvin.

"I was just walking back to Madison. I had to work in the stables today," I say, my voice unsteady.

He emerges from the trees ahead of me, one of the bloodhounds trailing behind him. I flinch when I see him.

"Then what are you doing out here, next to the woods? You aren't thinking of making a run for it, are you?" he asks pointedly. His stance is wide. The way he looks at me, it's like he's daring me to run. He wants me to give him a reason to beat the shit out of me.

"Of course not. I'm just going back to Madison. I don't even have anything with me to run away," I say. All I've got are the clothes on my back. I couldn't make a run for it right now if I wanted to.

"So you've planned it, then?"

"I'm sorry, what?" I ask, confusion pinching my words.

"You know you can't run away because you have no provisions with you right now. So, you've planned what you'll need to run away." His words are so smooth, so confident, it takes me a moment to make sense of them.

My stomach twists as I look between him and the lights slowly flicking on throughout the rest of the grounds. No one knows that I'm out here. Sayid may not realize I'm gone for hours. Melvin could drag me into the woods and put a bullet in my head right now.

He takes a step closer to me as the silence builds between us. My pulse thuds in my ears, making me all too aware of every second that passes without my reply.

"I'm not planning anything," I manage to choke the words out, but they're too high, I practically squeak them.

Melvin reaches out and grabs me by the collar of my shirt. His forearm connects with my chest as he slams me backward into a tree.

My teeth clack together with the impact, and my skull sings from the pain. Bright spots explode behind my eyes, and I try to blink them away. I don't know what I did to get on Melvin's shit list, but I have to get away from him. Otherwise, I know I'll end up like the other boys who disappear.

I don't fight against his hold, but his hand still moves to my throat as he pins me to the tree. He doesn't press hard, but the pressure is still enough to make panic claw at my guts. Sweat blooms under my arms, as I have to force myself to stay still. The pressure on my throat fills my mouth with bile. I want to throw up, I want him off me, I want out of this god damned nightmare.

"Please," I force the word out, it's practically a growl.

"Please *what*? You piece of shit runaway. Did you really think you could slip past me?" He's so close, I can see the wrinkles in his face, despite the darkness edging around us.

"I promise, I wasn't." It takes so long to force the words out around the grip he has on me, each word sounds like its own sentence.

He pulls me forward, his nails digging into my flesh, then slams my head hard against the tree. He does it again, and again, until the tree is warm and red with my blood, and I go limp. At least in the darkness, Melvin can't reach me.

26

BEFORE
Date Unknown

Though he's brandishing a knife between us, I know he's not going to hurt me. Not *yet*. He followed *me* through the city. He'll always choose to follow *me*, no matter how enticing the bait I give him.

"Where is she?" I ask. I'm just toying with him, I know exactly where she is. He hasn't found her yet. If he's here, he hasn't seen her. Every time he follows the same path: I'm always first. It takes so long for him to pin us down together. After all, he has to kill us at the exact same time if he wants to find us easily next time. If he jumps the gun and kills us separately, he might have to search for us on separate sides of the planet. My goal is always to make him angry, get him to come after me first. But these past few lives, he's gotten much more patient.

"I was hoping you'd tell me." His shoulders squared, he's ready to pounce again, to come after me. If I keep him talking though, he won't.

"You know I'm not going to do that," I say, and I can't help the smile that creeps across my lips.

"Of course not." He glowers at me. "You'll never change. You'll never evolve."

I laugh. "That's where you're wrong."

Behind him, I see her face peek out from behind a mausoleum. She's not close enough for him to see, thankfully. When she's sure I'm looking at her, she nods. She's hidden the journal. Now I don't need to toy with him any longer. Tonight's stash has been hidden. We need to leave enough fakes around the city to keep him busy long after we're dead. I give the slightest of nods back, not enough that he'd notice. She disappears into the night.

"Can I make a request?" I ask him.

He runs his hand along his slicked-back red hair, making sure each strand is in place. For a moment, he considers it. That's the distraction I want. The distraction I need. I take the dagger from my jacket. Lunging forward, I slice his neck. With the blood covered blade, I slice my arm. His blood burns when it mixes with mine. Exactly as I had imagined it would. In a few seconds his wound will be healed—mine, however, will take a little longer.

She wants me to collect his blood, to use it against him. But I know of a much better way. My hope is that using his blood might make me stronger. I haven't tried it before, but something tells me it might give me the edge I need.

Clamping down on my arm, he twists it behind me. It forces the wound to open further, I groan in pain. He presses his body to mine, the crook of his arm holding my neck. I won't fight this time. This is exactly what I was hoping for. Every time, his anger gets the best of him. Or maybe it's been so long this time that he's actually forgotten that she has to be here, too. It doesn't matter though, he's giving me exactly what I want, what I need.

That's it. Try to kill me.

27

AFTER

As darkness falls, a cold wind digs its claws into Dozier. The horses huddle in their stables, and though I know I should get dinner, I can't pull myself away. I climb to the loft and sneak back to the window. I light a cigarette and lean back against the wall. My eyes drift across the waving trees, and something catches my eyes.

White pops in and out of the branches, coming into view when the wind blows the hardest. I try to focus, but it's impossible to tell what's lurking out there. Goosebumps rise on my arms. A bad feeling nags at the back of my mind. There's someone out there. I can feel them watching me.

"Asher." My name hisses through the trees. I'm not sure if it's the wind or my imagination.

I scoot closer to the window. Someone moves in the trees, their movements are slow, jerky. When they reach the tree line, I hold my breath. I recognize the long black hair. Eden stares up at me, her eyes wild, face streaked with blood.

"Eden?" I call out, as my hand digs into the window frame. My pulse quickens, and I push myself off the floor.

She stares at me—through me—with a stare so cold, it could bring snow to Florida. I run toward the ladder. Halfway down, impatient, I jump to the ground. When I reach the back of the stables, she's gone. She's disappeared.

"Eden?" I yell.

I can see the spot on the ground where she stood, the imprints of her bare feet in the sand. The trees engulf me as I run into the darkness. She's got to be out here, she has to. Something scared her, that's all.

Moonlight filters through the trees and gives the path an eerie, green glow. Spanish moss grabs at my arms, and sticks to my hair. Thirty feet into the woods, her footprints disappear. There's no sign of her. It's as if she never existed at all. Maybe she never did.

I feel someone staring. I turn. A face peers at me through the trees, curly red hair seems to glow. He cocks his head and offers me a half smile. A few feet behind him, I see Eden.

"Dominic?"

The wind whips at my legs, behind me something snaps. I turn, but only the empty woods stare back at me. My heart is lodged in my throat as I turn back to Dominic and Eden, but they're gone.

Ahead of me, nearly thirty feet away, I see Eden again.

How did she get over there?

I bolt down the path, and she melts into the trees. Though her steps sound like they're only a few feet ahead of me, I can't see her. Eden's bled into the darkness, like the new moon is swallowed by the starless sky. My heart hammers, and my head swims as I stop to scan the trees. A nagging pain in my side spreads with every breath I take.

"Eden?" my throat tightens.

Down the trail ahead of me, I hear footsteps. I take a slow step forward, as I listen for her. No part of me wants to chase her any further into the woods. And I shouldn't have to.

Why is she out here? Why is she running from me? This can't be real.

"Eden, please?" I beg.

She steps out from behind a tree, and takes a step toward me, her face slick with tears. I start to close the distance between us, but she holds out a hand to stop me. Her eyes scan the trees.

"You have to go," she says, her voice is thick, strained.

"I'm not leaving you out here," I argue.

"You have to. You have to go. It's a trap, Asher."

My mind is a blur of confusion. What the hell is she talking about?

"A trap?"

She crosses her arms, her eyes still on the trees. Her teeth dig into her lip, and she nearly trips as she tries to step backward. Even from here, I can see she's shaking.

"He's out there, waiting. He brought me here to try and lure you out. You can't let him. Please, Asher. Please, go." Her voice cracks, and fresh tears spill across her cheeks.

"I'm not leaving you," I say as I step toward her.

Her wide eyes scan the trees, her arms tighten around her chest. "Pay attention to the dreams, the memories. You need to learn from them."

"How did you..."

"Run!" She screams at me, her voice so loud it makes my ears ring. I shake my head as my ears throb, and Eden disappears into the trees again.

"Eden, stop, please! Together we can get away from him. We can run," I say as I chase after her.

"I can't, he has Blake," she calls back to me. "If I run, he'll kill Blake."

I try to follow her, to keep pace, but my limbs grow heavy. Her footsteps grow farther, and farther away. A hand pops out of the trees and grabs me. My heart is stuck in my throat when I see Olivia. She balls my shirt in her hands as she holds me steady.

"You're such an idiot," Olivia says as she pushes me into a tree.

Bark bites at my shoulder blades as I stumble backward. I slap her hands away. I need to go after Eden, I can't let her get away. Olivia grabs me, and stands in my way.

"Move," I say as I try to step around her. But every time I move, so does she. My temple throbs as I glare at her.

She holds her palm out and presses it to my chest. "Let her go."

Anger rises inside me. *Why is she getting in my way?*

"Move, you're not real. Just get out of my way," I growl at her.

She pushes her palm hard into my chest. I take a step back, and wince.

"If I'm not real, how did I do that?"

I shake my head. "I don't know. Maybe this is a dream." It has to be a dream. This can't be real. This can't be happening.

She tilts her head and flashes me a grin she reserves for idiots. "I told you to be careful. To stay away from him. If you follow her, he'll kill you both. That's exactly what he wants. Don't you remember?"

I shake my head. "What are you talking about?" My eyes dart between her face and the woods. "I have to go after Eden."

"No, you're safer here. There's too many people," she says as she crosses her arms.

The woods grow quiet, the sounds of Eden have all but died in the night. I missed her. I'll never be able to catch up to her now.

"Go back to the school and stay there," Olivia says, turning me around and shoving me forward.

I take a few steps and turn. Only the trees stare back at me.

Surrounded by the darkened forest, the night thickening around me, I've never felt so alone.

It wasn't real. It couldn't have been.

28

AFTER

Though I woke up in my bed this morning, I'm as tired as if I ran all night. The nightmares have me on edge. It felt so real. But it must have been a dream.

My mind won't let it go, so I decide after breakfast to look behind the stables to see if there's any sign Eden had actually been there. The more I think about it, the crazier I feel. Though my food steams in front of me, calling to my grumbling belly, I can barely touch it. There's so much on my mind, I'm not sure there's room in my stomach.

My lip is numb, I've nearly chewed a hole through it. So lost in thought, I don't even notice Becks sit down, nor do I hear any of the "tip" he's come by to offer. His tips, all of the words, are worthless anyway. And likely, all lies.

"Pony up boys," he says as he slams his fist on the table.

A parade of hands with offerings spring out in front of me. Instead of handing over anything, I grab my orange, and shove it into my pocket. I stand from the table, nod to Sayid and walk out the cafeteria door. The heat hits me as soon as I step out of the shade. I look back a few times, to be sure he didn't follow me. I'm blissfully alone as I walk across the campus, and with each step I take, my stomach starts to untangle.

Behind the stables I barely make out the footprints of Eden's bare feet. It's easiest to make out the small impressions of her toes. A few feet away, toward the tree line, there's another set of footprints leading into the forest. Where the sandy soil meets the trees, it's damp, and the imprints are clearer.

Was she really here? That's not possible.

I follow the footprints. A few feet into the trees, the humidity grows thick. The air is so dense, it's hard to breathe. In the woods, completely alone, my chest tightens. Every creak of the ancient trees, and each bird call make me turn so quickly, I nearly get whiplash.

Her footsteps weave through the trees. At the end of the narrow path, they end. A few feet away I see something shimmering in the dirt. I reach down to find a thin gold chain. On it are tiny gold trinkets in the shapes of a shooting star, a moon, and Saturn—Eden's necklace.

She was here. How is that possible? A lump forms in my throat, and a bad feeling creeps up my spine. I shove the necklace into my pocket. I'll have to try to sneak into the office and use the phone. I need to make sure my sister is okay.

Until then, there's work to do, I can't focus on the necklace, or my sister. There's no way for me to help her. I swallow down the questions, the anxiety, and walk back to the stables. As I sweep, I notice droplets of brown atop the concrete. I follow them, cleaning the straw away. Beneath the straw, streaks and smears cover the concrete. A trail of dried blood leads to the ladder to the hayloft. The droplets lead up the ladder. My guts twist, like they're being clenched. My mouth and throat go dry. I force myself to climb. But I find only hay bales up top.

It isn't until I reach my nook that I find more blood. And the bloated corpse of a guard. My stomach twists as I look down at Melvin.

Bile claws up my throat. His pale skin is pulled taut over black veins, like worms caught beneath cheesecloth. His mouth hangs slack, a trickle of blood dried to his mouth. Purple rings circle his neck. His uniform is pocked with stab wounds.

I stumble backward. *I couldn't have done this. I didn't kill a guard, I couldn't have.* My breath catches in my throat, tears burn my eyes. *This can't be happening again.*

The memories of Sayid showing up with bruises, his words about Melvin forcing him. Raping him. Anger blooms inside me. I could have... for Sayid, I could have done it.

A deeper voice, one I don't recognize intrudes in my mind. *Who else could it have been? You killed Olivia, you killed this guard. Accept it, you're a killer.*

The bell rings for lunch. I stumble down the ladder, and put away the shovel in the tool closet. My body moves automatically, but my mind is locked away in thought. The cold fingers of guilt spread inside me. Ginger nudges me as I walk past her stall. I rub her head and tell her I'll see her later. Her ears fold back, and she stares daggers behind me.

When I turn, I see Becks and his cronies standing a few feet away from me. I sigh. *Not today. Not now.* My body tenses, I'm tempted to run. He's bulky, I doubt he'd be able to catch me. His cronies are long and lean, they could.

"You know why we're here," Becks says as he cracks his knuckles.

"Fuck off, Becks." I stare him down and try to push my way past him.

For a long moment, he glowers at me. His face grows redder by the second, teeth grinding so hard, I can hear it. He steps forward, the cronies flank him, and rub their hands together in anticipation.

I throw a bucket at them and try to make a break for it. If I hadn't put the shovel away, I might be able to defend myself. The bucket clatters to the ground behind me, and I hear Becks curse. They're so surprised, I make it out of the stables without hearing so much as a shuffle. Adrenaline burns when it hits my blood stream. The burst of energy hits my heart, and it's thunder in my ears.

Above me, thunderheads dot the sky, purple masses clot together. There's a storm brewing, and by the looks of it, it might be a nasty one. Ahead of me, the tree line beckons. If I can reach the trees, I may have a chance. My legs are heavy, out of practice, but fear propels me forward. My heart beats so hard, it may rip through my chest.

Their pounding feet grow closer. I want to look back, see how much of a head start I have. But I don't. I'm feet from the trees, so close I can make out the rough cracks in the bark, the tangled roots, the swaying moss. The air seems to cool as I reach the shadows. Engulfed by the forest, I feel the slightest relief. They're still loud behind me. I can't stop yet.

Years of practice allows me to run around the trees with speed. That's one thing I can thank Olivia for, after they kill me. Sharp ragged breaths shudder through my lungs, my knuckle cracks against a sharp piece of bark. I grit my teeth. A bleeding hand is a small price to pay to escape them. When all I can hear is my heart thundering in my chest, I slow. But I don't stop. Not yet. Fifty more yards pass beneath my feet, and I slow to a jog. Then a walk. Still, all I hear is the rush of my blood, quick breaths, my own steps.

I fall against a tree, breathless. The fear unwinds, and relief trickles over me. Less than three heartbeats pass before I hear them. I stand, alert, ready to run. Hands wrap around my waist, as a hot, sweaty hand claps over my mouth. The taste of salt slips through my lips. I struggle, and fight against the grip.

His cronies grab me. Becks tries to come closer, but I'm ready. I'm not going down without a fight. I use the arms binding me as leverage to bring my left leg up and kick Becks hard in the chest. He growls and stumbles. It takes a moment for him to steady himself. His size makes him unsteady on his feet. Every drop of fear drains from my body, fury bursts through me.

You can do this, you can fight them.

Though I struggle against the cronies, their nails dig into my arms, and they grip me tighter. I can't even make myself see them as people, they're just appendages of Becks. As he lumbers back toward me, a rush of noise in the trees draws my attention, and everyone else's. Footsteps, someone is running just outside the clearing where we're gathered.

"Don't let him go," Becks warns the cronies as he flashes them a deadly glare.

The moment Becks disappears into the trees, hope creeps in. All at once, it's as if all the sound rushes out of the woods. The cricket songs die, the soft twitter of birds, even his footsteps are silenced. I watch the trees for any sign of movement, but there's nothing.

As the cronies are distracted, their eyes on the trees, I try to pull away. Their grips tighten, but not with the same intensity as before.

"Who's there?" Becks' voice cuts through the silence.

My heart thunders. *Did a guard find us?* Maybe this will finally be the stunt that puts Becks in the white house. I can't imagine how much it'd cost to buy his way out of this. His voice echoes through the trees again, but it's silenced so quickly, I can't make out a single word.

"Fuck this," one of the cronies says to the other. He drops my arm, and runs into the trees. A few seconds, and a confused expression later, the other crony disappears.

I take off into the trees in the opposite direction. Ahead of me, I swear I see the hem of a white dress. I stop, and stare up the path ahead of me.

"Olivia?"

She steps out of the trees fifty feet ahead of me. Her dress is bloody, a line of limp curls is stuck to her neck. For a moment she smiles, and then something hits me hard in the back of the head.

29

BEFORE
Date Unknown

Metal bites at my throat. Though deep down I hope he takes the bait, I know he won't. He hasn't in years. Even with the knife, there's no real way for him to kill me, not out here in the middle of the city anyway. The warmth of his breath hits my ear. A face, rough and hot touches my neck. The book is heavy in my jacket. I know he'll find it. That's what I'm counting on. I force the smile creeping across lips away.

"This is the last time," his voice warns, spit hits my ear.

I know it's a lie. He doesn't know our plan. After all, he hasn't managed to kill us before. I know he won't manage it now. Likely, not ever.

"You promise?" I ask, trying to provoke him.

The knife presses harder, but my windpipe doesn't give beneath it. He holds me, but his grip is weak, he's focused too much on the knife. He always has. Holding me this close, I know his thoughts stray. The way he presses into me, it's a dead giveaway.

"Come on, give it to me proper, for old times' sake," I beg, and push back against him, toying with him.

The moment he lifts the knife, I know his intention: he's going to stab me. I feel it in the way his breath shudders, in the way he hesitates. When he inhales sharply, and gathers his strength, I make my move. I pull my head forward, and then force it back as hard as I can. The cartilage of his nose bends, I can feel it against my skull. There's a wet pop, and he growls as he falls backward, stunned. I turn and face him.

His red hair is gathered, slicked back. It's been a long time since I've seen him like this. Somehow he manages to look put together and scattered at the same time. I look down at him, he's crouched next to a small monument to the dead. The tiny statue of an angel can't be any bigger than the body buried beneath it.

"I'm going to kill you," he promises. His jaw is clenched, the usual pale color of his face is gone, cheeks flush. He narrows his eyes.

"Not today," I smile.

30

After

"Asher, wake up," Sayid says as he shakes my shoulder.

"Where is she?" I almost ask. But I smother the question before it creeps out.

My face and my throat ache. The straw rustles, and a horse snorts. My thoughts are so scattered it takes ages to gather them.

How did I get back to the stables?

I look toward Sayid, and he sits next to me, concern painted on his face. His hand rests on my shoulder. The stables stretch above us, Ginger hovers, her head hanging out of her stall. Though pain nags at me, all of me, the stench of horse shit is so comforting, I almost cry. Sayid brushes the hair from my face, and stares down at me. Emotion swims in his eyes. I sit up, my body lurches forward automatically, and I hug him. The warmth of his body, the smell of him, it eats away the sorrow welled up inside me. My hand wraps around the back of his neck as I cling to him. His breath is hot against my neck.

I pull back, my eyes on the ground. My cheeks hot with embarrassment. "I'm sorry." I choke the words out.

He reaches out, his hand rubs my shoulder gently. "It's okay, it's fine." A soft smile curls his lips.

"What happened?" I ask him.

"I was ..." he looks behind me, "going to ask you the same thing."

I turn to see what he's looking at. The body of one of the cronies lies behind me. His hair is disheveled, his face bruised, his throat has a strange black pattern across it. I kick, and propel myself backward, away from the body. Huddled next to Sayid, I stare at the lifeless body, unsure how he got here.

"Becks and the cronies came after me." I look down. The physical pain may be numbing, but my mind is still raw with confusion.

What the hell happened? How did I get back to the stables?

"I figured that much. I saw Becks rushing away from the stables. I was worried he came after you again. Did you kill this one?" He motions toward the crony, not looking nearly as concerned about the body as he should.

I shake my head. "At least, I don't think so."

Shock starts to fade, and panic sets in. *What's going to happen when the school finds a body smack dab in the middle of my work detail?* There's no denying this. It looks bad. If I try to explain, no one will believe me. Why would they? If they think there's another murder on my hands, they'll send me to prison. Even my father won't be able to save me from this.

"I have to get out of here. Where's the nearest town, where can I go?" I ask him.

His brows furrow. He considers for a moment. "You can't run away." His words are strained.

"How am I supposed to explain this?" I gesture toward the body. Then I remember the body in the hayloft. Two bodies, two more people dead, because of me.

There will be more. You have to get away from him before he's next.

"There are options," he says, the words are slow, his eyes lost in thought, but it looks like he's as stumped as I am.

"There's a dead guard in the hayloft," I blurt out. The guilt building inside me must have pushed the words out. My throat feels tight, my head swims.

His jaw drops, and he blinks a few times. "Fuck, Asher," he says as he clenches his jaw and looks away. "If you killed a guard that's a whole world of trouble that I can't help with."

"I don't think I killed him, he's got stab wounds. I don't have a knife." The way the words tumble out of me, I'm afraid it might be clear that I'm trying to convince myself that I didn't kill the guard.

You did have a knife. You might have another one.

Sayid climbs the ladder, I follow behind. "Where?" he asks, once he's in the loft.

"Back in the nook," I tell him as I point toward the nook at the back.

He walks over, but I don't budge. The shame welling up inside me has glued me to the floor. He stops when he gets to the nook, and turns slowly to look at me.

"Asher, there isn't a guard here. There isn't anyone here," he says, his brows fall, and he looks at me like he's concerned about me. Like, just maybe, he thinks I'm crazy. "Are you sure that's what you saw?" *Maybe I am crazy.*

I run over, weaving between the hay bales as I close the distance between us. Where the guard had been, straw is scattered. But there isn't so much as a drop of blood remaining. I sweep the straw out of the way. *Nothing.*

Did I imagine the dead guard? What else have I imagined? My thoughts are a jumbled mess.

"We need to go back down, I've got an idea to deal with him." He dusts the straw off his jeans and heads back down the ladder.

For a moment, he looks like he's going to walk toward one of the horses, then he thinks better of it. Slow steps lead him back way from Ginger. He offers me a cig, but my hands are shaking too badly to smoke it, so I wave it away. I cross my arms, and hold my elbows.

He looks toward the horse behind him, Ginger. "Are you, um, friendly with any of these things?" The way he cowers away from her, you'd think she was a seven-foot-tall spider.

I'm friendly with all of them. They're horses, not barracudas. I try not to roll my eyes at him. I walk over to her, and rub her snout. The warmth of her body seeps into my hand, calming me. She nuzzles me.

"Great," he says. But the way he says it, his voice falters. I'm not sure if it's fear, or disgust. "We're going to need her to carry the body into the woods so we can hide it. It hasn't been dark long, so we should have plenty of time."

"Are you up for it?" I ask Ginger. She can't agree, but she's always thrilled to get out of her stall. I grab a bridle and slide it over her head, open the lock, and lead her out. Once she's out, she stomps twice and snorts. Her ears perk up immediately, and her brown eyes search the night. The way she twitches, and nudges me, I can tell she's excited. I tie her lead to one of the support posts.

The way my body aches, I'm not sure I'll be able to lift the body. Sayid steps toward it first. I follow, he grabs the feet, and I grab the wrists. The skin of the corpse is cool, it sends a chill up my spine. Even though I doubt I'm responsible for his death, it weighs on me. I don't even know his name. He might have a family, he might have his own Eden waiting on him. I shake my head, and try to snap myself out of it. There isn't a single reason I should feel guilty this sack of shit is dead.

This guy wasn't worth a shit. There's nothing to feel bad about.

It's much harder to lift and maneuver a corpse than I expect. Several times the body slips from our grip and slaps to the floor with a hollow thud. Finally I decide to I hold the corpse under the arms, only then are we able to sling the body over Ginger's back. She gives me a look, guilt makes me think for a moment she might be judging me. I shouldn't be making her do this. It's bad enough Sayid is helping me hide a body. Cigarettes are one thing, but this is in a whole other universe of favors.

Sayid is too scared of Ginger to take the lead, so I do. She follows me through the stables, and around back. It's only twenty feet to the tree line. Under the cover of night, and the trees, I feel a bit better.

"I owe you," I say to Sayid.

"Yes, yes you do." He sneers at Ginger, and falls back a few steps.

Lingering behind, Sayid kicks the roots that protrude from the ground as we pass them. Ginger and I avoid them entirely. I'm not sure if Sayid is doing it on purpose, or if he's just clumsy. Every time he hits one, my jaw clenches, and my nerves flare.

"Just up here, we should be good to drop him," he says.

I look up ahead, and see a small clearing. That must be where he wants to stop. The moon pours into the clearing, somehow it's the only spot in Florida the Spanish moss hasn't managed to invade. It's all but abandoned, there isn't so much as a lingering footprint in the dirt here. Ginger walks into the clearing, I pull on her lead to stop her. Sayid walks toward the body, then thinks better of getting closer.

I tug on the shirt of the corpse. He falls head-first onto the ground. A wet pop echoes through the trees, the sound sickens me, bile creeps up my throat. I shudder. Ginger shakes her head from side to side, I guess she's happy to be free of the weight. I lean against her, my arm slung over her neck. In the woods, beyond what I can see, I hear the branches snap as someone stomps through them.

I can tell from the panic in Sayid's eyes, he heard it too. I hold Ginger still, not wanting her to make a noise that might draw attention to us. For all I know a guard is patrolling the woods, searching. The footsteps grow closer, louder. Sayid ventures closer to me.

"We're going to have to ride her, get out of here and away from whoever is out there," I whisper to Sayid. My hand rests on her neck. Her ears are perked up, watching the trees.

"I'm not getting on that *thing*," he says looking at Ginger with disgust.

"Have you ever had a dog?" I ask him, my voice as low as I can manage.

His eyes squint, brows furrow. "No, why?" he asks, barely above a whisper.

"Well, do you like dogs?" I ask, trying to find some comparison that might get him to understand.

"Yeah, why?"

"Horses are no worse than dogs. If you ask me, they're better." My whispers are hushed, barely audible. Dark hands made entirely out of tension claw at me. Whoever it is out there, they're almost to the clearing. They can't be more than ten feet away.

"A horse can kill you," he argues.

"A dog can kill you just as easily," I snap back.

I pull myself up on Ginger's back. Thankfully, I have years of experience riding bareback. Going without a saddle will be nothing new for me. As sore as I already am, chances are I won't even feel it tomorrow. I hold my hand out, and wait for Sayid to take it.

The footsteps are so close now, they threaten to breach the clearing. Sayid looks toward the sound, and takes my hand. I pull him up. Just as I pat Ginger on the neck, and nudge her side with my foot, I see the gleam of a knife cut through the trees.

Ginger rides through the forest like an expert. She works around trees, avoiding roots and stumps. I close my eyes, lost, letting the wind hit my face. I can hear someone chasing us. But with Ginger's speed, there's no way they'll keep up. When we reach the stables, we both hop off her back, and I open the stall for her. She wants to argue, she wants to be free, out for a ride. Still though, she does as she's bid.

Sayid and I run through the orange trees back to Madison. On the back porch, Sayid grabs my arm. Where he touches me, my skin tingles in response. I turn to look at him, and where I expect a smile, instead his brows are creased, his mouth a thin line.

"What's wrong?"

He pulls away and lights a cigarette. He paces the porch, glancing at me every few steps.

My guts knot, and my mouth goes dry. "Come on, spill. What's wrong?"

"What *isn't* wrong? That was really close, and really stupid. We shouldn't have done that."

I nod. "I'm sorry. You didn't have to help. I don't want you to end up in the white house because of me."

"I can't get in that kind of trouble. Contraband, that's one thing. I wouldn't spend months in the white house for that. Hell, I might even get off with a warning from the right guard." He shakes his head and takes a drag. "But killing another inmate, even someone like that, it's too risky. I can't be a part of that."

I look down at my feet, confusion prickles at the back of my mind. "What are you saying?"

He looks away, toward the trees.

My nose tingles, and emotion floods into me. The frustration and sadness nearly knock me over. The look on his face says it all. The silence builds between us. I swallow hard as I say a silent prayer that his words don't mirror my thoughts.

"I can't do this," he says as he points between us.

I sink beneath the weight of his words. All the life rushes out of me at once. Tears sting my eyes. Sayid turns, I reach for him, but he pulls his arm away and disappears into Madison. I walk toward the office, my arms crossed over my chest. Eden. I need to talk to her. The further I walk, the more I pick up my pace until I'm nearly jogging. Light pours from the windows, pooling on the dark ground. Inside, a guard stalks from one side of the office to the other. I duck out of view, my heart pounding. If I'm seen out at night, I'll get dragged to the white house.

31

AFTER

"Asher, come on, let's go." Olivia calls.

She's way ahead of me, already up the stairs in the mansion. The wood bows under my feet, it creaks and groans under my weight. It feels so brittle, I'm sure it's rotted through. I creep carefully, testing my weight on the battered steps before I climb. Clinging to the banister, afraid I'm going to fall through this ancient house. Beneath my feet squeaks, moans and a snap echo.

Every step sends a fresh wave of fear through me. I hold my breath when my weight shifts onto the step, like the air in my lungs will make me too heavy. The second I reach the landing, I let it all out at once.

The halls are littered with plaster, torn wallpaper and shredded newspapers. Old brittle leaves cling to the walls, decaying. The house is so old, and in such a bad state, I swear I can hear the termites chewing away in the walls. Each step atop the piles of debris cracks and crunches. Olivia managed to pad through as silent as a cat, not even a whisper of a sound when she walked. At the end of the hall, I see her standing in front of a broken window. Moonlight streams in what's left of the gauzy curtains, there's a glow behind her, like a spotlight.

Her blonde curls twist and twirl on a gentle breeze that I can't feel. Even the shards of glass clinging to the window frame seem to glitter and glow. I hear something rustle downstairs, probably a raccoon desperate for food.

"Olivia, come on, it's not safe up here," I say from the door frame, my hand clings to it, like it will save me from anything in this decaying heap.

She doesn't speak, she holds her arm out behind her, milky fingers extended, searching for mine. I take a step inside the room, the breeze inside is frigid, colder than the air should be in Florida. Wood bows beneath my feet, I step to the side hoping to find a safer place to stand.

Beneath my shoes, the floor starts to give way. There's a thunderous crash, and I dive forward trying to avoid falling through. Dust clouds the room. I hit something as I fall. A burst of splinters and dirt flies in my face, burning my eyes, drying out my mouth. I sputter out a cough, spitting mouthfuls of dirt to the floor. There's a rush, and something warm. Rain.

Droplets stream down my face, I rub my eyes trying to see through the blur. Once the haze fades and I look down, my hands are smeared with red.

Blood? Am I bleeding?

I look up to the window and that's when I see what I hit. Olivia's stuck, shards of glass from the window piercing through her neck and abdomen. Her eyes are wide, pleading as she searches my face.

"Oh God," is all I can manage to say, the blood pours from her body. My voice cracks.

I pull myself from the floor, as soon as I reach her side, her cold fingers search for my hand. I survey her body, trying to figure out a way to lift her off the glass, there has to be a way to save her before it's too late. If I drive for help it will be at least an hour before I'm back—she'll be dead by then.

"Just hold on, I'll get you out of this." Tears sting my eyes. I know it's a promise I can't keep.

She shakes her head at me. Somehow, even now, she manages to smile.

Wood groans and snaps. Creaks and pops surround me. The rest of the room is about to collapse, maybe even the whole house. But I don't care. I'm going to stay with her. Panic wells in her eyes, she mouths, "Go".

I shake my head. "I'm not leaving you." The tears pour down my face. She's barely hanging on. Her lips are no longer fleshy pink, they're blue. She struggles to breathe, gurgled haggard breaths shake her body.

"I love you, Olivia." I lean over to give her one last kiss, as I pull away she flashes me one last smile. The sweetest one she can manage as she slips away.

There's a groan far off in the house, and outside I hear laughing. In the darkness, beneath the full moon, Dominic is watching us. Laughing.

~

I wake up panting. A cold sweat slicks my body, emotion wraps its cold fingers around my throat. Sayid is still asleep. In the corner of my eye, I see the slightest glimmer of white fabric disappear down the hall. Tears burn my eyes. I have to get out of this room, out of this house, sorrow tightens throat, begging to get out. The weight of my grief caught in this room suffocates me.

I creep down the stairs and follow the white dress as it disappears around the darkest corner. The smell of sweat is heavy in the air. There's a groaning, rocking sound coming from the recreation room. I walk to the back and follow Olivia to see where the sound is coming from.

In the darkness, I can make out two figures. A guard and a student. Though I say nothing, I don't even breathe, they see me. There's a rush as they try to cover themselves and pull their pants back on.

I'm not interested in them. I just want to see her. Before they even zip up, I'm on the front porch. The door opens behind me, and before I turn, I say, "I didn't see anything."

A large hand grasps by bicep as I try to get away. I pull and twist. But it's no use. The guard overpowers me. Behind him, someone runs up the stairs.

"Stop, now," the guard demands.

"I said I didn't see anything," I repeat.

"That's convenient, but we have to be sure." He twists me around and holds me by both arms, a sinister smirk across his wide face. Buzzed blond hair pokes out from his skull, shiny with sweat. A large brow swoops over his dark eyes. His face, his whole body is so square, it almost doesn't seem possible. He drags me across the yard, and I know where we're going.

The closer we get to the white house, the more I kick and dig my heels into the wet earth. As we grow near, my heart threatens to beat straight through my chest. An invisible hand tightens around my throat, and each breath is harder to take than the last. When I trip him up, he grabs me around the waist, and drags me. Rocks cut into my flesh, and I claw at the ground, trying to stop him. We're still a hundred yards or so away but I can hear the muffled screams, the churn of an old fan, the moans. Fifty feet away, there's a sour smell in the air, but I can't place it. I stop struggling, and go limp. Outside the white house there's a stack of what looks like bodies wrapped in white sheets. The moon light shines bright enough that I can see the blood seeps through in spots.

The guard trips and drops me. I freeze, he picks himself up and sits on the small of my back. Cold metal presses into the back of my head, he grabs a fist-full of my hair and yanks my head back. The gun is sharp against my skull. I hear a click, and my whole body goes tense.

He's going to shoot me. Maybe that would be better than dying slowly in the white house.

"You are going to fucking walk in there or I'm going to knock your fucking teeth out. Then I'll fuck the hole where they used to be. Do you understand?" As he asks, the gun in his hand shakes, and the rage seethes through every word. The way he drags out each and every word, you'd think he wasn't sure I could even speak English.

I try to nod, but I can't. He's still holding my head back.

"Yes, yessir." I manage to say, but I can't keep my voice even. My whole body shakes, panicked tears pour from my eyes. My body doesn't want to move.

He pulls me up by the back of my shirt. I stand, my legs barely able to hold me. Fear quakes through my body. It's nearly eighty degrees, but goose bumps rise on my flesh, my teeth chatter. The scuff of his feet behind me reminds me to walk.

The stench inside nearly knocks me over. Shit, vomit, and ammonia swirl together. I dry heave. I stumble forward, my foot slips on the grimy concrete. Behind me, he holds a flashlight. The stream moves to the left side of the room. What looks like twenty naked boys are huddled on the floor. They're stained with blood and bruises. Frightened eyes call out to me in the dark. My insides may as well be lead. I can't help you, I can't even help myself.

I'm forced to a back room. The guard shackles me face-first to a wall. He walks away for a moment. When he returns I hear the clink of metal. Something dangles in his hand, the gleam of steel catches my eye. He takes a deep breath and winds up. I hold my breath, my whole body tenses. The steel bites into my flesh, opening it. Pain surges through me. Blood pours from the wound. He lashes again, and again. With each impact, white spots explode behind my eyes, my teeth grind together. Tears pour from my clenched eyes. As he beats me, my mind is far away, and I slip into the darkness.

When I wake, the muscles in my arms burn. They've been chained up for so long I can't feel my fingers anymore. I stand. There are shuffles and coughs behind me, but I can't see the boys. Though I don't think any guards are present, no one speaks. No one dares speak. The fan churns. Guttural moans cut across the low hum of the fan.

I want to know how long they've all been locked in here. How often they're beaten. If once you're in here you stay until you die. It isn't until the sun fades from the sky that I hear footsteps again. He beats me again, and again. Metal digs into my skin, blood pours from my body. For what feels like days, he returns to take out his frustrations on my flesh, each time he beats me until I lose consciousness. Though I try to count the days, the hours I'm in the white house, I find myself weak and disoriented. The only states here are pain and darkness. One blurs into the other, one becomes the other. A cycle that seems it will never end.

Please just kill me.

A beeping far off lulls me. I'm stuck somewhere, not awake, but no longer asleep. The rhythm pulls me slowly from the darkness. A needle sticks out from my arm, tubes snake up to bags that hang beside me. I sit up as much as I'm able with the things I'm hooked up to.

Sayid sits next to me. Empty hospital beds stretch as far as I can see in every direction. His brown eyes are saucers as he looks at me. The mess of jet black hair, all tangles and knots, tells me he's been here for a while. Black stubble clings to his jaw. His mouth is slack, like he tried to speak, but lost the words. He grabs my hand, and squeezes it softly. My eyes flutter closed, and I suck in a sharp breath.

"I was afraid you weren't going to come out of there," he finally says, he can't look at me when he says it. Once the words are out he rests his elbows on the bed, and his head falls between them.

"Me too." My throat is hoarse, dry, speaking hurts more than I could have imagined. I reach over and rest my hand on the back of his head. Slowly, I brush the hair from his face. He looks at me, his eyes raw, pink with emotion. I hate that he's upset, I hate even more that he's upset because of me.

"What happened?" he asks, his eyes fall to the floor and his mouth droops.

A tall, blonde nurse, lingers near, too close for comfort. I shake my head, my voice drops. "I'll tell you some other time. How long was I in there?" I hold my throat as I talk, hoping it will help the pain. It doesn't. The days bled into one another, with no lights, no meals, it's impossible to tell how long it's been. All I knew was the shift between pain and darkness.

"A month. That's why I was so worried. When you're in there that long, you don't usually come out alive." He looks down at his feet, like he's lost someone that way before. Maybe he's lost several friends to the white house.

When he lifts his head, my hand falls limp to the bed. His words lost in my mind. The confusion is still so thick it traps my thoughts in a fog. He takes my hand, and holds it gently, a soft smile curls his lips.

"A month? That long?" Time seemed to stop while I was there. All I can wonder is how long those other kids have been in there. Or how much longer they have left to live. In the back of my mind, I can almost hear a clock ticking down the minutes, the few heartbeats some of us have left.

He nods. Sayid looks down, his mouth pressed into a tight line. "I'm really sorry about what I said before." He looks up at me with darkened eyes. His shoulders are hunched like something heavy is weighing on him. "When Brandon told me you were in the white house, I was so scared I'd never see you again. That I'd never be able to say I'm sorry."

I squeeze his hand and offer him a smile.

"Will you let me make it up to you?"

I look down, my cheeks burn. "You can try."

He smiles, and a soft laugh escapes him. For a long time, we sit in silence, his hand in mine. I wish we could be closer, but the eyes of the nurses are still on us.

"Have you heard from Eden?" I ask, I feel like I've asked him a thousand times. She should have written back, we should have heard *something* from her by now.

He shakes his head. "Nothing."

A bad feeling grows inside me with every breath I take. There's something wrong. I need to find out where my sister is.

32

AFTER

I sit at the end of my hospital bed with my knees pulled up to my chest. Leaning against the window, I stare out at the inky sky while everyone else on campus sleeps. Sayid warned me not to go out tonight, not that I would anyway, they haven't released me yet. Apparently, this is one of the few nights the guards are on duty. Some officials from the Department of Corrections are coming to investigate tomorrow. Or as I've heard it, to come pick up hush money. Even so, things have to be above board for a few days, just in case.

From my window, I can see the guards moving about beneath the scant moonlight and stray street lights. The guards have been scattered, but now they're starting to congregate, like spilled BBs collecting at the low point in the room, pooling in front of the white house.

A few go in while the others stand together outside. It's the most I've seen in one area before, there must be fifteen. Slowly, people emerge from the white house, but they're not guards. Emaciated students hobble out. Many are naked, some still in school issue clothing, now stained, smeared with God knows what. Many of them are so pale they nearly glow. I'm far enough away that I can't make out the bruises, or their faces.

Twenty or so inmates file out and line up in front of the guards. A man in uniform steps forward and raises his nightstick, then, picking a student at random, hits them until they fall to their knees, and land first in the dirt. Together the guards move as a unit, like a hive of bees, then I hear gunshots and the bodies slump one, by one.

They're executing them.

I see someone move quickly, darting away from the white house. Sprinting for freedom. A hand raises, a gun fires, and he falls to the ground. I turn away, the sour burn of bile in my mouth. I can't watch. But, at least now they won't be suffering, starving to death. Or worse.

33

AFTER

I wake up gasping. Fresh nightmares of Olivia's corpse haunt me. A large warm hand rests on my shoulder. I flinch away from the touch. As I gulp the air, I look over from the hospital bed I'm still in. Sitting next to me is a tall, lanky guy I know is friends with Sayid, but I can't place his name. He sat at the table my first full day at Dozier, and probably every day after that.

David, maybe?

"You okay?" His large blue eyes assess me as he leans in. His blond eyebrows are furrowed with concern. When he's this close, I notice lines in his face I hadn't seen in the dining hall. He has a long straight nose, and high cheekbones. There's a scar across his right eyebrow, a bald spot where the hair doesn't grow in. It's deep, pink, and still a bit puckered—like it only recently healed.

"Yeah, I'm fine," I lie as I sit up. I try not to be rude as I ask, "What are you doing here?" I'd hoped to see Sayid when I woke up again, not one of his friends. But I know Sayid can't spend every minute beside me while I'm in the hospital. He'd still be expected to go to work detail.

He shrugs as he scratches his stick straight nose and brushes his long hair away from his eyes. He leans back in a metal folding chair, one of his long legs is crossed over the other. By how comfortable he looks, I'd guess he's been here a while.

"Needed some quiet and an excuse to get out of work. I'm Cameron, by the way." He extends his hand.

"Asher," I say as I shake it, careful not to tweak the needle still taped against my skin.

"Yeah, I know. But I could tell by the look on your face you had no clue who I am." He laughs. "How much longer they keeping you?"

"Not sure, no one's bothered to fill me in on anything. I'm not in any rush. I can live without shoveling shit for a few days." I fluff the pillows behind my head and try to get comfortable. Though I do prefer to skip most of the stable duties, I do miss the horses. I haven't even seen Ginger since she helped bail me out. *Who's taking care of them while I'm gone?*

"Yeah, I'd take a few days off detail, if I could." He smiles and leans back further on his chair.

"What's your work assignment?" I ask to be polite, but I don't particularly care.

"I work in the kitchen with Brandon. Won't be long, I'm counting down the days now." He teeters on the back legs of his chair, propping his feet on my hospital bed.

I recognize the name Brandon, one of Sayid's other friends. The one who always gives me piles of bacon.

"Then what?" I'm curious what anyone plans after leaving here. I still can't imagine having a life without Olivia. Maybe, it's because I'm *not* planning a life without her. If I do ever get out of here and have to come up with a plan, the first thing I'm doing is getting the hell out of Florida and never looking back.

"Going back to Gainesville, finally going to marry Marleen."

He smiles, he's looking off in the distance. His eyes lost in thought. "She's my girlfriend, been together for five years. Got her pregnant before I left. Was so mad I could only go to the first appointment. I'm hoping I'll get out before the baby comes." He sighs, he looks so happy, blissful. Jealousy pricks at me. "I want to be there, even if she's not going to let me in the room."

The life I wanted, the life I'll never have. I keep my face straight, I lock down the jealousy before it can claw its ugly head all the way to the surface.

"Do you want a boy or a girl more?" I ask, because I'm really not sure what else to ask when someone talks about babies.

"A girl. If it's a girl, we're going to name her Sadie."

"What if it's a boy?" I ask, only to keep the conversation going. The days in the hospital get long, lonely, talking to Cameron is a nice distraction. Even if it does make me miss Olivia.

"Not sure yet, she likes Davy, but I hate The Monkees." He shrugs.

The happiness on his face crushes me. Ahead of him is the future I wanted. A future I'm not so sure I want anymore.

His chair clinks to the floor and leans onto my bed on his elbows. "So, what's your story?" he asks.

"What do you mean?" I know what he means, but I want to know what information he's looking for specifically. If I know what he wants, I can give as little information as possible.

"What are you in for?" He looks at me like he's trying to guess. Like he can pin down the likely reason I'd be in here. He probably thinks I stole a car, skipped a class, maybe even got caught with a joint. I wish I could see the list of everything people expect I'm guilty of.

"Sayid didn't tell you?" A few months ago, I'd be surprised. I figured since murder is so rare around here that the news would have spread fast. But now that I've grown to know, and trust Sayid, I know he's about as tight-lipped with information as I am.

"Nope. He's zipped it up and thrown away the key." He mimes zipping his lips.

"I don't really want to talk about it." I look away. This kid will not understand. He has his own Olivia. He'll imagine if he could kill her. That's when he'll see the monster I am.

He leans even further onto the bed and drops his voice, like we're sharing a secret. "You wanna know what I did?" he offers.

"Sure." I don't really want to know, but I can tell by the look on his face, he's going to tell me anyway. The more he talks about himself, the less I'll have to talk about myself.

"So back home in Gainesville a couple years back, Marleen told me she'd caught her stepdad peeking at her while she was changing, getting out of the shower, stuff like that. Well one night she calls me because he touched her. I go over and I lay the law down. I tell this puny fuck if he ever touches her again, I'm gonna waste him." He's really animated when he's talking, like he's directing traffic.

I raise an eyebrow, "Why didn't Marleen's mom get involved?"

He shrugs. "Drugged up, asshole. She didn't give two shits about Marleen. Anyway, after I threaten this shit biscuit, a few weeks go by, all is fine. Then he grabs Marleen when she's getting out of the shower. Prick picked the lock. Long story short, he tries to rape her. She fights him off, but calls me frantic. I come over and nearly beat him to death with a crowbar. If it weren't for Marleen stopping me, I'd be looking at life." The way he puffs out his chest, the smile that crosses his lips, you can tell he's proud of himself.

I pick my jaw up and manage to say, "Wow."

He shrugs like it's no big deal. "I'd do anything for her, ya know."

I nod. I do know. I would do the same thing for Olivia. And for

Sayid. No questions asked.

"So come on," he nudges me, "will you tell me now?"

Knowing his history now, I think it's an even worse idea. "Look. I'm here for murder, I really don't want to talk about it though. I told Sayid, so if you have questions, please just go ask him." My tone isn't harsh, but I still feel like a jerk after I say it. I know even if he presses Sayid, he won't tell. My history, my secrets, are safe with him.

He looks me over, like he's inspecting me. Then he looks me straight in the eyes. "There's no way you killed anyone." he says, his voice is so sure that I'm envious of it, "I can see it in your eyes, you're not a killer."

"You'd be correct," I confirm.

"Were you set up?" His eyebrows are perked up as he leans on his right hand, peering at me.

"I have no idea. I can't remember anything about what happened that night."

His face drops, he leans in further. "Seriously? You don't remember anything?"

"All I know is that they found me next to..." I pause, considering my words, how much information I want to give him. I give him the usual run down about the memory loss. I leave it at that. No information about Olivia, no hints who the 'victim' was.

"You seeing the shrink?" he pries.

I nod.

"You know," he drags out the words, "he can pull some strings. If he thinks you're bad enough off, he can dismiss you from work detail, I mean, you still have to go sometimes. But mostly you can just stay in your room."

"Really?" I love the stables, but some days I'd rather just hide in the library.

"Yep." He looks toward the clock, and one of the bells sounds outside. "Crap, I've gotta get going. Dinner calls. Was good chatting with you Asher."

"You too."

34

BEFORE
Date Unknown

The night thickens around me as I walk through the empty streets. This close to dawn, the city is all but abandoned. The fake journal is heavy in my jacket. She's already planted one. Dominic didn't take it from me like I'd expected him to, so now it's my turn. We have to throw him off our trail, we have to keep him from knowing how close we are. Well, how close she thinks we are.

There are so many obvious choices, so many places that I know he'd look. But it can't be in the first place he looks, or the second. The real journal I've already tucked away, it's important that I'm the only one able to find it. Every lifetime I've detailed things I've learned, things that might not come back to me right away. Normally, the first mortal wound should release my memories, but this time it didn't happen that way. Each time, it's been easier for her to get her memories back in pristine detail, while sometimes mine aren't as clear, and lately it seems to be getting worse. She's always stronger than me for some reason, and she keeps getting stronger.

As the row houses give way to the cemeteries, I know I'm running out of time. I don't have more than an hour to plant it. If I don't get back soon, she'll be vulnerable. Now that he's here in the city, we're on borrowed time. A cold breeze slips through the streets, it's so sudden, so out of place that I stop walking. My eyes sweep the street. Darkness hides the secrets of whoever might be out there, but I can feel them. I can feel him.

I choose one of the shotgun houses on the edge of town that I've used as a decoy time and time again. He's seen me here before, it won't be much of a surprise. I climb the steps and sweep through the front door. Slowly I walk through every room in the house, once I've found every room empty, I stash the journal in a hidden compartment in the fireplace.

The second I step onto the front porch, I see Dominic waiting for me in the street.

35

AFTER

I stand outside Dr. Lennox's office. I can't do it anymore, I need answers. But how can I trust him when he lets these things go on here? Beneath his nose kids are disappearing, being beaten, or worse. How can he sit here, with his booze and his cigarettes while he lets the rest of us die around him?

He may not know.

How could he not know? He had to have noticed that I've been missing for weeks. But he doesn't mention a single time that I missed our sessions, like it doesn't surprise him.

He knows.

Someone had to send those boys to those small rooms that Sayid told me about. Someone had to decide they were too crazy to be with the rest of us. Will he do that to me? If I share the wrong information with him, if I share too much information with him? I have to decide how important the truth is.

Frustration pools inside me. For weeks, months, now, Olivia has haunted my dreams. I need to try the regression again. The answers are locked inside my mind somewhere. Not knowing, the questions, the guilt—it's killing me. And then, after I have the answers, I'll never have to see him again. I'll never have to see Dozier again.

My hand trembles, barely able to knock. My blood boils and my breaths quicken, fear coils inside me. Today I might finally know for sure.

"Yes?" he calls from inside, his voice is muffled by the door, like he's underwater.

I open the door slowly, just as Dr. Lennox closes a book. He shifts in his chair and slides the book onto the side table. He looks over his glasses and says, "Hello, Asher, how can I help you today?"

"I want to try the regression hypnosis. I need to know what happened." I try not to beg. My voice quavers.

"Are you sure you want to try so soon?" he asks.

I nod. "I'm not going to change my mind."

"Are you sure you don't want to discuss anything else? I'm still here to listen, Asher. You don't have to lock yourself away." He tilts his head to look at me over his glasses, his milky eyes bore into me.

"I'm only here for the regression."

He motions toward the couch, displeasure clear on his face. "Please lie down, then. Make yourself comfortable, you're going to have to relax." His voice is deadpan, and edges on frustration. I know he doesn't want to try again, he thinks my mind will just keep failing me. Maybe it will. But I have to try.

I walk over and fall backwards into the plush couch. Rough tweed fabric digs into my arms, and the scent of stale cigarette smoke hovers around me. The pillow on the end is too thin. I fold it over and shove it under my neck.

"I need you to close your eyes," he directs and I follow his instructions. "Take slow deep breaths."

My eyes close, and I breathe as deeply as I can. Before we start, in the moment before he speaks again, I can see myself next to her. The

AFTER YOU DIED   213

blood oozing from her body, the gray color of her skin.

"Count your breaths, in and out."

One, two, deep breaths shudder through me. He keeps directing me, the darkness ebbs in.

Even beneath the shade in the stables, the afternoon heat blankets me. It hasn't rained in days, yet it's still so humid you could hard boil an egg on the sidewalk. Though it's a thousand degrees out here, the horses still snort and stomp, as happy as if there were a breeze. It's been still outside for so long, I can't even remember the last time I felt wind. Florida's got the kind of heat that wraps itself around you, holding you so tight you feel like you're being smothered beneath it.

Since Olivia's been out shopping with Eden all day, I've been out here, reading. I'd have gone shopping with them, but Eden flashed me a warning glare. I knew if I followed, a funeral procession wouldn't be far behind. The smell of shit, hay, and dirt is as comforting as the escape I usually find in words. Truth is, I'm not really focused on my book. My favorite horse, Lady, is fit to foal. She's four days late, actually—not that I'm counting. As stubborn as she is, I'm not surprised. She's been late every single time she's been bred.

I look up from my book when I feel her eyes on me, her breath against my hair. The only thing hotter than Florida is horse breath. She's taking a break from pacing to stare out at me over the door. I reach up, and push her muzzle into the side of my head.

I set the book down and push off the wooden bench. She's paces and circles around her stall. She's got one of the largest stalls, giving her plenty of room. The hay in her stall is damp, riddled with blood. Her torso tightens, she's pushing. This is the fourth labor I've been through with her. There's a pop, a waterfall of fluid, and in two more pushes the foal falls to the floor. She turns and nuzzles the foal and moments later it tries to stand on shaky legs.

Lifting the wooden lever, I push the door in. I enter the stall to inspect the foal. He's tiny, almost looks like he came a little too early. I slide my hand across Lady's brown and white body. The foal's father is gray. But this foal is solid white. It's not often you see solid white horses, and I'm surprised she managed to make him. Every other foal of hers has been a tiny replica of her.

"Nice work," I say as I run my hands across her mane.

As I run my hands across Lady, her belly tightens again. She starts to push, and fear wells in my stomach. The vet never guessed Lady might be carrying twins. Twin pregnancies are dangerous for horses. She has the second foal out so quickly I'm barely able to process it. It's hard to even look over at the foal, I'm expecting it to be dead. They're always dead.

Then I hear shuffling, and Lady shifts to look at the new foal. This one is also white, with just a touch of chocolate brown on her mane. But she looks just as healthy as her brother. It's all I can do not to hug Lady.

I hear footsteps behind me. I expect it to be my father checking in on the horses. But the second I see the flaming red hair, I know it's Dominic.

"Hey," I say to him.

He nods but doesn't say anything for a moment, finally he asks, "Where's Olivia?"

"Out with Eden, shopping," I explain as I watch to be sure both foals are nursing.

"Olivia is obsessed with that Howey mansion, right?" he asks.

How does he know that? She never talks to him, and she wouldn't have told him. "Yeah, why?" I turn toward him, watching him light a cigarette.

"Old lady Howey got carted off to the hospital. Heard it was serious, she'll probably be gone a while," he says as he takes a slow drag.

My eyes burn when I come out of the vision. Quick breaths make my head spin. Dr. Lennox doesn't speak right away, he waits until I sit up. My head rests on my palms, and my elbows dig into my knees. After a while, my back complains; I have to sit up and correct my posture.

It wasn't real. Was it?

The vision was as clear as any memory I've ever had, clearer than the visions I know weren't real. *Was it real? Did we go to the mansion because Dominic told me about it?*

"Who's Dominic?" Dr. Lennox asks.

Though I know during the regressions I tell him everything I see, the question still takes me off guard.

"He was my friend," I say. "The best friend I had who wasn't Olivia." The words have a finality to them that I don't expect. *Was.*

"Was," he repeats, picking it out of my sentence. "Why, *was*?"

"Partly because I'm here. Partly because my sister thinks that Dominic has something to do with Olivia's death."

"And what do you think?" he asks as he tilts his head and crosses one of his legs over the other.

"I don't know." A leaden breath slips out of me. "I don't want to think that my best friend could have killed Olivia. And I feel horrible for even thinking it." But there's something that's nagging at the back of my mind. The fingers of a memory working their way into my mind.

"Had he ever hurt Olivia, or anyone else?"

I shake my head. "No, not that I know of."

"Is there any reason you can think of that he might have hurt her?"

"He was always jealous of Olivia. He hated her. And she hated him. But I never understood why."

His brow falls and he brings his hands together so that his fingers form a peak. "While it's possible that someone else hurt her, you need to understand that your guilt and depression may be working together to shift blame. I think we should try regression again in a few days, or whenever you're comfortable."

A lump forms in my throat, and my eyes tighten.

"There was another set of footprints at the scene. Did I ever tell you that? There was someone else there that night. There was someone else who could have done it. But that doesn't matter, does it? You think I did it. You think I killed her." I don't know why I'm so surprised, so disappointed. Part of me expected that if we spent all these sessions together he'd see that I'm not a killer.

I push a shuddering breath out of my nose, and some of the frustration brewing inside me slips out with it. Right now, I can't even look at him. Part of me doesn't want to come back.

36

AFTER

A weird prickly feeling haunts me. There's a crisp and cool fog hanging in the air this morning. Mist pools on the ground, and creeps across the lawn. A chill slithers up my arms. The campus is all but abandoned, except for a few boys that sneak off into the cornfield. I feel like my mind is giving me hints about the memories that are locked there. My mind is trying to tell me I'm a killer. That I did it.

As I wander, I avoid the dining hall, sneaking a cig in the orange trees, before heading to the stables. The smell of hay is heavy in the air. Even though the horses can't smile, when they nuzzle into your shoulder you know they're happy, you know they love you. I have a handful of hay when I reach my favorite. Her soft, rich, chestnut fur folds beneath my hands, she nuzzles me before she takes the hay.

"Sorry I couldn't sneak you an apple," I say as I rub my hand across her nose. I skipped breakfast, but the hollow feeling in my stomach isn't because I'm hungry—I feel bad for not bringing her a treat.

A few of the other horses are not as happy to see me, they simply tolerate me. Years of mistreatment has likely made them numb to humans. Two others, black and white paint horses show me a bit of affection, but I haven't bonded with them like I have Ginger. When I let her out of the stables, she follows me around like a puppy, nudging me when I turn away. Most of the time that I should be shoveling, or cleaning, I'm actually brushing her.

I've got the brush in my hand working through the knots in her mane when Sayid jogs up.

Out of breath he says, "Hey."

I nod at him. He's hunched over, with his hands on his knees as he catches his breath. Stray strands of hair are glued to his face with sweat. My eyebrow perks up as I watch him, he never runs anywhere. *What's the rush today?*

"Your dad's on the phone, says it's an emergency. They sent me to get you," he says and pauses between each word to suck in a breath.

"I thought we weren't allowed phone calls," I say, and glance at him, searching his face. It's not that I don't believe him. But I'm wondering if the news is really *that* bad, or if he pulled strings because he's a judge. A bad feeling claws at the back of my mind, letting the darkest of thoughts in.

"We're not."

I take Ginger off the lead, and my hands tremble. She follows me into the stable, and gives me a disappointed snort as I shut the door to leave. Her head shakes from side to side. She stomps twice, and pulls her ears back.

"I'll be back later." I promise. Each breath I take in is sharper than the last.

In a blur, I run to the office. Sayid follows, keeping pace with me. I burst into the office, the metal door quakes as it slams behind me. I grab the phone, laying on a desk, as soon as I see it.

"Dad?"

"Asher?" His voice is flat. Though he's speaking directly into the phone, his words seem far off, hollow.

"What's wrong?" I ask. Something must be wrong, he hasn't spoken to me since he sent me here. There has to be some reason for him to call, and it can't be good news. He never wanted to talk to me even when I was home.

"Your Mom... Eden..." He pauses to suck a drag off his cigarette, and I hear ice clink in a glass in the background. "They're missing."

I feel for my pocket automatically, her necklace is still there. I should have tried to call her when I had the chance. Guilt pummels me. *What if I never see her again?* My eyes burn, my throat tightens, dry as a bleached bone.

"What do you mean, missing?" The words are rejected by my mind. They're so impossible, I can't process them. A pit forms in my stomach, weighing me down. It spreads, my limbs turn to lead. I might never be able to move from this spot. I know it's been a while since Sayid heard from her, and her necklace...but she can't be missing, she can't.

"Eden's been gone six weeks, your mom disappeared last night." His voice cracks.

Six weeks? She's been gone six weeks and no one told me? No one wrote me?

A rush of anger flares up inside me. But it's crushed beneath the weight of sadness a few moments later. The thoughts twist in my mind. I have to find her. I'm no use to her in here.

Did Dominic do this?

I've never heard my dad upset before, I've never even seen him cry. But I can't pity him now. I hate him for this. I hate him for not telling me.

She's really gone. I didn't imagine it. I had a chance to save her, and I didn't.

"Did you call the police?" I ask, because I'm not really sure what to say, what to ask. Fear coils inside me, and I feel like I'm going to throw up.

Eden can't be missing. My Mom can't be missing. This can't be real.

"Of course I called the police. They're working on it." His voice falls and he sighs. It's clear he has no faith in them, but I knew that already.

I don't want to ask the next question, but it slips from my mouth anyway. "Do you think they're dead?" My voice is barely a whisper. I'm aware of Sayid's eyes on me, the stricken look on his face. I turn, and face the wall.

There's a long pause. A rustling, like he's moving the phone. I hear the clink again of ice cubes in a glass, followed by a slow sip.

When he doesn't speak I say, "Dad?" I pause, "Please," I beg, my voice cracks.

"Yeah," he mumbles. "I mean, it doesn't look good. I know how it turns out for most missing persons cases. Especially since they both disappeared separately. Asher, I don't think they're coming back." He blows his nose.

"Are you going to be okay?" I ask. I'm not sure why I ask, I'm not even sure I care. But if they're gone, he's really the only family I have left. The only family in this state anyway.

"Yeah, I'm fine." His voice is distant. "Look, I've got to go. I'll talk to you soon." I know he doesn't mean it, it's just something he says.

"Yeah, bye, Dad." I hang up the phone, and turn to leave the office. As I walk away, it feels like part of me is still stuck in the office next to the phone, like I'm leaving part of myself behind. My eyes burn, and I wipe my nose on my shirt.

Sayid follows me outside, but I can't look at him. My eyes fall to the ground. There's a gaping hole inside me, so raw, it burns. When

I reach the bottom of the stairs, I stand on the sidewalk and stare at him for a moment. Every word is weighted to the bottom of my mind, and I can't pick them up. I can't find a single thing to say.

"Hey, you okay?" he asks as he nudges me. "Everything alright?"

I shake my head. "My mom and sister are missing. My dad thinks they're dead." I take a deep breath as I try not to break down. I sniffle, avoiding eye contact. Each burst of air shudders through me, I cross my arms hard across my chest, and try to keep myself from hyperventilating.

Eden is gone. She's gone. This can't be real.

"You want to talk about it?" he offers as he squeezes my forearm.

"No. I just want to be alone right now." I start to walk away and he grabs my arm. My eyes water. I've never felt so lost, so alone in my life. Eden was the other half of me. *Who am I without her?*

"Wait, before you go." He holds out his hand and gives me a pack of cigarettes.

"Thanks."

"Anytime." He gives me a half smile, shoves his hands in his jacket pockets, and turns toward the laundry. He looks back for a second to say, "If you need to talk..."

37

AFTER

After everyone is asleep I sneak down the stairs. Though fears that the guard may be downstairs are fresh in my mind, something is propelling me. When I reach the bottom, I listen carefully, not wanting to run into the guard and his toy again. Greeted by silence, I continue to the bathroom on the first floor. Thoughts weigh me down, I'm shrinking beneath them. Olivia is dead because of me. Eden and my mom are probably dead, and I wasn't there to save them. *Why do I get to live? I don't deserve to be alive.* I don't *want* to be alive. Every day is slightly more painful than the last.

The door squeaks when I open it. The smell of mold, and crappy shampoo heavy in the air. Beige tile lines the floors, the walls, dirty grout sticks out between them. Six shower stalls line the right hand side of the room. On the left side, three urinals stand with three stalls holding toilets beside them. Along the back wall that I face, there is a trough-like sink with four large mirrors above it.

Surrounding me, consuming me, the thoughts dig at me. I push the bathroom door shut and lock it. For a long time I stare at myself in the mirror. My features are dark, I don't recognize myself. The face staring back at me is so foreign I don't even see Eden in it anymore.

Everyone is gone, everyone that mattered. I'm completely alone.

It's your fault they're gone. You'll end up killing Sayid too. You'll kill anyone you get close to.

Without understanding what I'm doing, I pick up a plunger, but I'm not sure why; my body seems to move on its own. The wooden end slams into the mirror, it shatters. The shining shards shower around me. The air burns my skin as several of the mirrored daggers pierce my flesh. The sound cuts through the silent night. But I don't care anymore. By the time anyone could burst through the door, I'll be gone.

There's a *drip, drip, drip* of blood on the floor. The shards crackle beneath my feet as I shift, and stare at them. One large piece in particular calls out to me. When I hold it, look at it, it's not pain and a rush of blood I see. It's a way out. My way out. My way back to Olivia, Eden, and my mom.

I should feel panic, I should be scared. But all I feel is how much I miss them. How much I miss me, and my old life. There's no going back. That life is gone, and this new life isn't one I can stand to live in anymore. If I live, more people will be in danger. It's only a matter of time before I kill someone else.

It's like I'm standing outside myself, watching. My body moves a few feet away, on auto pilot. I feel nothing as the shard drags across my wrist over and over. Blood starts as a trickle then turns to a stream, a pool forms around my feet.

My breaths become shallow as darkness ebbs into the corner of my vision; then it engulfs me. Olivia and Eden are the last things to cross my mind, I feel words drift across my lips.

"I'm sorry."

38

A sly smile creeps across Dominic's face as he looks at me. He takes a long drag from a cigarette, and his eyes sweep the street. He plays it as though he's not quite interested. The truth of it is, he probably hasn't stopped looking for me since I escaped from him in the cemetery. My stomach twists as I watch him. He never lets it go on this long. He's so quick to act, to get it over with. His eyes narrow on the house.

What's changed?

"Really, here? You two should be able to do *much* better than this," he says as he shakes his head.

We *do* much better than this. I know he's trying to get information out of me, to get a clue. He's been able to find me just fine, but it's killing him that he can't find her.

"It's not the two of us, anymore," I say. There's no way it will ever be true. We'd never split up, we'd never be apart for long. But I need to lie, to convince him that he'll have to start looking elsewhere. It's our only chance for next time.

He cocks his head and his lips purse. The way his eyes tighten,

I can tell that he doesn't believe me. He's searching my face for the truth. But I don't look away, I don't shift, I hold steady.

"Shame," he says without an ounce of empathy.

I take a step closer to him. He doesn't move, he watches me. Another step, I need to get closer. I need to distract him, get him to trust me again.

"I've missed you," I say, the lie heavy on my words. "I've missed *us*." I close the distance.

His eyebrow perks up. It's what he wants to hear. I know it. But there's so much history between us, I doubt it will do anything other than serve as a distraction for a few minutes. But that's all I need.

39

After

Sayid hovers over me. His long dark hair covers most of his face. But I can see the thin line of his lips. Dark bags hang beneath his eyes, and the stubble collecting on his chin seems to have grown half an inch since I last saw him. He's close enough, the warmth of his breath hits my face, the smell of cigarettes lingers on it. He brushes the hair out of his face, panic in his eyes, searching me, evaluating me. I notice a strange bundle of long metal objects in his hand. They disappear quickly, shoved into his pocket.

"Are you okay?" he asks in a rushed, hushed voice.

I'm groggy, out of it. Mind blurred and far off. I grimace as he picks up my arms, and looks them over. I pull them from his grip and look up at him. My face is scrunched up, the light stings my eyes.

"Whose blood is this?" His eyes are wide. He's grabs towels from the laundry bin, and paces around me. There's a sucking sound with each step he takes on the wet floor.

For the first time I look down and notice the streams of dried blood on my arms. Shards of the broken mirror float in red pools around me. The dirty grout of the bathroom tiles stares back at me. *Did I sleep in the bathroom?*

"Mine?" I'm not sure. But I think I remember it being mine. *Or was that a dream?* The memories slip back to my mind slowly, like I'm reeling them in. One slow frame at a time. *It's impossible though, isn't it?* Otherwise, I'd be dead. Sayid wouldn't be pacing around me, panicked. I'd be in a body bag.

"What did you do?" he asks in a pained voice as he pulls me up from the floor. "Wash your arms off, hurry." He pushes me toward the sink.

I'm not sure why he doesn't want me to shower, but I follow his instructions. There's too much confusion clouding my mind for me to argue. Shards of glass crunch beneath my feet as I stumble forward. I slide, and grip the porcelain trough to steady myself. Though I scrub, the blood doesn't come off, not easily anyway. While I try to clean myself up, he mops the floor and gathers the shards of glass. A whisper of panic crosses my mind, it slithers in, and blots out the confusion. Each time I replay last night, or what I think happened last night, the panic swells from a whisper to a roar.

"Let's go," he says as the last of the evidence swirls and is swallowed by the drain. His hand grips my shirt, and leads me to the door.

My heart beats furiously and cold sweat clings to my neck. I'm still disoriented as I follow him across the dew-covered lawn, I stumble a few times, even though there's nothing in the way, it's my thoughts I trip over. The orange branches pull at my shirt as we plunge into the cover. I waiver on my feet, and take branches to the face more times than I'd like to admit. Once there's nothing around us but branches and tiny green oranges, Sayid throws the bloody towels onto the ground.

"Strip," he demands, pointing to the pile.

I shake my head. Heat slaps my cheeks, and I know I'm blushing. "Your clothes are covered in blood, take them off." He grabs my shirt.

"I'll get you clean ones." He promises.

I pull my shirt off, followed by my pants and throw them onto the pile.

His eyes appraise me, "Blood soaked through to your underwear too."

I sigh, and pull them off, and toss them on top.

He squirts something on the pile, strikes a match, and throws it. The pile is consumed by flames in seconds. He leads me further into the trees, away from the smoke, nearly to the back edge of the orange orchard. Once we're far enough from the fire, he drops my arm. My hands fall automatically, to cover myself.

"Stay here, I'm going to get you clothes." His words are slow, and careful, like he doesn't expect me to understand them. He looks me in the eyes, and waits for me to nod before he leaves.

After he disappears, I look down at my arms. The fuzzy memories of last night flood into my mind again. They're so clear now, I know they're real. They have to be. I'd cut deep gashes, but not so much as a scratch remains. My arms are pristine, no cuts, no scars. Sayid finds me in the dirt, sitting on my feet, still surveying my arms.

"What are you doing?" He squints, head tilted, as he looks at me.

I look up at him, carefully taking the shirt he holds out.

"There aren't any scars." The words are nearly a question. "How is this possible?" There has to be an explanation, something logical that I just haven't considered.

I slip the shirt on, then the jeans. I'm unsteady on my feet, as uneven as my thoughts.

"So you did try..." he trails off, not even looking at me.

I give the slightest, quickest of nods. Guilt gathers inside me, it feels like an anchor threatening to pull me under. My head lulls forward as I lean into one of the trees. The scent of oranges envelope me as the branches scrape my skin.

"Why?" he asks, anger taints his voice.

I shake my head, and cross my arms. "It's all too much. Olivia, my sister, my mom. I've lost them all." My eyes burn as tears stain my cheeks. "I just couldn't do it anymore. It's too much, it's too hard."

He kicks the toe of his shoe into the ground. When he looks back at me, his brown eyes aren't friendly, welcoming, like they usually are. It feels like I'm withering beneath his stare.

"I told you I didn't want to lose you again. How can you be so selfish?"

My fists are balled at my side, and my temple throbs. "This isn't about you. And I'm sorry that it was selfish that I couldn't take it anymore."

He crosses his arms and looks off into the trees. Anger flares inside me, and I have half a mind to yell at him. But instead, I look at my feet and cross my arms.

He looks down for a long time, his teeth against his lip, almost chewing it. The space between us disappears, as he steps closer to me. I feel his eyes on me, I meet them. The deep pools of brown are so sharp, so intense, I feel them stare straight through me. My eyes focus on his lips. My heart picks up into a gallop. Deep down, I know what I want. It's something that I haven't wanted since Olivia. But the feeling is stronger, sharper. My head swims, and I lean against a tree for support.

"Please," he pleads. "Please, don't do it again. I know it's hard that you lost them. But you still have me. I'm still here." He brings his hand up, and I hold my breath, until the hand rests on my shoulder. Then he leans in and hugs me. Though I know it's meant to comfort me, I want more, but I know I don't deserve him. When he lets go, a wave of guilt crashes hard into me, and I can't look at him. After what I did, are we ever going to be the same? Will he ever even kiss me again? We're silent for a long time, the tension grows between us, but I'm sure only I can feel it.

Guilt twists my insides. I can barely keep myself up, I'm slumped against a tree. I'm too drained to fill the void between us with words. I'm uncomfortable beside him, wishing we were closer, but I'm not brave enough to close the gap. I know I *shouldn't* close the gap. After this, he's not going to be able to forgive me. He's not going to want me.

"Wanna go watch the newbies come in?" he offers.

"Yeah, I guess." A distraction would serve me well. I flick my cigarette to the ground and follow him. Part of me knows he's asking me along to keep an eye on me, but I don't care. It's probably best I'm not alone. So far, I haven't seen any new students come in, I'm ready for some entertainment, maybe it will take my mind off…everything.

We work our way through the trees, I drag my fingers across the branches. Fallen oranges squish beneath my feet. When we reach the office, there's already a line waiting to see the newbies. We fall behind the line of spectators, and watch them file off the bus. The first two kids look so young, I'm surprised they were sent here at all. They can't be older than eleven.

"Is it me, or do they just keep getting younger and younger?" Sayid asks.

A brunette and a blond file off next. Followed by a halo of curly red hair that's hauntingly familiar. His eyes lock on mine, like he was searching for me, expecting me. I'd recognize his smile anywhere, it lights up his face.

"Do you know him?" Sayid asks me and flashes me a look. There are other questions in his eyes, but for now, he doesn't ask them.

My thoughts turn sour as dread spreads through me. A bad

feeling prickles at the back of my mind; the tingle of a memory lingers there, but I can't grasp it. My eyes narrow and my mouth goes dry.

"Used to be a friend back home, Dominic." I reply. I haven't talked to Dominic since before everything happened with Olivia. Since then he's appeared in my nightmares, and never as the friend I remember—it's like he's stalking my dreams. Olivia's words creep into my mind, *there's something wrong with him.* According to Eden, Dominic was stalking her.,

If he's here I know it's not good news. But why would he be here at all? Rage smolders just beneath the surface as I think of my sister. My missing sister. *What did he do to her?* He was following her, he must have had something to do with it.

Despite the handcuffs, Dom gives me a little half wave. I don't wave back, a mind heavy with questions paralyzes me.

Sayid eyes me, "You okay?"

"Fine," I say a little too quickly. I realize my fists are balled at my sides. I unclench my hands and cross my arms as I debate how to get Dominic alone. Something warns me that he's dangerous. But my sister is more important than anything he could do to me. He knows something about where she is. He must. She was terrified of him.

I wait outside with the others while the new kids get searched. Hot afternoon sun beats down on me, even the brick wall behind me radiates warmth. Everything in Florida is always hot, sticky and wet—like you're trapped inside a sponge. The procession of scared, searched and shaken souls march out. They work their way through the grounds, and disappear into their cottages.

Sayid and his friends hover outside the office as they wait for the lunch bell to ring. Consumed by a million questions, I can't find an excuse to leave. Sayid eyes me like he knows something is up.

"Asher, my boy!" his words are so sharp they practically snap.

"What are you doing here?" my words edge on accusatory.

"I couldn't just leave you in here all alone, now could I?" he asks with a sly grin.

"What did you do to get here?" I look at him, trying to read his face for clues.

"You know," he laughs and shrugs, "does it really matter? I mean it's no worse than what you're here for."

That's not comforting. The creeping feeling claws its way back to the pit of my stomach.

"So, what's the deal with this place? No fences? How do they keep anyone here?" he asks looking around like he can see the boundaries of the place, despite them being acres away, buried in the forest. Something tells me he's been here before. A strong feeling of déjà vu crashes into me.

Though I want to dig into him, I wait to pummel him with questions. I can't do it here.

I keep my voice impossibly calm. "We're in the middle of 1400 acres of *nothing*, around that is swamps, even if you make it through that, congratulations you managed to escape into the middle of nowhere. They also love to hunt kids down with bloodhounds. They leave with dogs, sometimes you hear shots in the woods, most of the time they don't come back with the kid." I explain.

He smirks. "Sounds like that could be a fun game."

My eyes scour Dominic for a sign that it's a joke. But he doesn't so much as chuckle. It'd be a fun game to be hunted down by bloodhounds in the woods? To be killed by guards? This Dominic is nothing like the friend I had back home. This Dominic is a stranger.

He rolls his eyes at me, "You're content going along with the rest of the world, aren't you? You'll never dig your heels in, never cause a fuss."

"I don't like change," I say as I grit my teeth. There isn't a reason to fight, if I fight I know where I'll end up. I know what will happen to me, and it's worse than death.

Stay calm. Get him alone.

"Clearly," he says with finality. "What's the stance on smoking?"

"Not allowed, but not really enforced. If you smoke behind buildings, or in the orange trees, you'll be fine." I gesture toward the trees.

He smiles, but by the look on his face, I can tell it's not genuine. "Glad you've gotten so accustomed." Sarcasm drips from each word. He runs a hand through his hair, the red curls fall for a moment, then spring back.

I look away from him, toward Sayid. He's talking to Gordon. Gordon's arms are flailing while Sayid's arms are up in surrender, looking like he's calming Gordon down, or trying at least.

"You should probably go get your work assignment," I say, so that I can get him away from my friends, so I can get him alone.

"I already got mine." He grins.

"What'd you get?"

"Waste disposal." A twisted smile curves his lips.

"What?"

"Nothing." He steps closer to Sayid and Gordon. "Let's go see your friends." There's something menacing behind his words.

I'm tempted to step between him and Sayid, but Gordon storms off when Dominic tries to break into the conversation. Sayid is chewing on his thumbnail when I get close. I'm not sure why he bothers, all his nails are chewed down to nubs. He's stiff, arms crossed, looking after Gordon when we get close.

"Hey," I say, trying to get his attention.

He nods, but doesn't speak.

"What's wrong?" I ask.

He looks at me for a long moment, then his eyes fall on Dominic. I can tell he doesn't want to talk in front of him. "Cameron is missing," Sayid finally says.

"What?" He isn't the runaway type, he's only got a few months left. He's got a pregnant girlfriend, he's the type to go straight. "Do they have any—"

"No." He cuts me off. "He's just gone. He didn't say anything to anyone." A pack of cigarettes appears in his hand. He glares at Dominic, then disappears behind the building.

For a few minutes, I stare after him, torn. Every part of me wants to follow. I want to be with Sayid. One of his friends is missing, I should be there to support him. Though I'm not sure where we currently stand, seeing him through this should be more important.

Dominic has me weighted to the spot. I feel torn between the answers I need and being there for Sayid. The answers are more pressing. My intuition tells me Dominic knows where my sister is, and I'm going to find out, even if it kills me.

"I've got to get to work detail." I edge away, in the direction of the stables, hoping that he'll follow me. There are answers I need from Dominic before I can give my attention to Sayid.

"I'll come with you," he says, without skipping a beat.

Good.

My head is bowed as I work my way to the stables. Ginger nudges me as soon as I'm close enough, I pat her head gently. I swear, for a moment, I think I catch her glaring at Dominic. He leans against the wood, and watches me as I clean.

"So, how were things after I left?" I ask as I try not to give myself away.

He shrugs. "Stupid."

I'm going to have to be more direct. "Have you seen Eden?"

His eyes tighten and his lips twist. *He has.*

"I really miss her, it's been forever since I saw her," I add. My last question might have been too direct.

"You know your sister hates me. So I haven't exactly sought her out." He doesn't look at me when he says it. He scans the tree line. He's a fucking liar.

I open my mouth, but a horn cuts across the campus. The choir of bloodhounds rise. I turn my head to look toward the sound. A group of seven guards head toward the stables. My knees shake, and I swallow hard. When I look back toward Dominic, he's gone.

40

AFTER

While the guards search the woods for Cameron, I head to my appointment with Dr. Lennox. Though I try to shut off the frustration of the last appointment, I'm on edge, uncomfortable when I get inside.

Don't trust him. He thinks you're a killer.

But it doesn't matter if I trust him. It doesn't matter what he thinks of me. He's no better than anyone else here. He doesn't care what happens to us. All the matters are the answers I need, and he's the only way I can get them.

Dr. Lennox waits for me, sitting in one of the arm chairs with a notepad in his lap. He's wearing a gray suit with a light plaid pattern. Beside him on the small glass table is a glass filled with amber liquid.

"Hello, Asher," he says as I fall backward on the couch.

We exchange small talk before he finally asks, "How are you doing today?"

"Not so good," I admit.

His eyebrows pull together, and he looks down his long crooked nose at me. "Oh?"

I'm not here to talk to him. I'm not here to heal, or to feel better.

He sits in this room with his plants and his cigarettes while the rest of us disappear or die. My thoughts are bitter, acidic. There are a million pointed questions I want to ask him, but I swallow them down. The memories of the boys trapped in the back of the hospital is raw in my mind.

If you tell him too much, that could be you.

"Can we try another regression?" I hate to admit, today I'm hoping for answers about Dominic more than Olivia.

His eyes tighten, and I know he wants to argue. To deny me. But he doesn't. Instead he shakes his head slightly and lights a cigarette.

"Lay back, we'll get started."

It takes nearly two hours to drive to the Howey Mansion from Ocala. When we finally turn down the street, I notice something strange. I see someone for a split second before they run behind a tree. A shadowy figure that feels vaguely familiar. It's probably a spooked kid, scared to get caught sneaking out. I push it from my mind.

To be sure we aren't seen, I park a couple streets away. Old lady Howey, or her watchful neighbors, love to call the police. The property is covered in about forty thousand no trespassing signs. Kids are caught constantly sneaking in here. I don't want our trip cut short. I want Olivia to enjoy every second of tonight. Olivia practically jumps from the car, a spring in her step like she's on a pogo stick. I catch up with her quickly, and she takes my hand. Her warm fingers wrap around mine. We walk along the road's edge, moonlight streaming down through the tree branches.

A breeze kicks up as we walk. The scuffs of Olivia's feet echo through the night. I'm surprised by how quiet she is, especially on a night like tonight. She's obsessed over the Howey Mansion for years. I'd expected her to rehash the entire history of mansion trivia she's collected during our car ride. But her mouth was a thin line of nothingness.

She fidgets beside me, crossing and uncrossing her arms as she walks, until I finally ask, "Is everything okay?"

She nods, but it seems forced. Silence falls between us again, and in that silence a bad feeling blooms. She seems to look everywhere but at me. I've seen something on her face all night, but I have no clue what it might be. Olivia isn't the type to keep anything bottled up. The moment a thought pops into her head, it comes right out of her mouth.

Finally, after nearly five minutes she says, "Hey, Ash?"

I look at her, she's hiding behind her blonde curls. "Yeah?" I ask as smoke pours from my lips. This timid, shy side of her is strange.

"I was thinking..." She doesn't look at me, instead she looks at the houses, the trees, anything to avoid eye contact. Olivia never has trouble communicating what's on her mind. That's one of the reasons I love her, I always know exactly where I stand with her. "Do you still..." she continues.

I stop walking and look at her. When she finally makes eye contact I say, "Just spit it out."

It takes two drags from my cigarette before she speaks again, just long enough for me to think I sounded too harsh.

"Do you still love me?" she asks, and her voice trembles.

I balance the words carefully in my mind. And finally settle on asking, "Really?"

She nods as she chews her lip and tugs on one of her stray curls.

"Where are we going right now?" I ask. Deep down I know she's going to think that I'm avoiding the question, which, I have been known to do, but not today, today I have a point to prove.

She squints, but finally humors me. "The Howey Mansion?" she says, as if she isn't quite sure. Even though the mansion looms at the end of the street.

"That's right, because ever since you were little, all you could talk about was that damn house. The rock walls around it, the ivy, Hell, you even obsessed about Spanish architecture for two years because of it. You told me all about how it was built, speculated what it looked like inside. You even built a little dollhouse to try and mock it up. You planned how you'd one day be rich enough to buy it, and you'd have me and Eden move in with you. But you called dibs on the turret," I explain.

She bites her cheek and kicks the toe of her shoe into the ground. A hollow thump, thump, thump echoes through the empty street with each kick.

"That mansion is your dream. The second I heard about old lady Howey getting hauled away, all I could think about was the look I'd see on your face when I told you." I smile, and take a drag from my cigarette. "You lit up like a bottle rocket." I step closer, close enough that there's less than a breath of space between us. Close enough that I can smell the scent of oranges on her skin.

She looks down, and says, "That doesn't answer my question." As dark as it is, I can still see her pink cheeks flush.

"Yes," I say as I wrap my arms around her waist and pull her into me.

"Yes?" She looks up through her eye lashes at me.

Sometimes, on the rarest occasions, the smartest people you know can be so dumb it's actually painful. This is one of those times. I roll my eyes playfully, knowing what it is she wants to hear. "God, Olivia, yes, I love you."

She reaches up, her hand circles behind my neck. Olivia pulls me down, stretches up on her tip toes. Her breath is hot on my lips, but I refuse to close the distance between us. The first kiss is gentle, barely a kiss at all. It shouldn't make my stomach leap, or flutter, or my blood *rush—but it does. Then she kisses me harder, her soft lips press against mine, I taste her mouth, and she presses her body against mine.*

She pulls away, her curls bouncing as she stands flat on her feet again. A wide smile is set across her face. "I love you, too," she says.

A fire spreads through me. I've been waiting for her to say that for fourteen years. Every-fucking-day I've wanted her to say it. I pull her back into me. "Are we finally going to do this? Go steady. I mean." My hands rest on her hips, my fingers twitch begging to venture further.

She wraps her arms around my shoulders, and pulls me down. Her breath hits my ear, she whispers, "Yes." Her face against mine brings heat to my cheeks.

"So, what is this? What are we?" The question sounds stupid once I've said it. But her face doesn't fall. That smile is still plastered to her face.

Pink tinges her cheeks. "Well, you're my... boyfriend," she says coyly, it's almost a question.

"Yes, I am," I say, and then kiss her gently. My mouth falls on her lips, cheek, neck. When I reach her collarbone, I feel her shiver. Goosebumps rise under my lips.

She giggles, "We have a mansion to get to, don't we?"

I relent, I don't want to. I may have been after her for fourteen years, but she's been after this mansion nearly as long.

Though the walk should only take ten minutes from where we parked, we've been out here nearly an hour. Ancient crooked trees, heavy with moss, stand sentry around the fence. We reach the rock wall, the iron gates are weighed down with locks and chains. Bound to the gates are several no trespassing signs, we ignore them, everyone does. It's never made sense to me why they bother locking it up, the wall around the perimeter isn't even four feet tall. A dog could jump over without batting an eye. It's not keeping anyone out. It certainly isn't going to keep us out.

I climb over first, and offer my hand to help Olivia. She straightens her dress, and dusts it off before continuing. The tile roof of the house glows in the moonlight, slick with dew. Layers of ivy creep from the ground, covering the turret on the right side of the house. It's so dark, the usual light pink color of the stucco is barely a faded beige. White arches stick out from the walls framing three floor-to-ceiling windows. Unkempt topiaries grow around the front door, like they're guarding it, or maybe hiding it. A long winding driveway curves across the overgrown yard, past the front door. I watch Olivia as she stares in wonder at the house, smiling from ear to ear.

"One day, we're going to get married here," she says, her words are heavy, like a promise.

Halfway across the dew-covered lawn, we stand in the shadow of the house. I'm on my fifth cigarette. Olivia has spent the last four minutes staring up at the ivy-covered stucco—not that I'm counting. I stand watch while she stands in wonder, like a kid in a toy store for the first time. My eyes are on the street when I see movement. At first, I'm not sure I saw it at all. But as I watch, I'm sure I see a figure in the distance, watching us.

"Ash?" she asks, she's a few feet behind me now, close to the backyard.

"It's nothing, let's go," I say automatically, I don't want her to worry if it's nothing. I don't want anything to ruin this night for her.

I click the metal lid of my lighter open and closed. It at least drowns out the sound of frog croaks that are putting me on edge. The pit of my stomach prickles. Olivia walks in front of me, finally she's meandered into the backyard. Once we can't be seen from the street, I feel the slightest bit of relief. Still, I start smoking my sixth cigarette.

That's when I see it again. I'm sure I saw someone run down the street and hide behind the fence. Maybe Dominic followed us. He knew we were coming tonight, I know he'd love to see the inside of the mansion.

"Hello?" I call out. But only the crickets answer me back. I turn around and follow Olivia.

"Who are you talking to?" Olivia asks as she glances back at me.

"Didn't you see that?" I ask her.

She stops and peers at me over her shoulder. "See what?

"Never mind, maybe I imagined it."

A towering tree weeps next to a small pond, it's so large it looks like a tower. The spindly branches are as restless as my hands, moved by a breeze I can't feel. Spanish moss clings to the branches, and grazes the surface of the water. At the edge of the pond a marble statue is slowly being consumed by green moss. It's an angel with open arms. Only the palms and face remain white. Orange trees huddle in small pockets before a forest springs up, forming a natural wall around the property.

Next to the pond is the only thing here I don't want to see, the mausoleum. The idea of burying your dead relatives on your property is the creepiest thing I can imagine. It's carved from marble. The edges of the structure are precise, perfect. Black veins creep their way up the marble, like tendrils. The mausoleum has avoided the fate of the statue, no moss has begun a trek up its walls. The wrought iron door curves clutching an ornate stained glass feature.

Olivia creeps closer, I catch her fingers. "Please don't tell me you're going in there," I say, my feet planted firmly in the ground. I want it to be clear there's no way I'm going in that mausoleum.

"Fine, I won't tell you," she laughs.

I sneer at her playfully.

"Oh, come on, Ash, it's no worse than a cemetery. You don't even have to go in. Just stand at the door." She points to the left of the door, there are a few pavers gathered, like some idiot just couldn't be close *enough to these corpses. Like they were building a patio to have their coffee on, right outside the mausoleum. "If you stand right there, I bet you can't even see inside. The ghosts won't even know you're out here."*

I shrug and say, "Fine."

She comes closer, her arms wrap around me. A gentle kiss falls on my cheek, then on my neck. Heat rushes through me each time her lips brush my skin. She pulls away and beams at me, waiting for me to smile back. I offer her a half smile in return. I brush away the curls from her face. The heat between us grows. She pulls me tighter, into a deeper kiss. The way she pulls me and wraps herself around me, it's hard to tell where I stop and she begins.

She breaks away. "Can't you feel how exciting this place is?" she asks.

I shrug. "Nope, all I can feel is someone watching us," I admit, looking toward the front of the house. I feel the heat of eyes against my skin.

"Ash, there's no one watching us, we're alone out here," she says, but then again, Olivia doesn't ever see danger.

"If you say so," I say, there's no sense in arguing with her.

"Maybe it's old man Howey's ghost," she offers.

I roll my eyes at her and a forced laugh escapes me. A scraping sound cuts through the night as Olivia pushes in the gate on the mausoleum, it's so loud, it might wake the dead. She disappears inside, and I survey the backyard as I smoke my cigarette. I look over the pond, behind the angel statue a dark figure stands, watching. Fear races through me, my heart beat a furious warning.

Run. My mind screams, but I know we can't. We'd be better off getting into the house. I won't rob her of tonight.

"Come on, Olivia, let's get inside," I say, but there's an edge to my voice.

She comes to the door, her face deathly white, like all the blood has disappeared from her body. Her eyes are impossibly wide, saucers. That's when I hear a twig snap behind me.

I look behind me, all I see is the Howey Mansion towering about thirty feet away. I must have stepped on a twig, snapping it. Olivia clamps her hand to her chest, her mouth a tight line, her eyes, milky saucers with blue baubles in the middle. Even her curls seem to expand with fear, like the way a cat's fur stands on end.

"Sorry, that was me," I say, heat rushes to my cheeks. Nothing feels worse, quite as embarrassing as making the girl you love fear for her life.

Her hand clutches her stomach as she spends a few moments catching her breath. Even though she seems to breathe easier, the fear still courses through me, a fire in my veins. I still feel someone watching. Even though they no longer linger behind the statue. They're out there, somewhere. They may not be behind me, but they are close. I feel them.

"Let's get inside," I say, not wanting to alarm her, but the house would be safer.

She hops from the mausoleum, and laces her arm in mine. I light another cigarette as she stares wide-eyed at the back of the house. It's more ivy than house, if you ask me. She unlaces her arm from mine and bounds up the steps to the porch. Porcelain tiles cover the entire patio, which is larger than the entire first floor of my house. Ornate concrete pillars circle around the entire length of patio, creating a decorative and functional barrier. A shallow, screened-in porch covers the back door and a row of windows.

And just our luck, every single one of them is locked. After we test every dusty doorknob and rusted window, Olivia notices the lattice leading up to the second story. It's buried in ivy, and I fear it's rotten beneath the layers of foliage.

"I'm going to try climbing up," she says as she motions to it. She bounces off the ground onto it.

"Good idea," I say, but immediately follow it up with, "but, be careful. No telling how old that is."

We've been climbing trees nearly as long as we could walk. It's not her abilities I'm concerned with, it's what's hidden beneath the ivy that has me worried.

"Yeah, yeah," she says playfully.

Once she's up, I follow. I pull myself up to the roofline and find myself looking over the second story patio. It's a flat, sparse expanse. A simple stretch of flat concrete roof with a couple benches. Two dead potted plants sit on either side of a bench, long since abandoned. Up here, everything is covered in a thick coat of moss.

When was the last time anyone was up here?

There's a small landing near the edge of the patio, behind that, up a few steps, there's a door. Olivia reaches it first, she rests her hand on the knob for a moment, probably willing it to open. The handle turns and she sighs. She disappears into the house, and I follow. Once inside, I take a deep breath, relief. Aged wallpaper, tobacco, and the faint smell of something rotten curls into my nostrils.

Yellowed walls seem to glow. The moonlight pours in through the moth-eaten curtains. Somehow, the glow seems to pool in the middle of the room, like it's being cast by a force we can't see. White rectangles leave echoes of where paintings used to hang. The paintings now lean against the walls on the floor, muted by thick layers of dust. This room hasn't been used for some time, or so it seems. Dusty white sheets hide furniture pushed against all the walls. Small cracks snake through the plaster, and seem to gather around a forgotten fireplace.

"This place is magic," she whispers, she beams as she looks around in awe.

I step carefully through the room, following her, dust billows around my feet. We step through double doors. She walks in each and every abandoned room, tracing her fingers through the thick layers of dust. The entire second floor is lost in time. We weave through bedrooms draped in cloths, bathrooms adorned with ornate mirrors and claw foot tubs. A library greets us at the end of the east wing, an ornate wooden desk in the middle of the room. Piles of books, bloated by humidity, cover every inch of the desk, the floor, they're even piled in the chairs.

A curved staircase leads us downward, the first floor is much more lived in. But down here the rotten, earthy smell grows stronger. It's something I've smelled before, but I can't quite place what it is. On the first floor, she heads into what looks like a ballroom, I stand in the hall, footsteps echo down the stairs. Olivia doesn't hear it. But fear flickers through me so fast, my whole body goes rigid. Whoever was outside, is in the house. And soon, they're going to come down those stairs.

"What are you doing?" she asks, her eyebrows perked up. She's not smiling now, she looks concerned. I think it may be her mission to make me love this house as much as she does.

"We're not alone Olivia. We need to leave, now." My voice is barely above a whisper.

She rolls her eyes at me, like I'm not serious. Like I'm playing a joke on her. She takes my hands in hers, tilts her head to the side and flashes me a soft smile. Her hand brushes across my face, hair, as if to calm me. It doesn't work. Instead, it only intensifies the feelings that I need to protect her. To keep her from whoever might be upstairs.

"You're hearing things, there's no one here. There's just one more thing I want to see, okay? Then we can go."

My teeth are on edge, locked. My whole body is tense, ready to fight. Ready to do whatever I have to, to keep her safe. I relent as she pulls me down the hallway toward the kitchen. There's no talking her out of anything. And I won't drag her from this house kicking and screaming.

She opens a door along the back wall of the kitchen, the rotten smell is so thick in the air, I can taste it. I think old lady Howey might have had a cat that someone forgot about. Olivia looks in the doorway, like it's exactly what she was searching for. I follow behind, and see it's a stairway leading down. Basements are rare in Florida, they tend to flood during hurricanes, or rain, or just because.

My guts twist into knots wound as tightly as her curls. Every step further into the basement, makes me more nauseated. My skin crawls. Olivia stops at the bottom of the stairs, her hand claps over her mouth. I turn, and that's when I see the pile of bodies beside the stairs. The bloated bodies are piled on top of one another, like a pile of old, dirty socks. Black veins bulge beneath tight skin, black eyes stare. A swarm of flies buzz around the pile.

I grab Olivia's hand and pull her up the stairs. She gags and vomits. As I pull her, I see the silhouette of someone standing at the top of the stairs.

When I come out of the vision, bile creeps up my throat. I can still smell the death, taste it. Dr. Lennox shoves a trash can toward me. It takes me twenty minutes of puking before I stop tasting the corpses. Cold sweat clings to my face, my neck. My throat is raw it burns with every ragged breath I take.

I open my mouth to speak, but I can't find the words. My mind is heavy, thick with thoughts of her, of us. She finally said it back. Or, at least she might have, if my mind is telling me the truth. She *was* my girlfriend, if even for only one night. She chose me, she wanted me. And it got her killed.

The voice nags at the back of my mind again. *It's all lies. She didn't love you. How could anyone love you?*

"Are you alright?" Dr. Lennox asks as he hands me a glass of water.

I take slow sips, not wanting to throw up all over again. The bitter taste of fear and vomit are still strong in my mouth. My eyes burn. These visions, not knowing if they're real, or if they're all my imagination is killing me. I don't know what to think, what to feel anymore. Inside, I'm hollow, numb. But I'll keep going. After all, what else do I have to lose?

41

AFTER

After meeting with Dr. Lennox, I need to be alone. I try Madison first, and find several younger kids skipping dinner to drink schnapps. Instead, I head back to the stables. At the very least, there's somewhere to hide should the guards still be looking for Cameron after lights out. As I walk closer to the stables, I hear barking in the distance. The closer I get to the stables, the louder the barking grows. A bad feeling brews inside me, and I look back toward Madison. I should have just stayed there.

A group of guards and dogs break the tree line. I'm frozen a hundred feet from them. Two of the guards drag a sagging body, the moment I see it, I know it's Cameron. All my resolve to be alone floods out of me, I have to find Sayid and tell him. I don't want him to find out from someone else.

I jog to the cafeteria and find Sayid sitting across from Brandon. He looks at me the moment I come through the doors. As soon as I'm close enough I say, "I need to talk to you."

He nods, and pushes up from the seat. Outside, the darkening sky looms above us, storm clouds hang on the horizon smothering the sunset. Dread pools inside me.

"What's up?" Sayid asks as he leans against the wall.

I cross my arms and shift on my feet as I consider the best way to tell him what I saw. Standing this close to him, even with the bad news between us, I want to reach for him. To be with him. But I shove the feelings away.

"I just saw the guards pull a body from the woods. I think it was Cameron," I say as I try to soften the blow as much as possible.

His lips pull together, and he looks away. "God dammit," he says, refusing to meet my eyes.

I reach out and rest my hand on his shoulder. But he shrugs away.

"I'm sorry," I say.

"Yeah, me too." Sayid grabs the door, and I reach out, my hand on his forearm.

"Are you going to be okay?"

"Yeah, fine," he says, but it sounds forced. His eyes flit back to the dining hall, like he doesn't want to look at me. Maybe he can't stand to look at me.

"Want me to come have dinner with you?"

He shakes his head. "You don't have to do that."

I don't have to, or he doesn't want me to?

I pull away, though it stings, I understand. For a few seconds, I stand and stare at the door he just walked through. Though I want to go in and make sure Sayid's okay, I don't think he wants my company. Through the window, I see Sayid sitting next to Brandon; he sags in his seat. It kills me to pull myself away, but it's for the best. He may not say it, but I can feel that he doesn't want me there.

∼

While everyone else sleeps, I lean against the bowed wood on the back porch. The night is eerily quiet, even the mosquitoes have taken the night off. I watch the trees for her. I haven't seen Olivia in so long, I'm starting to think I may be sane after all.

The boards creak next to me as Sayid steps out of Madison. A smile curves my lips when I see him. But I look away.

"You should be asleep," I say as I turn my attention back to the trees.

"I could say the same to you," he says as he nudges my shoulder, and takes a seat next to me. I scoot close to him, my side pressed against his. For a moment, I lean my head on his shoulder.

"Bad things always happen when I sleep. I've decided to give it up."

"You're giving up sleeping?" he asks incredulously as he slides a cig from a pack.

"Sure am," I confirm.

After he takes a long drag of the cigarette, I hold my hand up, and he passes it to me.

"Thanks," I say, smoke trails on my words.

I brush my empty hand against his, I want to hold his hand. He offers me a half smile, but doesn't take it. The disappointment is so strong, I'm nearly crushed beneath it. He doesn't want me, he must have moved on.

"Are you doing okay?" I ask.

He shrugs. "I guess," he says, but I suspect it's a lie. "I'm sorry about earlier."

"Don't worry about it."

He stares off into the orange trees, and I pass him back his cigarette. He takes a long drag, flicks the cigarette into the dirt, and crosses his arms.

"It's my fault he's dead," he says with a deadpan voice.

"How do you figure?" I ask.

He looks down, and pulls his knees up to his chest. "Most communication here goes through me. Except for some of the richer kids, like Becks. He could make calls out if he gives the guards cash."

"I'm not following."

"Cameron's family, they sent word that his girlfriend had the baby early, so early, they weren't sure the baby was going to make it," Sayid presses his eyes into the palms of his hands. "I shouldn't have told him, if I hadn't told him, he wouldn't have tried to run."

I put my arm around him, and pull him closer. "It's not your fault."

"Yes, it is," he says.

"You can't control what he did. You didn't know he would run away. And there are smart ways he could have done it. No one knows those woods better than you. Chances are, you could have gotten him to town."

He shrugs. "I guess." He looks toward the trees. "I should have offered."

I lean against him and offer him a hug. It kills me to know he's upset. But being this close to him, I feel guilty for how much I like it. And I feel like a complete asshole that all I can do is think about kissing him.

Sayid sniffles and I pull away. It feels like he's slowly building a wall between us. But I won't let him, I have to break through. I push off the porch and crouch in front of him. He looks up at me, his eyes darkened, sadness tainting his face. I brush my hand against his cheek, and rest my hand there. His eyes meet mine.

"It's not your fault," I say, my words barely a whisper.

He looks down. It's not going to be that easy to convince him. He clenches his jaw, and his fists ball on his knees.

My pulse quickens, and I lean in. His breath hits my face, and I breathe in his woody scent. Sayid looks up, his face inches from mine, a smile creases his lips. An invitation.

I close the gap between us, his lips are full, wet, salty. My hand moves to the back of his head, his hair tangles in my fingers. His tongue brushes against mine, and I stiffen. I'm drunk with how much I want him. Every thought fades away, and the only thing left in my mind is the persistent throb of desire.

My hands seem to move on their own, exploring. I pull his head back, and kiss his neck. Slowly, my teeth graze his flesh. A low moan rolls from his lips, and I twitch with yearning.

"We can't do this here," he says as he halfheartedly tries to push me away.

"I don't care," I say as I slip my hand up his shirt. Sayid's abs are firm beneath my touch, his skin slick with sweat.

I kneel in front of him, and unbutton his pants. Sayid's eyes are wide as he looks down at me.

"Are you sure?" he asks as he runs his hands through my hair.

I nod as I look up at him.

The sound of someone clearing their throat makes me freeze. My heart leaps and beats so hard it may burst straight through my chest. A fist of fear tightens around me, and my head fills with static.

"Move it along boys," a guard says from the right side of the house, his eyes on Sayid. "I'm sure you can find somewhere more fitting than this."

"Y-yeah," Sayid stammers. He pulls me off the ground before buttoning his pants.

As the guard steps closer, I recognize him. It's the guard who helps Sayid with the shipments. Sayid grabs my arm and yanks me into the house. The moment he closes the door, his lips are on mine again. I pull away.

"I can barely breathe right now," I say as my hand rests on my chest.

Sayid looks down and purses his lips. "You okay?"

"Yeah, I'm going to, uh, need a rain check." I say. I'm still too jolted to get my head back in the game.

He smiles at me. "Alright." He leans in and gives me a soft kiss before we head up the stairs together.

42

BEFORE
Date Unknown

Dominic turns and strolls down the dark street without a word, without a look back. I glance back at the house where I hid the journal. A few seconds later, I follow him. He weaves through the city until we reach a three-story house on the edge of the canal. The house rises above us, the roof ends at a high peak. The Victorian touches of the house are perfect. It's typical for Dominic. He's always had a penchant for the extravagant, the grand.

"It's beautiful," I say as I follow him up the stone path to the house.

He doesn't say anything, instead he looks back and offers me a soft smile. The inside of the house is pristine. But I know there's somewhere in this house where he has his research. That's the only reason I came willingly. If we can get our hands on what he's found, we might stand a chance against him. After all, he's been searching for the same answers we have. He must know *something*.

I follow him through the house until he finally thrusts a door open on the first level. Olivia would kill me if she knew I was doing this. Stairs lead down into the darkness, and I know better than to question him. I know it's unlikely he'll kill me without her. He lights the candles one by one, and slowly his study comes into view.

"This is what you wanted, right?" he asks as he sweeps across the room.

"What do you mean?"

"You aren't here for me. I'm not stupid. We spent so long together, you should know by now that I am anything but stupid," he growls the words at me.

I step closer to him and brush my hand against his arm as I try to diffuse him. "No, that's not why I'm here." I run my hand along his cheek, over his hair, down his neck. "I'm here for you." My words are barely a whisper. Something cold twists inside me. I lean closer and kiss his cheek softly. His body tenses and instead of responding like I expect, he grabs me. In a flurry of movement he moves behind me, a knife to my neck.

"What are you doing?" I ask him.

"You know what I'm doing," he laughs at me.

Dominic drags me across the room and straps me into a chair. He ties ropes tight around me. And after he's satisfied that I'm secured, he takes a step back and glares at me.

"I've seen you two here."

A lump forms in my throat. If he's seen her, our plan won't work. My mouth goes dry as I stare at him in disbelief.

"I'm going to go get her, and then I'm going to kill you both. Maybe next time you won't think I'm stupid enough to fall for this," he says as he rolls his eyes at me.

Moments after he sweeps out of the basement, I begin trying to free myself from the ropes. I'm careful as I slip out of them, I'll need to try and make it look like I never left.

Dominic always thinks he can keep us tied up. He never learns.

He never figures out a better way. He doesn't expect much of us and still looks at us like we're humans. I pull my arms from the ropes, the top layer of my flesh is left behind on the ropes as a sacrifice. I take a deep shuddering breath as I swallow down the pain. In a few seconds, the skin heals.

I look over the papers that Dominic has gathered. He's got beakers atop the table, burners flickers beneath them. He's mixing something, he's creating something, but I can't tell what it is from looking at it. Instead of trying to figure it out, I remove the burners. Whatever he's got in there will be ruined by the time he gets back.

Two at a time, I bound up the stairs. When I reach the top, the door is locked. Panic prods at the back of my mind as I search the rest of the basement. There has to be a way out. I have to get to her before he does.

In the far corner, hidden away behind the stairs, a small window leads to an overgrown backyard. With the help of a chair, I slide through it.

I run through the streets as I try to make my way back to her. By the time I reach the house, I'm breathless. The house is empty, abandoned. But she'll be back. He couldn't have found her already.

43

AFTER

My eyes burn, and my limbs are heavy, like they've been since I peeled my eyes open this morning. All night my nerves gnawed at me. After being caught by the guard, adrenaline burned in my veins for hours. And just as I had begun to drift to sleep, thunder rolled in, splitting open the sky.

As I trudge to the dining hall, nearly a hundred yards away I can smell bacon. Last night's storm had knocked one of the few remaining shutters into the flower bed. The way they've accumulated, it looks like the few spindly bits of greenery are growing shutters, not flowers. Sayid jogs up beside me, and I'm grateful it's not Dominic. He bumps his shoulder against mine and smiles at me.

I hate walking into the dining hall alone, and it's impossible to feel bad with Sayid at my side. We walk together through the line, Brandon is working today. He gives me a few extra pieces of bacon, an orange, and carrot slices, which he knows I'll pass along to the horses.

I slide my tray onto the table, and Sayid sits down next to me. He prods his fork into his eggs a few times, and glances at me. "You okay after last night?"

I shrug. The memory of being caught by the guard still makes my throat tighten. We're lucky it wasn't worse, that it wasn't a different guard. His eyes lock on mine for a moment, and he offers me a smile. He reaches for my hand, and offers it a quick squeeze.

"I was hoping we could duck today, but I've got a shipment coming in through the laundry." His voice drops when he says it, I can see the disappointment darkening his eyes. "You want anything?"

"I'm good with cigs," I say, though I'm still uneasy about it.

"You sure? Girly Magazines? Booze? Nothing?" he presses as he pops a browned potato into his mouth.

I shake my head. "Those, I can live without. You're all I need," I say, my voice barely a whisper. "I need to talk to you about something," I say as I eye the rest of the table. Once I'm sure that no one is listening, I continue. "It's about Dominic."

Sayid's eyes are wide, hungry.

"I think he had something to do with Olivia's death, and with Eden's disappearance." I know it's likely that Eden is dead, but I can't bring myself to say it. Because she can't be dead. Though Sayid was there when I spoke to Eden about Dominic, I'm not sure how much attention he paid to our conversation.

He nods slow and smiles at me. "I'll help with anything you need."

I dig into my breakfast. It's a relief that none of Sayid's usual group of friends have arrived. I survey the cafeteria, out of habit. That's when I see Becks. I try to look away, to not see him. But in that split second, of course, he noticed. His eyes lock on me, and he saunters over. He chews on the end of a toothpick as he sits down. I recoil. My whole body tenses. I hope he doesn't notice. He does. A laugh born deep down bubbles up to the surface, like a wet burp.

"Good to see you, boys," he says it to both of us, but the way his eyes bore into me, it's clear he's only talking to me.

My throat tightens and my heart thumps hard in my ears. I stand, tray in hand, ready to escape before Becks demands tribute. But his massive fist hits my tray and knocks it back to the table. The slick wooden surface is showered in scrambled eggs, a couple of the carrots tumble to the floor. My eyes dart to the guards, hoping they noticed, they didn't. After all, he's probably paid them off.

"Where you off to in such a hurry?" Becks asks as he cocks his head to the side.

"The stables." My voice is stiff. The moment after the words leave my mouth, I regret them.

"I'll see you there?" He grins, his tongue flicks across his teeth, and his hand moves to grab his crotch.

Without thinking about it, without even feeling that I move, the metal tray flies from my hands and hits Becks in the face. I'm so stunned, I miss my opportunity to run. Frozen, practically a sculpture, I stand waiting for my body to do something else. The only thing I can feel is the fear clawing at the back of my mind and the panicked beats of my heart. Becks' nostrils flare, he glowers at me with his clamped fists on the table. His shoulders are square, he's fit to pounce. He grabs the tray, and throws it toward the wall. It clatters to the ground and ensures every eye in the dining hall is now on us.

My mind screams, *run*, but my body will not obey. I don't move a single inch. He jumps across the table and knocks me down. Every bit of air is knocked from my body, I gasp, and gulp at the air. Fists clench my wrists and pin them to the cold tile floor. I kick, trying to wrestle him off me. When that doesn't work, I struggle to free myself, wiggle my way out from under him.

Voices rise and fall around me, but I can't make out the words. They bleed together, like a song. But the beats that would be the drum, are the fists against my face. One sound in particular mutes all the others, the thunder of my heart in my ears. One of my wrists comes free, before I can move, a wet hollow thud cuts the air. His fist pounds into my face, over and over. My eye screams in pain, and throbs after every impact. Explosions of light blind me each time he hits.

The guards take their sweet time breaking up the fight, or the pummeling, as you could call it. My face is bloody, my nose is broken, and one of my teeth feels loose against my fat lip. I dig at the tooth with my tongue, feeling the wiggle. Two of them drag me out of the cafeteria. The other two grab Becks. As I'm dragged out of the dining hall, I see him slip something to each of the guards.

I don't even get the chance to fight when I realize they're taking me to the white house. Tears pour from my eyes and I beg for them to let me go, to take me anywhere but there. The moment I smell the stench of shit, piss, and vomit, my stomach turns. My eyes are nearly swollen shut, I can't see anything as they drag me. They throw me face-first into a crusty mattress that reeks of whiskey, iron, and pee. The last thing I remember is something hard, maybe a gun, hitting me in the face.

44

AFTER

"I don't think this one's going to make it. They just pulled him in from the white house." A high, soft voice trills, but it sounds like she's far away, or underwater. The woman's voice is stricken, pained.

Though I try to open my eyes, I can't. No control over my body remains. The world seems to rush around me, like I'm moving. There's the sound of metal. Something pricks my arm, my veins run cold. Icy plastic presses against my face. There's a hissing sound to my right. An uneven beeping marks the seconds beside me.

"He's hemorrhaging. I need a pint of O negative," a rough voice says.

I feel a tugging, something snaps. Though I'm no longer moving, my head swims. Warmth rushes from my head. A salty coppery taste fills my mouth, then it's cut by bile. My chest heaves, like I'm being tossed, thrown around. But I'm not in control of it.

"Make that three pints," the voice says, again, urgency hovers there.

I hear a trickling, like rain dripping from the roof into a puddle.

"He's coding, get me a crash cart."

There's a rush of movement I try to look, to see what's going on. I still can't open my eyes, I can't even move. Somehow, I'm aware when I hear the last beep.

45

AFTER

I unravel myself from unconsciousness. Pain is hidden away so far in the recesses of my mind, it takes a long time for it to creep in. It laps at me, waves of discomfort spread through my body. As I become more aware, it grows into a crest of crippling agony. My muscles are locked, rigid. Throbbing pools at the back of my head. The air around me is unusually cold, it tastes crisp, sterile as I breathe it in.

Realization floods to me all at once. The pain, most of it, is from how hard I'm shivering. As I breathe, my hot breath hits my face. A sheet is pressed to my body, covering me. Cold crusted blood makes it cling to my nose and chin. I sit up, and rip it off. Confusion twists my mind into a frenzy of clouded thoughts. A dimly lit, damp room surrounds me. Metal tables, surgical instruments, walls covered in small doors. The air is so cold, I can see my breath.

What am I doing in a morgue?

I stand, my bare feet curl when they touch the concrete floor. I see myself reflected in the slick metal of a cabinet. Confusion clouds my mind and slows my thoughts. Blood and iodine paint my chest. A trickle is dried, and forms a red river down my face. My stained clothes lie on a table near the door. I pull them on, and drape the sheet around my shoulders. My breaths quicken as panic flares through me.

What the fuck happened?

When I open the door, it squeals, a strangled grinding sound. The heat outside is like a punch to the face. Pain in my muscles melts away with the warmth. The way the light falls across the campus, I'm not sure if it's early morning or late evening. Purple and black clouds roll in front of an orange horizon. I find myself behind the hospital and work my way around the building. I cut through the cornfield, sneak past the stables, through the rows of orange trees, and finally take a deep, unsettled breath when I reach the back porch of Madison.

The living room is abandoned as I climb the stairs to find Sayid. He's still asleep. Face pressed into a pillow. His hair splayed across it, like a black squid. It must be morning. I sit on the bunk next to him, and give his shoulder the lightest nudge. His eyes pop open, his hand automatically wipes the drool from the corner of his mouth. He looks at me and all the color drains from his face. Like he's seen a ghost.

"What's wrong?" I ask him.

He sits upright and shifts. His back presses against the wall. There's an ocean of white around his brown irises.

"How are you..." he points to the bed and his voice shakes, "here?" I notice the raw red edges of his eyes, the way they protrude, swollen. Pink clings to the edges of his nostrils. It looks like he's been crying. Not a few tears, but a night-long sob.

I recoil away from him, his reaction makes my heart drop. Dread gathers inside me. After a hard swallow, and a few second to compose myself, I ask, "What do you mean?"

"You were in the hospital, they said you weren't going to make it," he looks down when he says it, his face falls. Tears crowd his eyes.

"Clearly they were wrong." My voice shakes. I know they weren't wrong. But I can't admit that out loud. It's too crazy. It can't be real, it can't be true. There has to be another explanation, a sane one.

"One of my customers works in the hospital. There was a hole in your skull. They had to cut you open, there was internal bleeding... and complications," he explains, his eyes never moving from the spot they're glued to the floor.

"Maybe they lied?" I offer. There has to be an explanation, an explanation that isn't what I'm thinking. Because it can't be possible. It can't.

"You were dead. You *are* dead."

I shake my head. It's not possible. This had to be a dream, a hallucination, *something*.

"Asher, what the fuck is going on?" Sayid asks as tears gather in his eyes.

I reach for him, but he inches away. My hand shrinks back, and the sharp sting of rejection cuts through me. His eyes wide, his jaw set. My head swims, and my thoughts bleed into one another. Tears sting my eyes, and I look away.

"I don't know." I manage to choke the words out. "Does it matter? I'm here now. Does it matter what happened?"

He looks down, balls up the sheets in his hands, and wipes his face. "Yes it matters. You were dead, Asher. You were dead." His voice cracks. "Don't you get it?"

"Stop saying that." Every time he says dead, my mind rejects the word. Before he can pull it away from me again, I grab his hand and hold it firmly in mine. "I'm here. I'm real," I say.

But the way he looks at me doesn't change. I may as well be a ghost. When he doesn't try to pull his hand from mine, I move closer. I crawl onto the bed and wrap my arms around him. Sayid lets me hug him for a moment, his arms pinned at his sides. A shuddering breath slips from his lips, and his tears are slick against my neck. He hugs me and pulls me closer.

"I love you," the words slip out before I can stop them. My heart swells, and regret slams into me. It may be how I feel, but I shouldn't have said it. Sayid holds his breath, and then sobs.

"You were dead," he says as his tears soak through the sheet around my shoulders.

"I'm not."

"I can't lose you. I can't," he sobs.

"You're not going to."

I can't die. A foreign voice is low and insistent in the back of my mind. I shake my head, and push back against it. No. It can't be true. *That isn't possible.*

"Why are you wearing a sheet?" he finally asks, and tugs on the edge gently.

I pull it open, and expose my bloody shirt. His eyes tighten.

"How do you explain that?" he asks, challenging me with Dominic's words.

"No idea, I don't really care. Can you just come stand watch while I shower, please?" I'm too exhausted to care. Mentally, I'm worn, beaten down. It feels like I've been wrung out.

"But what if—" he starts.

I hold my hand up, and silence him. I shake my head. The way he looks down, sullen, it crushes me. Sayid grabs my arm. I'm ready for him to argue. What I'm not ready for is the hug he gives me.

His hair is soft against my face, neck. The smell of lemon laundry soap is thick on his skin. As he pins me beneath his embrace, a warmth spreads through me. Like a fire slowly building. I lean into it, rest my shoulder on his, breathe in the scent of him His neck is so close, inches from my lips. Each beat of my heart billows the flames of desire, and I find myself leaning further into him. He shifts, the warmth of his neck is close enough to brush my lips. I'm painfully aware of his body, his movement, his breaths. My hands fall to my sides.

With Olivia, I fought for so long for her attention. For her affection. It's still jarring that with Sayid, my feelings are returned.

"Sorry," he says when he finally lets go. He won't look at me.

"It's alright," I say, the words uneven.

With each step I take toward the bathroom, the desire edging inside me slowly slips away. Sayid disposes of my bloody clothes and the sheet while I wash the evidence from my body. My fingers search my chest, my skull, for any signs of injury. But there's nothing. Not a stitch, not a bruise, not even a scar. Sayid is painfully quiet while I shower, though I try to talk to him a few times.

He's scared of you. He doesn't want to be around you. If you tell him the truth, he'll never talk to you again.

After I've toweled off, and wrestled my clothes onto my damp skin, Sayid finally talks.

"You coming to breakfast?" he asks.

"After what happened last time, I think I'll skip it," I say, and walk out onto the porch. There's also the pesky matter that rumors saturate the campus that I'm dead, I should keep a low profile.

Sayid turns toward me with his arms crossed. He tilts his head as he looks at me. "Do you want me to bring you something? Or come with you to the stables?"

I do. I want him to come have breakfast with me in the loft like before. But I know we can't. It's too risky for him, it's too much to ask.

"It's fine, I'll see you later," I say as I give him a little wave.

"Suit yourself," he says, and jumps off the porch toward the cafeteria. A few feet out, he turns back to me. "No ducking today, guards are out in full force. More kids have gone missing," he offers.

"Thanks."

"Anytime," he calls back, and waves.

Ginger isn't happy when I get to the stables. She's got her eyes narrowed, ears back. She even flicks her tail at me. I curse myself for not at least getting her an apple from the cafeteria.

"What's wrong, girl?" I ask, and reach out to pet her.

She pulls away, bristling, and tousles her mane. Her large brown eyes follow my every move. She's tense, I notice every single time her skin twitches. Ginger's always had a bit of an attitude, but this is an angst I'm not used to. It's never been directed at me.

"Fine, you win." I grab her lead from the post next to her stall.

The moment the metal jingles, her ears perk up. Her head shakes back and forth as she snorts happily. I slide the lead over her head, and open her stall. She trots out, her head held high. It's exactly what she wanted.

I've been trained by a horse.

I tie the lead loosely to a post, and grab a brush. It slides through her hair, her skin ripples. Outside the stables, the wind kicks up. Dry branches pop and snap. Across the campus, I hear dogs bark. I'm not surprised, those will be the bloodhounds. After all, they have a chase to conduct. Deep down, I know the missing kids are probably in the white house. Or they were already killed.

Footsteps on the concrete, shuffling, and a rush of voices draw my attention. There's no surprise when Ginger pulls against the lead. Two guards stand at the other end of the stables, they eye the horses. As they walk closer, I recognize one. He's the guard I saw with the student, the one who dragged me to the white house twice. His holstered gun bounces as he walks, there's a jingle, keys on a key ring. Eyes focused on me, he holds his belt as he saunters toward me. The way he squints his eyes, it's like he didn't expect to see me here.

"You," he says, the word trails off, saying more than he means for it to. "I thought they said you died."

My pulse is frenzied. I swallow hard and search my mind for what to say. "You must have me confused with someone else."

His eyes narrow, and he looks at the guard to his left. "We need three horses saddled and ready to go." I'm relieved when he drops it. How do I explain away that I should be dead?

"Okay, I'll have them ready in a few minutes," I say, far more cordially than he deserves.

I take Ginger, and usher her back to her stall. She pulls against the lead, angry about being forced back into her stall so soon. This isn't going to help her sour mood.

"Why are you putting that one away?" he asks, annoyance cutting into every word.

"She gets spooked, she's not going to be good with the dogs," I say. Or the gunshots, I don't say.

Thankfully the guard doesn't question me about it. In a few minutes I have three of the other horses saddled for him. With the bloodhounds beside them the guards disappear into the tree line. Something inside me shifts, this is all a charade. They're *looking* for students. Students that they probably know are dead. I shift my attention back to Ginger and listen as the barks of the bloodhounds disappear into the distance.

46

AFTER

While the other inmates sleep, I sit on the back porch chain smoking like my life depends on it. *What's the harm after all? It seems nothing can kill me.* My eyes are locked on the rows of orange trees as I will myself to see Olivia again. Really, even if I don't see her, just avoiding Dom would be a win. Since our interaction in the stables, he's all but disappeared, which is just fine, if you ask me. Soon I will have to find him. But I need answers first. After I know for sure what he did, that's when I'll find him.

This is where I always imagine her. It's like the miles of orange trees surrounding our houses where we played when we were little. I've got ten years of memories with her disappearing into trees like this. But tonight, no matter how hard I try, I can't see her.

There's a void so deep within me, I feel like I'm collapsing into it. I look down at my feet when I expect the tears to come again, but they've run dry. My face is hot, but this time at least, I don't cry.

A flicker of movement in the trees catches my attention. A burst of excitement explodes through me. But instead of her white dress, school issue jeans and a t-shirt emerge on a lumbering figure. Though I'm a good fifty feet from him, I know who it is before I can see his face. It's Becks. And based on his stumbling, it's obvious he's drunk. I can see it when he notices me, even though I'd extinguished the glowing ember that would have given me away. His eyes narrow and he stops walking as he stares me down. My body tenses. Despite his missing cronies, I know there's no getting away. If I go inside, he'll follow me. Running is out, too, my legs are heavy.

"Flemming," he says like it's a curse. Like, I'm so far beneath him I'm lucky he even knows my name.

I should ignore him, look the other way and pretend I never saw him at all. But I know no matter what, he's not going to leave me alone. So I say, "Becks," and nod to him, far more politely than he deserves, like he doesn't bother me a bit. I won't to show my hatred, my disgust. No matter what he's done to me, I will not give him power over me. I will not let him win.

He wavers on his feet for a moment. My guess is he's trying to decide if he wants to go on his way, or if he wants to bless me with more of his presence. While he's unable to decide, I light another cigarette and move my attention back to the trees.

I sigh when he's made up his mind, and comes closer. Once he's only a few feet from me, the stink of alcohol is so pungent, it makes the air smell sharp.

"You know what your problem is, Flemming?" He stumbles as he shakes his finger at me.

I could name a thousand. Though I don't particularly care what he thinks my problem is, I say, "What?" because I know he's going to tell me anyway.

"You think you're the only person in here who's in pain. You can't see anything beyond yourself. No one else's struggles, no one else's pain could ever amount to yours, could it?" He spits the words at me. Then literally spits at me.

It takes a lot of effort to not roll my eyes. I can't imagine what struggles a rich boy like Becks could have, and I don't care to know. So, I shrug. He's not one to lecture anyone on pain. By my count, all he causes is pain. Pain and misery.

"Typical, real fucking typical," he says, irritation thick on every word. The harder he hurls the words at me, the more he wavers on his feet.

"Just go away. Don't you have anything better to do?" I ask to try and get him to move along or make a decision to fight me. I just want to get it over with. This time there won't be any guards to break it up, or drag me to the white house. He won't have anyone to help him. I may not be able to kill him, but I'll welcome the chance to try to cause some damage.

I glare at him. I force my fists to my side and hold the edges of the wood planks. The tension keeps my hands from shaking.

"You're just like me, you know?" He slurs the words out.

I shake my head. We are *nothing* alike. I can't find my voice to argue. Anger has wrapped its hands tight around my throat. Thoughts about the night he attacked me slither into my mind. My eyes clench shut as I force them out. Do not let him win. Do *not* let him get inside your head. You can do this, you can stay strong.

"I know all about you," his tone is mocking. "Rich judge father, race horses, old money." Each word is like a punch to the gut. That's not my life anymore. Chances are, it will never be my life again. Those things, all the things I grew up with do not define me. They're not a part of me, they did not make me who I am.

"Are you done?" I ask, proud of how strong my voice sounds

His eyes snap forward, looking through me. Every muscle in his body has gone rigid. Even his fists are clenched tight. "No, I'm not." He wants to torment me. "You think you're so much better than everyone else here."

"No, Becks," I manage to keep the words calm, even. Like I'm correcting a child. He looks down at me, with that look I'm so used to now. He doesn't believe me. I continue before he's able to argue. I tell him the details I've told everyone else a thousand times.

"I heard about that girlfriend of yours," he laughs. "I bet you did it."

I shrug. Anger flares within me, but I won't show him. I won't let him win.

"Funny, since you got here, 'lotta kids gone missing. 'Lotta kids killed. I suppose you don't remember any of that either?" He's toying with me, trying to get me to swing first.

I roll my eyes at him and look back at the trees. I'm done with his game.

"Guess we'll know for sure if I end up dead." He laughs, and then decides to finally move on.

47

There's dirt in my mouth when I wake up. I push off the ground, my hands sink into the moist soil. Moonlight filters through the trees and bathes the forest in a gray glow. Olivia sits atop a fallen tree beside me, my heart skips, and terror traps a breath in my throat. Up this close, the gash on her throat is so deep, I don't know how she's not bleeding. Then again, there's so much blood soaked into her dress, it's likely there's no blood left in her body.

"What are you doing here? You can't be here. This isn't happening," I say as I press my eyes closed and shake my head. Confusion blankets my mind.

I need to wake up.

"Watching over you," she says with a smile as she looks down at me. The way her mouth curves shoots a shiver up my spine.

"You're haunting me," I say automatically. Nothing about her presence feels comforting, or protective.

She tilts her head and presses her lips together. "That's not what I would call it." She bristles and brushes her curls back.

I'm not sure if it's because I know it's not real, or because of Sayid, but seeing her makes me nauseous.

"What do you want?" I ask, hoping that doing something, anything, might make this hallucination end.

"To help you, to protect you."

"Please, just let me move on." Pleading edges on my voice.

"I can't do that," she says as she offers me a hand to help me up.

I don't take it, I don't want to touch her. Instead, I use a nearby tree to stand. I waver on my feet. The earth seems to move around me, wavering from left to right.

"How did I get out here?"

"You followed me," she says like it should be obvious.

"You're not real, you're dead," I say as I look toward the trees. I just want to wake up, to get away from her.

"I'm not dead. I just needed to *look* dead," she says as she runs her fingers along the gash on her neck.

"How?"

She makes a tsking sound. "You have your secrets, I have mine. Maybe one day, once Dominic's dead, then I'll tell you." She smiles at me and taps her finger on her chin.

I only glance at her, but it's enough to make bile creep up my throat. Maybe if I leave, if I just walk away, then I'll wake up.

"Before you go, I want to show you something," she says as she holds out her hand.

"What?" I ask.

She smiles. "I can't tell you, I have to show you. It's a surprise."

Olivia walks from the clearing, and for a few minutes I follow behind her. She points to something in front of her. I have to look around her to see it. At the base of the tree, Becks slumps, his jaw is slack, his eyes stare off at nothing.

"I killed him for you."

My guts knot, and I take off into the trees. I have no idea where

I'm going, this is a part of the woods I don't recognize. But I don't care. I'd rather run into the unknown than spend another second near her. It takes at least ten minutes for me to find a path, and by the time I reach the tree line, there's a cramp in my side that threatens to take over the rest of my body. I collapse onto my bed, my skin slick with sweat, and force the night from my mind.

48

AFTER

Something touches me, waking me with a start. A nightmare haunts me, I'm dizzy, disoriented. I try to move, but I can't. I'm pinned down. Furious blinks shutter my tired eyes, I try to make them adjust to the darkness. That's when I see him. Dominic on top of me, he straddles me, and holds me down.

"Shh..." he whispers so close, his hot, moist breath hits my cheek.

Goosebumps erupt from my arms, neck. Panic shoots through me when I see the bunks in my room are empty, the door is shut. Sayid is gone.

Where the hell is Sayid?

Dominic pets my hair gently and hushes me. His fingers slither across my cheek, they're impossibly warm. I recoil, and pull my head away from his touch.

Did Dominic do something to Sayid?

"It's okay," he whispers, his fingers run through my hair.

My skin goes cold beneath his touch. I try to shift beneath him, trying to find a way to throw him off me. My hips are the only part of my body I can move. He pins me down. Dominic is too strong, much stronger than he looks. My body is frozen, paralyzed beneath him. Short shaking breaths erupt from my lips.

"I'm not going to hurt you," he coos. "Not yet, anyway." His fingers dance gently along my cheekbone.

Where he touches me, my skin seems to shrink away. It takes me what feels like forever to clear the fear caught in my throat. The words I seek are hidden in my mind beneath a fog of terror. Finally, with a shaking voice, I ask, "Dom, what are you doing?"

He leans back so that he sits on my hips, his fingers drag across my bare chest. When he moves, I try to take the opportunity to shift, knock him off me. That's when I realize my arms are bound above my head. I try to tug against the restraints, and pull against them as hard as I can. They won't budge.

"There's something I need to know. And there's something I need to apologize for." He strokes my face, then his fingers brush my abs, one by one. "Ugh, I'd kill for these abs." A disturbing laugh slips from his lips, somewhere between maniac and schoolgirl. "You're always so muscular."

Light hits me in the eyes, I recoil and squint. Realization floods my mind, the gleam of metal. A knife. He traces the tip from my sternum to my belly button. Not enough to cut, he's toying with me. I shrink away from the knife, sucking in my stomach. I hold my breath. Each jagged breath gets caught in my chest, one on top of another, they pile until my lungs are bound with chains of fear.

"Dom, please, what are you doing?" My words are steady, strong. The panic has reached a point that I've started to feel calm, settled. I can talk my way through this. It will be fine. It has to be.

"I need to know if you're who I think you are. If you lived because you're him, or if there's some other reason." His eyes are wide, hungry. "Something gives me a feeling you're just like Eden."

"What do you mean, just like Eden?" I growl. Something snaps inside me, realization and anger at the same time. It was him. I was right. He has Eden. He took her. *Why didn't I listen?*

His face scrunches up like he's going to cry. Even in the dark I can see how red he is. He turns, refusing to look at me.

"I'm really sorry I hurt you, Asher, I love you. But I just got so mad. Always coming in after Olivia, she didn't love you the way I do. She didn't deserve you. No one else deserves you. I was just so angry that you betrayed me again. It's a shame you don't remember." He tsks. "You normally do. That first mortal wound usually does the trick," he says as he runs his finger across my neck.

A twisted smile darkens his face.

"But when I realized you didn't remember, that you didn't get your memories back like you normally do—" His face brightens. "I thought it might be another chance for us."

"Did you kill her?" The question slips out of me in a strangled growl. "Where did you take her? What did you do to her?"

"I killed her," he cocks his head and smiles at me.

Rage strangles every single thought in my mind. I struggle against the restraints. I'm going to get free, and I'm going to kill him.

"Oh, darling," he says as he rush is hand across my cheek. "Don't worry, she's fine."

"If you killed her, how is she fine?"

"I killed you, and here you are, fine," he says as he pokes me softly in the belly.

Eden is like me. She can't die. Relief washes over me.

"I've killed you both hundreds of times, Asher." When his eyes meet mine again, there's a spark in them, an intensity that scares me.

My throat is dry. I'm lightheaded. I don't know if Dominic is insane, or if he's telling the truth. It can't be true.

But I already know the truth.

He smiles at me and leans down, his face pressed next to mine. His bare chest sticks to mine as he takes a long, deep breath. "You smell so good," he purrs. Then his lips brush my neck.

My jaw tightens, and I turn my head away from him.

"See, here's the thing. You were hurt. You bled to death so quickly. I was so sad to see you like that, lifeless, pale. I spent sixteen years finding you, and since you died, I was convinced you weren't him. I mean you couldn't be. You died. But then I had to take over that ugly business of killing Olivia. Can't have any witnesses, or survivors." He wipes a tear from his cheek. "But the next morning I heard they arrested you, uninjured. Then they locked you in the hospital for a month, always with a guard, so I couldn't get to you. "

Anger wells inside me. He's talking about killing Olivia as if it's as trivial as breaking a dinner plate. Like she didn't matter at all. If he hurt my sister too, hell even if he didn't. I will kill him. Even if I have to chew through whatever he's tied me up with. He deserves to die.

He continues talking, though his far-off eyes show he's lost in thought. "It's amazing though, no matter what I did to Eden, when I came back in the morning, there she was, lively, unharmed. I mean, I knew she would be, after all," he laughs, then smiles like she's a favorite pet that's made him proud.

"Where is she, Dom?"

"At the Drew Mansion. Don't worry, she's safe. And you'll see her soon enough. I have to kill you two together, remember. Otherwise, you're both very difficult to find. Eventually you always find one another. But it's in my best interest to kill you as early in your lives as possible," he says as he pets my cheek.

The Drew Mansion? Where the fuck is that?

"What the *fuck* are you talking about?" I spit the words at him.

He pulls the knife up, running it across my stomach again. No matter how I twist and turn, I can't get him off. My breaths quicken as my anger rises. Then he pulls back, and drives the knife into my chest.

49

BEFORE
Date Unknown

The flickering candle casts a shifting glow around the room. A breeze I can't feel breathes through the room. I've been waiting for her for too long. Long enough that I suspect I'm too late. Fear creeps in that Dominic already has her. Wind licks the flame, the shadows twist around me. Before she enters the room, I feel her. Her presence comes with more energy than the sun. A buzz, a life, something I will never understand.

In front of me a worn wooden table holds the daggers. She's talked me into this, but I don't agree. Then again, it may be our best chance. Most of all, it terrifies me how long it will be until I see her again. She's made me do a thousand things I haven't wanted to. And in truth, I'd do a thousand more. Once upon a time, we thought Dominic's blood was necessary for the ritual. But Alaric told us the truth, all the power lives within the dagger. Dominic has none on his own.

She shoves a sobbing girl into the room. Her arms bound with rope and a dirty white cloth tied around her mouth.

"It's about time. He's coming for you," I warn her.

A smirk twists her lips. "We'd better hurry, then."

I look at the sobbing girl as she rocks back and forth on the floor. "I thought you said she was willing, a volunteer." I spit the words at her the second she sweeps into the room.

"The girl is," she says as she kicks her onto the floor. "Was, cold feet is all." She rolls her eyes. "Is it really important?"

I press my lips together. It's important to me.

"Don't want to get off on the wrong foot. We'll be stuck with her for a very long time," I pause and correct myself, "*I* will, anyway."

Her eyes tighten and she presses her hand into her temple. "He's getting closer, I can feel it. We need to get this over with," she says as she thrusts the dagger toward me.

"Wrong one, love," I say as I slip the decoy dagger back onto the table. Instead I grab the one I know is real. I slip the cloth away from her mouth and offer her a kind smile.

"Will it hurt?" the girl asks as her eyes well with tears, and her lips tremble.

"A little," I say as I stroke her hair. "What's your name darling?"

"Elizabeth," she says with a wavering voice.

I draw the blade across her palms. In a few moments I have my own cut. I press our palms together. I whisper to her as our blood mixes, "Not anymore."

50

AFTER

After Dominic's attack in the middle of the night, I can't risk sleeping in Madison. Part of me thinks it may not have been real. But the other half of me isn't so sure. When I woke up, there wasn't a single scratch on me, but the small piece of rope I found on the floor tells me it may not have been a dream after all.

All day I've laid low. The guards must think I'm dead, or at least that's what I figure since someone had to put me in the morgue. There are rumors swirling around the school that I ran away, I was killed, and a few that I'm locked away with the crazies.

I've hidden out in the labyrinth of hay in the loft. A few hours after lights out, I creep from the stables to Madison. I should have convinced Sayid to stay with me, but I was too chicken shit. There was no point in risking him.

This late at night, thankfully, I'm the only person awake. A chorus of heavy breaths, snores and crickets are the only thing I can focus on to keep thoughts from creeping into my mind. I need a map so we stand a chance of finding the Drew Mansion, where Dominic has Eden. There may also be information about Dominic in the school's files, I need to know what he did to get in here, and if there's any other information that we could use. This is the last night I'll spend in this place. No one will come looking for me anyway since the guards think I'm dead. Then I have to find Eden, if she's still alive.

I need to get into the office to get a map. Then I'll have to resort to calling my dad, maybe he can give me some clues, or at least tell me where or what the Drew Mansion is. Eden's necklace is nearly burning a hole through my pocket.

I have to find her. I have to get to her before Dominic gets back there.

All I can hear are the words of warning buzzing in the back of my mind. I could see the fear in Eden's eyes when she talked about him. Thinking of it now, the way her jaw was clenched, her eyebrows raised, her eyes so wide the white was an ocean around her brown irises. It makes goosebumps prickle on my arms.

I take the shortest shower of my life and pull on clothes from the dirty laundry that aren't as bad off as my old ones. I move through the dark cottage, as smooth as a snake across silk. This time of night, I know the guards are nowhere near Madison. But I can't risk waking anyone else. Crouching next to Sayid as he sleeps, I shake his shoulder gently. His eyes pop open.

"H—" he starts to say, but I clap my hand over his mouth.

"Shh, it's me," I whisper. I raise my hand and signal for him to follow.

Like shadows, we sneak across the carpet, work our way down the hall and the stairs. I don't even turn around until we're outside. I don't have to turn, I can feel Sayid behind me, inches from me. The ancient porch bows and creaks beneath my feet. Sayid stretches and yawns. The cool night breeze is as crisp as an apple.

"What'd you wake me up for? Are you okay?" he mumbles.

"I have to go. I need to find my sister."

Sayid bristles, and his eyes go wide. "You're leaving?" he asks as he crosses his arms.

I nod slowly. "I have to find her. I can't stay here anymore. Getting answers about Olivia, that's part of the reason I stayed. But saving Eden, that's more important." That's all I can tell him. It's too much to explain, it all sounds too crazy.

"So you woke me up to say goodbye?"

I shake my head. "I woke you up because I need your help, and I want you to come with me."

The tiniest smile crosses his lips. He looks intrigued, he creeps closer to me and drops his voice. "What do you need help with?"

"The office, we're going to need a map. I imagine if there's one here, it's in there. We'll probably also need money." I step toward the edge of the porch.

It's clear by the smirk that creeps across his face, he's in. "Pretty risky. But you're right, that's where they'd keep the maps. They're probably all marked up from searches, but they'll still serve the purpose." He walks toward the window and searches behind the frame until he dislodges a pack of cigarettes. He holds one out for me, and I take it.

"I'm in." He jumps off the porch.

"You sure?" I jump off after him.

"I don't have anything better to do." He shrugs and takes a drag off his cig.

The darkness is thick around us as we sneak across the campus, we hide behind the trees and building as we work our way to the office. There's no reason for it though, no one's out here but us. The guards don't bother patrolling, they don't care if we escape—after all, they love the chase.

The lights are still on in the office, but no one is home. The building is sealed up tight, doors and windows locked. I sigh, defeated, when we can't find a way in. Sayid just laughs.

"Like that's going to keep us out." He disappears around the building and comes back with a handful of shiny metal rods.

"Where'd you get those?" I ask.

"Ash, I've got stuff you've never imagined squirreled away all over this place." He smiles and bends down to peek into the keyhole. He digs away with the metal rods.

"Why?" It seems weird he'd spend so much time hiding things around the school.

"You never know when it will come in handy." He flashes me a wicked smile. "I've got lock picks, matches, cigarettes, drugs, weapons. Don't tell anyone, you're the only one who knows about my hiding spots." He winks at me.

"Really, you've never told the other guys?" Seems weird he'd have chosen to tell me. He's trusted me with other secrets, but the caches he relies on seem like a bigger deal.

"Nope." He smiles for a moment, then turns to me. "Want me to teach you?"

I don't know when, or why, I'd ever need to pick a lock, but I do want to learn.

"Yeah," I say as I close the distance between us.

Sayid grabs my arm and yanks me closer. He kneels down next to the door, and tugs on my shirt. I take my position next to him, and watch eagerly as he raises the tools.

"You slip in this first," he says as he holds up a bent metal rod. "Then you take this," he brandishes an L-shaped metal tool. "And slip that into the top of the lock to turn it." He shows me how to slip the tools in, but doesn't turn them. "Then, you're going to run the first tool up, toward the top of the handle as you try to dislodge the tumblers. It takes a bit, but eventually you'll be able to feel each of them click in and out of place."

Sayid pulls on my arm, and I edge closer to him. The heat builds between us, and I can't concentrate on the lock, or how to pick it. All I can think about is how good he smells, and how much I want his lips on my neck.

Stop it. Focus.

I press my lips together, and realize that Sayid is watching me. My mouth goes dry, and I swallow hard. He pushes the tools toward me, and I try to follow the same motions that he showed me. But my hands shake each time I try. My nerves are raw. Sweat blooms on my palms and makes it difficult to grip the metal.

"I don't feel the tumblers," I say as I run the metal rod upward like Sayid showed me.

Sayid stands up and positions himself behind me. His chest presses to my back, and his arm wraps around mine. My breath catches. I close my eyes as I swallow down my desire. His hand meets mine, and he pulls it upward.

"Feel that?"

I feel something.

"No," I say as he guides my hand. All I feel is the tool grinding against the lock.

He pulls my hand upward, and I feel something click. "How about now?"

"Yeah, I felt that," I say as we guide the rod against the other tumblers.

"Now, turn," he says as he twists my hand.

As he says it, there's a click, and the door swings in. Happiness rushes through me. I never imagined I'd be able to pick a lock. I hand the tools back over to Sayid, and he stashes them away. Once he's moved away, I feel his absence. But I push the feelings from my mind. There are more important things at hand.

We both slide into the room, quiet as housecats. I pull the door shut behind me and lock it. Once inside, I begin to go through each of the desk drawers. I make Sayid a nice stack of cigarettes as I find at least one pack in each desk I search. No matter where I look, I don't find a map. I don't find anything that will help us once we get away from Dozier. We won't be able to use cigarettes as currency in the real world.

There are so many knots in my stomach my guts might be a noose. We have to find Eden. And there's only one other way to figure out where the Drew Mansion is. My father would know. I walk to the nearest desk, and grab the phone, and dial the number to my house. It takes a few seconds for the phone to ring. Each time the ringer drops, I hold my breath, waiting to hear her voice. She doesn't answer. Of course she doesn't, she can't. But my dad doesn't pick up either.

Is it just me left?

"We have to go," Sayid rushes toward me, and grabs my arm.

I'm barely able to hang up the phone before the door opens. Sayid dives behind the desk, and yanks me down with him. Heavy footsteps fall feet from the desk. Aware how loud my breaths are, I clamp my hand over my mouth. My heartbeats are louder than thunder, whoever that is, they might be able to hear it.

The longest seconds of my life tick by before I hear movement again. The footsteps grow closer. I push my back against the desk, like I might be able to disappear into the cold metal. They're so close now, I can see the blue jeans peeking out around the side of the desk.

They walk in front of the desk, back toward us, but I can't see enough to tell who it is. I'm not even sure if it's a student or a guard.

They move out of view, doors open and close around us. By the time I hear the front door hiss as it opens, I'm about to burst from the tension welled up inside me.

I shift, about to make my escape, but Sayid grabs my arm again. Settling back down beside him, I look at him, but don't dare speak. He holds his finger to his lips. Then gestures toward the door, I understand his meaning right away. Whoever it was, they haven't left yet. They're toying with us, trying to draw us out.

We sit together, huddled under the desk, less than a breath apart. The lights switch off, the door opens, and we hear the metal grind as the door locks. I don't dare move, or breathe, until Sayid does.

"That was too close," he whispers.

I nod, still too on edge to speak.

"Do you smell that?" he asks as he sniffs the air.

I take a deep breath in through my nose. "Smoke?"

Sayid moves and springs up from the floor. I narrowly avoid hitting my head as I stand. A carpet of smoke creeps across the floor, its fingers drag along the fibers as it stretches out from the fire. Flames lick the windows. My throat tightens as the smoke billows around us. Heat fills the room, sweat clings to my skin, and though I try to breathe it feels like all the air has gone out of the room.

"Fuck," I say. Between us and the door, a wall of flames grows. *There's no way out.*

"That sick fuck set the building on fire," Sayid growls, anger flashes across his face in a way I've never seen before. It's furious, powerful, and makes me shrink back.

"Who?" I ask.

"Dominic." He flashes me a look that makes my heart sink. Guilt eats away at me. It's my fault we're here, it's my fault were in this position. My stupidity might get us both killed.

He deserves better than you. He deserves someone who won't get him killed.

"Is there another way out?" I ask, but I'm sure there isn't.

"There's a window in the back room, but we have to hurry, before anyone sees us. If they think we set the fire, we're dead." He looks back at me for a moment. I swallow and open my mouth to speak, but he shakes his head at me. Smoke rises higher, my lungs burn. The air boils as the flames eat away at the building. Sparks and pops echo as the fire consumes the file cabinets. Sayid grabs my hand and leads me, it's nearly impossible to see through the smoke. He lets go of my hand long enough to throw a chair through a back window. I urge him out first, then follow.

"We need to hide," he says. "We're going to have to leave, if they notice we're out of bed..." He starts to jog toward the orange trees.

"The stables, we can hide in the loft. The dogs won't be able to smell us over the horses," I offer. Eventually, they'll check the stables. But we might get a day or two. My eyes scan the trees, the buildings around us, anywhere Dominic might hide. I don't see him, but I know he's out there somewhere, watching.

Once inside the safety of the orange trees, we look back. The flames scorch the sky and send a spiral of gray smoke high into the air. A crowd grows around the office. The gathering makes me nervous. I grab Sayid's hand and urge him to follow me. I look to Ginger's stall and she shakes her head at me. Her tail flicks as she cocks her head. But I can't give her the attention she wants right now.

I grab a few handfuls of dried hay, and layer it around the edge of the loft. If anyone steps up here, we'll have a heads up. We work our way through the labyrinth of hay and reach my nook at the back. Here I've got some books, blankets, and food stashed. The only thing I keep forgetting to add is clothes.

I sit on the blankets and pull my knees to my chest. Sayid sits next to me. In the distance, we can hear a fire engine, the rush of water, a sea of voices. My heart still pounds, nerves raw, on edge. I can hardly sit still. Nothing feels real anymore, like I'm living in a dream, or nightmare.

"We have to leave tonight," he says.

"I know. Even after we find Eden, we can't come back here," I say as I look at him. "Where will we go?"

"I'm sure we can find somewhere better than here." He grins, like he knows something I don't.

He turns toward me, my head turns automatically. I open my mouth, before I can speak he presses his lips to mine. When he pulls away, I realize I've been holding my breath.

I close the distance between us. I kiss him slowly at first. Sayid's hand moves up my back, as he tugs at my shirt. I pull it over my head, and he sheds his own. His full lips press against mine, I feel the weight of him, his hunger as he kisses me back. With my palm against his chest, I feel the insistent *thump, thump, thump* of his heart. The rapid pace matches my own. Long black locks of his hair brush against my neck, he kisses my cheek, my jaw, my neck.

I don't care that I don't deserve him or that he can do better. All I care about is in this moment he wants me, and the only thing that I want is him.

I pull Sayid on top of me and breathe him in like air. The comfort of his smell washes over me, cigarettes and laundry soap. Dirty and clean at the same time. He presses himself against me, and I feel his excitement. My hands hover on his waist, part of me is too scared to venture further. He pulls away, as if he can feel my hesitation.

"Are you okay?" he asks, his words breathy and rushed.

I nod, and lean my forehead against his. My heart flutters as my eyes meet his. "Just nervous."

He grins slyly. "There's no reason to be," he says as he brings his hand to my cheek.

Though my thoughts are bathed with desire, longing, the reminder of my complete lack of experience nags at the back of my mind. His eyes are locked on mine as he moves his hand lower. My body responds as Sayid unbuttons my pants. As he pulls them down, I kick them to the side. He takes me into his hand, and my eyes close, a groan slips from my lips. His lips brush mine for just a moment before he whispers, "I love you, Asher."

51

BEFORE
Date Unknown

I leave the girls together, I have get rid of the dagger and to make it back to the house before Dominic returns. Weaving through the streets, I drop the dagger at Alaric's doorstep after only one knock. It's all the time I can spare. If Dominic knows I was missing, even for a moment, the plan won't work. Before I slide in, I scan the basement to be sure he's nowhere to be found. Once I'm sure it's empty, I climb through and sit back in the chair. My heart hammers as I work to secure the rope around my body again.

With my back to the stairs, anxiety grips me. I'm always jumpy toward the end, even though I know what to expect, even though I know what's coming.

After what feels like an eternity the lock on the door clicks. It flies open and rattles on its hinges. I want to turn to see if he's got someone with him, but the tell-tale sound of dragging lets me know he does.

"Could you take any longer?" I ask him, making it sound as if this is simply the biggest inconvenience there is.

"Do you ever shut up?" he snaps at me.

Behind me, I hear him drop something. A few seconds later, he drops something else. *No. Two bodies.*

"Someone thought I was stupid again," he growls. "Someone thought I wouldn't figure out they were trying to trick me."

A lump forms in my throat. *No.*

Her strangled moan slips out behind me.

No. He wasn't supposed to get her.

I try to look back, but I can't see with the way I'm tied. Dominic draws a circle around us, and squirts a liquid at our feet. In seconds, flames lick my feet.

No this can't happen. She needs to stay here. She needs to research. Otherwise this will happen again and again.

Dominic grasps the beaker from the table in the corner of the room. He takes a deep breath and throws it toward us. As the glass shatters the air around us glows a sparkling blue.

The flames rise and the pain turns to agony as they consume us. Dominic takes out a sheet of paper, unfolds it, and dangles a crystal above it.

As the world goes up in flames around us, all I hear is the word, "Florida."

52

AFTER

The spot beside me where Sayid slept is still warm when I wake up. For the first time in months, Olivia didn't haunt me in my dreams. I feel settled, grounded. My head, my thoughts, are alarmingly clear as I stare at where he slept. For a few minutes, my hand hovers there, his lingering warmth spreading into my fingertips. The weight of sleep lifts from my mind and I pull myself from the floor. I reach for the pack of cigs beside me, and light one. I take a long drag, and stretch as I stand up. Slowly, I work my way between the rows and rows of hay bales, there's no sign of Sayid.

Night blankets Dozier as I venture out of the stables. I cut across the orange trees and creep into Madison. My heart nearly bursts out of my chest when I find someone sitting in the living room. Relief washes over me when I realize it's Brandon.

"Hey," I say as I nod.

He raises an eyebrow when he looks at me. "I thought you died."

I'd forgotten that everyone thinks I disappeared, ran away, or died—the rumors seem to shift moment to moment from what I hear. "Nope, still here," I confirm. "Have you seen Sayid?" My eyes move to the stairs and I hope that he'll walk down.

He shakes his head. "If he's not upstairs, check the laundry, he might have gotten a late shipment."

"Thanks," I call back to him as I walk up the stairs.

Our room is silent, still. His bed doesn't look slept in. I doubt he came back here at all. I head back down the stairs. Before checking the laundry, I decide to check Dominic's cottage.

I scour each window of Washington, darkness welcomes me. The newer wood of the deck doesn't bow beneath my feet, like it does at Madison. I try the handle and find it locked. I search the nooks around the windows, I find three packs of cigarettes, a baggie of pills, a bundle of naked pictures, and a box of matches before I find a lock pick set.

I put everything back, minus a pack of cigarettes and the lock picks. My hands are shaking as I stick the bent metal rod into the keyhole. I pull the metal rod upwards, hearing it click against the tumblers. The last time I did this, Sayid held my hands steady. He guided me. Again and again I drag the metal across the tumblers, each time the knob won't give.

Digging through the kit, I grab another pick, slide it into place and start to glide the metal against the tumblers again. This time, I turn the pick ever so slightly to the left, the handle begins to turn. I hold my breath, my silent prayer, my hope. The door opens, I exhale. Creaking inward the door reveals a familiar layout, a twin of Madison.

I creep up the stairs and slide between the beds looking for Dominic. He's not in any of them. In the last room, once I reach the door, I see the empty bed. In that moment, in a flicker of weakness, I imagine the worst. Olivia's bloody body with my mother, Eden and Sayid lying next to her.

Leaping off the porch, I loop around toward the back, he has to be around here somewhere. The most obvious places need to come off the list first. The rows of orange trees are empty, three boys are hiding out in the laundry drinking, the way they're stumbling around, I don't even bother to ask about Dom.

From the front of the stables I see something moving at the edge of the corn field. Something being dragged.

I run closer, until my heart drowns out my thoughts, and my stomach knots. That's when I see it's Sayid. He's unconscious. I weave in and out of the corn, the rows are staggered, planted by lazy students. Sayid is being dragged with impossible speed, I have to jog to stay within sight.

Deep within the maze, Sayid stops moving. His limp body slumps to the side, like an abandoned toy. I hear a crack behind me. There's a rush, pain, then darkness.

53

BEFORE
January 7th, 1968

I stand at the top of the stairs with my arm wrapped tightly around Olivia. Dry heaves wrack her body. Between heaves, her body trembles. Her skin is slick with sweat. The smell of the bodies in the basement lingers in my nose, my mouth, my throat. Their empty eyes squeezed into their bloated faces, I still feel them on me.

"Someone just piled them up like old socks, like they didn't mean anything. They're *people*," Olivia says through a sob, her voice trembles. "Who would do that? Who *could* do that?"

I pull her into a hug and she cries into my shoulder. I don't know that I'll ever be able to get the image out of my mind. And the smell has seeped into her hair. It's not just the weight of their deaths we bring with us, it's their empty stares, the smell of them.

"Who would do something like that?" she asks as she pulls away. She looks down at the puddle of tears left on my shirt and rubs her hand over it as though she can erase it. "I'm sorry."

"You have nothing to be sorry for," I say as I wipe her cheek. "I think we should get out of here before whoever did this gets back."

She gives me a quick nod and grabs my hand. We turn down the hall, the front door is open and headlights pour in.

Whose car is that?

My feet are heavy next to hers. A hollow metallic thud fills the hall, like a boot hitting a metal pipe. Black spots explode behind my eyes, the world shifts, and I fall to the floor.

Afternoon light streams in through the moth-eaten curtains. My vision is tainted, swirled, blurred. Black edges in, until I see Olivia. Her head is slumped, smeared red. Limp blonde curls fall in her face.

Rough rope bites at my wrists. I try to move my legs and look down to find them tied to the chair I sit in. For good measure there's also a rope around my waist. Adrenaline and fear pour into my veins. My breaths quicken. My bound hands tremble. If we don't get out of here, we'll end up like those people in the basement.

My eyes scour the room searching for the person who hit us, tied us up. When I don't see anyone, I whisper, "Olivia."

She doesn't move, I try several more times. Though I'm afraid I might crumble beneath the fear quaking my body, I need to stay strong for her. The air is thick with death. With each agonizing moment that passes. I wonder if she's dead. She can't be dead.

"What?" the word slips out of her as a breathy sigh.

"Someone tied us up, I need you to see if you can get out of your ropes," I whisper to her as I try to see how well she's been tied. If she can get free, we can get out of here. We can escape.

Her eyes go wide as they sweep across the room. All at once her whole body contorts as she tries to slip free of her ropes.

Heavy footsteps echo from the back of the house. The boards ache and moan with each footfall. The closer they get, the higher my stomach and heart creep until they fight for room in my throat.

"Asher, someone's coming," Olivia whispers to me.

"I know," my voice is flat.

The first thing I see, is red hair. Dominic strolls into the room, his gait as smooth as an Atlantic City hustler.

"Dom!" I call out. "Hey man, someone tied us up. Can you help us before they come back?"

Dom laughs. "'fraid not." He pulls a pack of cigs from his pocket, shakes one out and lights it.

"Come on, I'm not joking," I say with an edge to my voice. It's only now that I see the darkness hiding just beneath the surface of his face.

"Neither am I." Dominic clicks the lighter closed. "You've always wasted your time with fucking morons like this one." He motions toward Olivia.

"Don't you *dare* talk about her like that," I growl the words at him.

"I was hoping your last moments would be a bit more special than this. But unfortunately, you had to come out here before I'd planned for you to and move up my timetable." Dominic makes a tsking sound as he walks toward Olivia. When he reaches her, Dominic runs his hand across Olivia's cheek. "I had something nice planned for you, too."

"What are you talking about?" Olivia jerks her head away from Dominic's hand.

"It's unfortunate that you two can never remember...after. At least you'd understand." Dominic smiles and cocks his head as he looks at me. "But you know, it doesn't matter. Whether you remember or not, I love killing you. Both of you." He smiles at us, looking between us.

In one fluid movement, Dominic is behind Olivia, there's a glimmer of metal, a knife. Dominic leans in and runs his finger across

Olivia's neck. She grimaces and jerks her head to the side, away from Dominic. That's exactly the opening Dominic wanted, he brings the knife up. And horror floods through me. He's going to kill her. He's going to kill Olivia.

"Don't!" My throat tightens as I spit the word at him.

He makes another tsking sound and drags the knife across her throat, blood shoots out of her in a fan. Her eyes are locked on mine, fear seizes her, then she's choking, red pouring from her mouth.

"No!" I cry, "Please, no." I growl at him, "I'll kill you." I struggle against the ropes.

Dominic holds his stomach as he laughs. His bloody hand staining his shirt. "Oh, love, that's rich. But no, no you won't." There's a hint of something to his words, like an accent that's started to bleed through.

He turns his back to me and looks at Olivia like he's waiting for something. Fear chokes me. I feel like I've been punched in the heart. I wish harder than I ever have for anything in my life, that she will be okay. If I could get free, maybe I could help her. Save her. There has to be something I can do. My body shakes as the tears pour out of me.

"Hmm," Dominic finally says. "That's strange, guess I was wrong." He shrugs, cuts Olivia free, and slings the body over his shoulder. Blood drips off her forehead onto the floor, leaving a trail behind them.

He's gone so long, hope creeps in. Maybe I'll live through this. I'm not sure I want to live in a world without Olivia. I sure as hell don't want to be bled out by a psycho. When he returns, he cuts me free. I lunge at him, but he holds the knife out. Olivia's blood still clings to the blade.

"Walk outside," he orders, knife inches from my eye.

"Or what? You'll kill me?" I challenge. I stand straight, as tall as I can manage, arms pressed to my sides.

"Either way, I'm going to kill you." He shrugs and takes a long drag from a cigarette with a bloody filter.

I turn toward the hall, starting slow, walking over the debris I avoided on the way in. When I see the sunset peeking through the door frame, I start to run and bound down the stairs. Adrenaline pours into my veins. But he catches me only a few feet from Olivia's body, grabbing the back of my shirt. He traps me, my neck in the nook of his arm.

"It's a shame, you two weren't who I thought you were. Now I have to start looking again. Can't believe I was wrong this time." He brings the tip of the knife to my throat. Then his lips are at my ear, "Don't worry, I'm sure you'll find each other in hell."

The knife is so sharp I don't feel it cut me, I only feel the air sting the wound. The spray of the blood hits the ground, it sounds like rain. When I go limp, he drops me and before the darkness takes me, I take my last breath and look into Olivia's lifeless eyes.

54

AFTER

There are voices around me in my dreams, but I can't make sense of them. I'm close enough that I hear the trail of whispers, but I can't make out the language. There's only one thing I recognize.

"Asher," a voice calls beside me. Fear ignites inside me when I realize the voice belongs to Dominic. He stands a few feet away, a limp, lifeless Sayid held in a headlock. "It's about fucking time you woke up. I swear in this life you're defective. You should ask for a refund."

"What are you talking about?" I ask as I sit up. My head swims as my brain adjusts to the sitting position. Dried blood flakes from the side of my head, but the wound is already healed.

"And you just keep getting stupider. Get off the fucking ground." He points down the row of corn with his knife, "Walk. That way. Otherwise, I'm going to kill your *boyfriend* here."

Anger rises up inside me. Though I want to lunge at him, I swear Dominic knows what I'm thinking, because he holds a knife out toward me, just long enough for me to see it. Then in a few seconds he has the knife pressed back to Sayid's throat.

"Where am I walking?" I growl as I follow his instructions. I should have known better than to trust this asshole. How could I have ever been so stupid?

Behind me, I hear dragging. When I look back, Dominic is dragging Sayid. My heart falters, and I stumble. Eyes locked on Sayid's limp body, my heart beats into a frenzy. He can't hurt Sayid, I won't let him. "Just walk, and keep your fucking mouth shut."

We weave through the cornfield and cross the small stretch of open field before the forest swallows us. The further we walk, the more the anger twists inside me. A silent flame smolders inside me, when I get the chance, the second Dominic lets his guard down, I *will* kill him.

By the time we break through the trees, the sun ignites the horizon. I recognize the large willow tree looming over the field ahead of us. This is the same place we met with Eden. Dominic must have known. He leads me to a new Buick. With one fluid motion Dominic pulls handcuffs from his pocket and tosses them at me.

"Put those on," he says as he winks at me.

Anger flares up inside me as I glower at him. If he didn't have Sayid, if he didn't have my sister, I'd fight him. He can do whatever he wants to me, it doesn't seem he can kill me anyway. But I need to protect Sayid. I can't let Dominic hurt him. I press the metal to my wrists and lock the handcuffs in place.

"Good, now get in the passenger seat," he says as he waves toward the car with his knife.

I slide into the car and the moment I'm in, he wraps me in ropes to hold me in place. He's drilled a loop into the dashboard. After he's bound me with ropes, he loops a chain over my hands and then attaches it to the loop on the dashboard.

"There we go, can't have you getting away from me," Dominic says as he smiles at me. I turn my head to look at him and Dominic cocks his head. He pulls his hand up and runs the back of it along my hair. "I've missed you," he coos.

Bile rises up in my throat. This Dominic isn't the Dominic I was best friends with. This is a stranger, this is a crazy person living in his skin. A memory prickles at the back of my mind, it swims together, it feels raw in my mind. I see the living room of the Howey Mansion first, Olivia strapped to the chair next to me and then his blade at her throat.

Dominic slides into the driver's seat next to me. I eye the back seat.

"What did you do with Sayid?"

"He's in the trunk," he says simply as he starts the car.

As the Buick begins to trundle along the cracked pavement, I shift in the seat. My mouth tastes bitter, my throat tightens as anger grips around me. But I have to ask him. This might be the only chance I have.

"I almost feel bad doing all this to you if you don't know why," he grins at me. "Almost."

"Can you please tell me what you're talking about?" I beg. My arms ache, the metal bites into my wrists.

He shrugs and slips a cigarette between his lips. He takes a long drag and then extinguishes it on his arm. In a few seconds the wound has closed up complete. He's like us. Panic writhes inside me.

"How?" I ask.

He shakes his head.

The questions are thick in my mind. But I don't know how many of them he's going to answer. His foot presses down on the gas pedal and the car lurches. We're going too fast down the narrow, two lane highway.

"Where are we going?"

"Ellaville," he says simply.

"Where's that?" Though I don't know where the city is, I imagine that's where the Drew Mansion is, where he has Eden.

"Not too far. East of Dozier. " He doesn't look at me. Though his eyes are straight forward, he doesn't seem to be paying attention to the road, or anything.

The question bubbles to the forefront of my mind. And I have to ask it. I have to try again.

"Why did you kill Olivia?"

He rolls his eyes. "You just can't let my *mistakes* go." He lights another cigarette and casts a glance my way that's a sharp as a dagger. "You didn't used to be like this. You used to be happy when it was just us. But then stupid girls like Olivia have to go and confuse you. She's a victim of circumstance. I thought she was someone else."

My jaw tightens as anger rushes through me. He's so nonchalant about killing one of the most important people in my life. I struggle against the restraints. Then I remember that Sayid is in the trunk. If I try to get free, Dominic could hurt him. There's another question lingering at the back of my mind, but I'm afraid to ask it.

Dominic turns the wheel sharply and pulls the car off into the woods. "The town has been shut down since the forties. The roads are destroyed. You might not believe me, but driving through the trees is actually much better than trying to make it through the roads."

He weaves in and out of the trees at a speed that makes my stomach creep into my throat. *Please don't hurt Sayid, please.*

"Why can't I die?"

"You can," a smirk creeps across his face.

"Not so far I can't," I argue. By my count, I should have died at least five times.

"You just haven't been killed the right way yet," he says as if to comfort me. He leans over and sets his hand on my thigh. My skin crawls at his touch. "Trust me, I've killed you hundreds of times."

He must be crazy because it's not possible. Even though I know I've healed when I shouldn't have. Even though I've lived when I shouldn't have—it still seems impossible.

"The key is making sure there's none of you left to regenerate," he turns his head toward me.

"So what's the right way, then?"

"Don't worry, I'm going to show you."

I can see the sickness brewing in him. There's something so dark beneath the surface of Dominic that it scares me. How was I so blind that I didn't see it in the beginning? Eden and Olivia saw it. Why was I so stupid?

I swallow my fear. The fear won't do me any good. But the answers might. "So, what, we get reincarnated and then you find us again?"

He nods with a smile.

"Why, though? Why do you keep hunting us? Why do you keep killing us?"

He pulls the car to a stop in front of a old, decrepit house with a sagging porch.

"Because it's what you deserve," he says as he pats my thigh.

Dominic slips from the car and grabs Sayid from the trunk. He carries him into the house. A while later, he opens the door, unties me, and I slide out.

I look toward the house, and back at the car. We're in the middle of the woods, I could try and make a run for it, but I can't leave Sayid and Eden.

"Don't even think about it," Dominic says as he glowers at me.

I walk slowly toward the house, my feet dragging in the sandy soil. This is the end, I can feel it. He's brought us here to kill us all.

Fear coils tightly around me, and panic swells in the back of my mind.

On the porch, I realize nearly every window in the house is broken. Shards of glass cover the porch. The door moans when he opens it and dry leaves crinkle as they're crushed. Black dirt clings to the seams of the dark wooden floors. Brittle leaves, grass, and dead roaches form piles that gather at the walls.

A wide rotten staircase stretches to the second floor. So many of the boards are missing, I'd never dare climb them. I hope that's not where he's taking me. Wallpaper hangs limp from the walls, like old sagging skin. But still, the house is hauntingly beautiful.

I look around for my sister, for Sayid. Dominic shoves me through open double doors. Above them is stained glass that looks like it used to be the last supper. This room used to be the living room. Light spills in from the windows, through the moth eaten curtains; there are so many holes, they may as well be made from Swiss cheese. Sayid and Eden sit tied to chairs in front of me.

The house smells like dust and mold; the musty smell of old people. I stand amongst the furniture covered in white sheets, and splinters of broken furniture. Dominic pushes me forward, and slides a chair behind me. He shoves me into it.

My chest tightens, fear's fingers digging into me. He wraps ropes around me and secures me to the chair. My eyes fall on Eden, her face is a mask of frustration, not fear, like I expect.

"Are you okay?" I ask her.

She offers me a curt nod.

I shake my head. None of this seems possible. None of this *is* possible. Dominic must be lying.

"Did he hurt you?" I ask her.

"Yeah, he really loves knives," she glowers toward the door. Dominic has disappeared for the moment and I use it to my advantage.

"Did he tell you anything strange about hunting us in other lives?"

"You don't remember?" she asks as she cocks her head.

Dominic's feet are heavy against the wood floor. Something sloshes in the can he carries. He whistles as he brings the can of gasoline close and splashes it onto the floor, and on us.

"Please let Sayid go. He didn't do anything," I plead. I know there's no chance of him letting me or my sister go. But Sayid isn't like us.

"He's seen too much. He's too close to you. He can't stay. If I let him live, I'd be breaking the rules." He smirks and winks at me.

The image of all the bodies in the Howey Mansion basement floods into my mind. I swallow down my disgust.

He stops, takes a long look at me, then a deep breath, "I just love the smell of gas. I could smell it all. Day. Long."

He sets the can down and pulls a gold lighter from his pocket. As he looks us over, he clicks the lid open and closed. For a moment he drops his eyes to his feet. His tongue slides across his teeth.

"This will be the last time," he says as he smiles at both of us. "I'm not sure what you did to become siblings this time around, but I'm telling you, this is the last time." He pulls a dagger from his waistband and moves toward Eden. He slices her neck and his palm in one fluid movement and holds the two together. Eden doesn't wince or react.

"Get the fuck away from my sister."

He rounds on me, his head cocked. "The two of you deserve much worse than this." He spits the words at me. He grabs my bound palms and drives the knife into them. Pain shoots from my hand up my arm. He squeezes my hand as he mixes our blood together. Seconds after he's done, the wound on my hand closes.

"What are you talking about?" I ask him.

"He thinks we killed his family," Eden says. "He hasn't shut up about it for weeks."

I open my mouth to question it. I've never met Dominic's family, neither has Eden. There's no way we're responsible for killing them, or anyone else.

"Enough," he growls. He strikes the flame, tosses it to my feet, and smiles at me. "See you on the flip side, Ash."

Dominic looks back one last time before he disappears. The fire grows around us. I kick my chair backward into the flames. I groan as the pain floods through me. The fire burns my back, my arms. But more importantly, it burns my ropes. In a few agonizing seconds, I'm free. The flames lick Eden's feet. But I have to get Sayid free first. He doesn't have the gifts we do.

I free Sayid and drag him to the edge of the room, far from the flames. But as I turn to Eden, she does the same move I did and kicks her chair backward. I pick Sayid up and sling him over my shoulder, he's heavy, but I don't feel nearly as weighed down by him as I should.

Eden's at my side in seconds, and we rush out the back door. My eyes sweep the sides of the house, the engine of the Buick hums from the front of the house. Directly in front of us the woods are close. I head for the trees and Eden follows. My heart hammers in my chest as fear floods through me. I have to get them both away from Dominic. I have to keep them both safe. There's nothing I could do to save Olivia, but I can save them.

We get far enough into the woods that I can no longer smell smoke, or hear the pops of the fire. I set Sayid down, he slumps against a tree. He's still out cold, maybe that's for the best. I turn toward my sister. There are a million questions I want to ask her, there are so many things I want to say, that I need to say. But instead I hug her. When I pull back, her face contorts, tears pool in her eyes.

"What do you remember?" she asks with her voice impossibly low.

I shake my head. "Scattered memories. But they don't make sense. There was a girl in all of them. I thought it was you at first, now I'm not so sure. What do you remember?"

"Everything," she says simply. Her face is tight, stricken. Her eyes drop to the ground. "Asher," she says as her eyes meet mine again.

"Yeah?"

Eden is never like this. She's being really weird. She sighs and presses her lips together before she says, "I'm not who you think I am." She looks down. "You knew me before as Elizabeth. That other girl, the one you thought was me, I think *that* was Olivia."

My mind is swallowed by confusion. It's not possible. Is it? That would mean...

"I think Olivia is still alive," she says.

Her eyes meet mine, and a shiver ricochets down my spine. My eyes move over the trees. If she's not dead, that might mean I'm not so crazy after all. If Olivia is out there, if she's still alive, where is she?

ACKNOWLEDGEMENTS

Thank you to the incredible editor who helped me with this book, Chantelle Aimée Osman. And thank you to the rest of the Polis/Agora team for helping me bring this book into the world. I appreciate your support, guidance, and all of your hard work.

Thank you to my agent, Jill Marsal.

To my incredible critique partner, Elesha, you are the best. Thank you for everything <3.

To all the people who read *After You Died* over the years and provided me feedback, without you this book wouldn't be possible. Thank you for your words and your time.

To all my readers who have bought my books over the years, thank you—I hope there are at least thirty more to come!

LETTER TO THE READER

Dear Reader,

Thank you for reading *After You Died*. I hope that this story has touched you in some way, like the story of the Arthur G. Dozier School did for me. When I first heard about the Dozier school in 2013, I started reading the stories of the boys who'd lived there—survived the school. I've woven some of their stories and their history into this novel because I think it's important that their stories are told.

In the state of Florida, the Arthur G. Dozier School for boys fought allegations of abuse, murder, and more for years. The school finally shut its doors in 2011. Yes, 2011. The school was open for over a hundred years, and there are unmarked graves still being exhumed on the property today. Many of these victims, we don't know their names, who their families were—if someone out there is still hoping they'll come home one day.

Many of these victims, their only crime was being unwanted. Orphans, truants, petty thieves, they were all locked away in this school and treated with the same cruelty. If you enjoyed this book, please do some research on this school and other schools like it that have been allowed to operate in this country. Please believe the survivors and honor those that did not survive.

Dea Poirier

(

9 781951 709419